D0651309

The Banner
of the
Passing Clouds

The Banner
of the
Passing Clouds

Anthea Nicholson

GRANTA

Granta Publications, 12 Addison Avenue, London W11 4QR
First published in Great Britain by Granta Books, 2013

Copyright © Anthea Nicholson, 2013

Anthea Nicholson has asserted her moral right under the
Copyright, Designs and Patents Act, 1988, to be
identified as the author of this work.

Armageddon Averted by Stephen Kotkin (2008) 8 words from p. 70.
By permission of Oxford University Press, Inc.

All rights reserved. No reproduction, copy or transmissions
of this publication may be made without written permission. No paragraph
of this publication may be reproduced, copied or transmitted save with written
permission or in accordance with the provisions of the Copyright Act 1956
(as amended). Any person who does any unauthorized act in relation
to this publication may be liable to criminal prosecution
and civil claims for damage.

A CIP catalogue record for this book
is available from the British Library.

1 3 5 7 9 10 8 6 4 2

ISBN 978 1 84708 756 0

Typeset by M Rules
Printed and bound by CPI Group (UK) Ltd, Croydon, CR0 4YY

for
Corinna Faith
Max de Wardener
Rob Gribbin
Mamuka Japharidze
და საქართველოსთვის

But the sky,
because of conversations under the banner
of the passing clouds,
heard not the prayer
in the silence dusted with snow,
drenched like a cloak,
like the dusky echo of threshing,
like a loud argument in the bushes.

  Boris Pasternak, Still More Sultry Dawn.

All previous life was revealed as a lie.

  Stephen Kotkin, Armageddon Averted.

PART I

the spools turn, the red needle stirs

It was raining and Givi's face was wet as he looked up to the high window of the maternity clinic where Vera stood in her dressing gown holding the swaddled bundle that was me. Other women stood at windows hugging their tightly wrapped infants and other husbands gazed up trying to pick out their wives with their newborn babes. Givi waved and Vera called out, How is she? But Givi could not hear from so far below, with the traffic rushing between him and the clinic, and so he just waved and nodded and tried to smile. Very soon a white coated nurse ordered the mothers away from the windows and the babies were put back into their cots and wheeled into line in the observation ward. The mothers went back to their beds and sat knitting and smoking, sucking sweets and chatting. But Vera could not join in with the general atmosphere of achievement. She could only think about her daughter who she had last seen lying like a rag doll on a high hospital bed next to the iron lung. The polio had taken hold within days.

Vera and Givi were not allowed to enter the isolation ward but had watched Tiniko struggling to breathe on the other side of the glass bricks in the partition wall. The glass was tinted green and they could not see her face properly. And then Vera went into labour and I was born in another clinic while Givi stayed watching over Tiniko.

Her little head flopped as they lifted her into the iron lung. The iron lung wheezed and clanked and Tiniko's chest rose and fell, and the nurse in attendance nodded to Givi behind the glass bricks, as if to say, You see, nothing to worry about! But the child was too in love with life to live forever inside an iron lung, at least that is what my parents told me, so she allowed herself to die, they said. Givi had seen the doctors bending over his beloved girl and each in turn placing an ear to her chest where they had lifted the faded blue hospital gown that had been far too big for her. One of them came out to say that the patient had died and that Comrade Dzhugashvili should go immediately to the deceased relative's office to fill out the appropriate forms.

So when he stood in the rain looking up to Vera who was holding me, the wetness on his face was tears. After a few days when he was allowed to go up to the maternity ward and see Vera, he had to tell her the awful news. She was calm. She said she had seen Tiniko in a dream and she had been with other children and was laughing. So she's alright, she's with God now, said Vera with tears running silently down her cheeks. And how's he? asked Givi looking down at me in the moulded plastic crib. Vera looked vague, blinked her tearful eyes and drew her shawl tighter around her breasts. A nurse said that visiting time was over and I was wheeled away.

Soon enough Vera came home to the apartment with her swaddled bundle. She had the funeral to see to. The pain hit her now she was home with Tiniko's toys and books. I was a quiet baby, gave no trouble, slept a lot, did not fuss at the regulated feeding times, or so my parents said. For a long time they just called me, The Baby, but eventually they started referring to me by name. It had been given to me by some anonymous comrade at the maternity clinic. Vera and Givi had been too dazed and sad to concentrate and had not been able to settle on a name in advance and there were birth-registration forms to fill out before I could be taken home. Some overworked official wrote down the first name that came into their head, and my parents signed the document without looking.

My father's lowly family tree of Dzhugashvilis were not directly related to the infamous Iosif Dzhugashvili, aka Stalin, who was considered a national hero by many ordinary Georgians. Perhaps that anonymous comrade named me in a fit of Patriotic fervour. The Motherland was in mourning for Stalin, who had died on the same day as my birth and my sister's death. His portraits were draped with black curtains, drawn open so his face was visible as it was in his coffin, while the endless line of weeping comrades trudged through the Hall of Columns in Moscow's Red Square.

If I am to continue hoping for the best in humanity, I must believe that I was named Iosif Dzhugashvili not for malicious intent, but in honour of a hero. But it does not really matter about the whys. By the time my parents began to notice me properly my name was a fact. My future was planned during that period of their grief and guilt at losing Tiniko.

Polio was a well-known killer and you had to keep your children away from stagnant water where it lurked. But the ancient yards of Tbilisi were pooled with tepid water. Old water dripped from old pipes, old water sat in the blocked gutters, it filled the abandoned metal trays used for cement mixing, it bubbled in the depths of bashed up empty chemical drums and seeped from the smelly grids of drains. In the summer when the temperature soared to almost boiling point and the night rain fell in torrents, all the children took off their socks and shoes and paddled and splashed in the green pools.

My sister Tiniko contracted polio and died before I ever knew her. But I contracted the complete living being called Stalin. My parents mourned for their private loss while the Motherland mourned for her Great Leader. He lay in the satin folds of his coffin far away in Moscow, smiling discreetly to himself as he found me out. Every eye was misty with tears so nobody observed the slight disturbance in the flowers massed upon his empty form as he slipped away to snuggle into the new fit of baby flesh that was the innocent me. Innocent that is, apart from the old familiar name. But I did not think innocent thoughts as a child. At least I cannot remember any. I worried that this famous Iosif, whose portrait hung four times on the walls of the nursery which I attended every working day, might be discovered in the hiding place he had chosen behind my ribs. I opened my mouth as little as possible. But the songs always let me down.

As soon as I was old enough to toddle out to the balcony, grip the railings and peer down into the dust-filled air, the wind tugging at my bare feet, the balcony trembling, the odour of sulphur from the domed baths rising sharp in my nostrils, I knew that my mouth could not stay shut for ever.

The tannoys perched on the posts like birds. A song came rattling from a distant speaker, gathering power as it tumbled through the electrical interference of poor quality broadcast. The song reached my ears and ran on in all directions, both instantaneous and delayed, sidling down the cables and warbling from the tin beaked tannoys. The words might have once made sense, but by the time they reached me they were a muddle of overlapping fragments and slurs, a stuttering, lisping defect which never failed to enthral me.

He squirmed in my lungs as I ran my tongue over my lips.

I had seen the cow's lungs on the butcher's slab, so I knew how the formless mass was pricked with minute holes where blood escaped. I stood on tiptoe, pressed my face to the rails, hoping that my name would not wake. But he always did and even as he perked up to smile his kindly admonition I had no choice but to open my mouth and let my voice come out to join the song. Even at that young age I was dimly aware that the sounds I was making did not nearly match the sounds that so enthralled me. When the tannoys fell quiet and I droned on alone, he continued smiling and crinkling his kindly eyes. Then would come the muffled tapping of his fingers on the inside of my ribs. I stood as straight as I knew how and pressed my burning lips shut.

You will not be a singer, he instructed, your voice will never ring true.

*

I see myself on the high balcony of our tower block apartment, but until I was about six we lived in the old quarter of Tbilisi, in one of the twisty wood and brick dwellings with earthen yards where ancient wisteria grew over everything. These two- or three-storey dwellings were wrapped with glassed Italian balconies or hung with wonky wooden shelves whose rails were carved to imitate Grecian urns in silhouette. They were divided into communal quarters now, with three or four families using one kitchen and one bathroom. Our home was a single high-ceilinged salon with the bonus of an extra small box room or dressing cabinet. In this tiny windowless space we had the luxury of a private kitchen. And pinned to the wall of this private kitchen, above the formica table, was a family portrait taken before I was born.

7

A photographic studio setting. Vera and Givi wearing traditional Georgian costumes, she in a heavily pleated black coat
and he in a tight-fitting high-collared silver-white jacket with
cartridge holders sewn across the chest and a silver dagger
hanging at his side. The costumes are decorated with the
colourful embroidered edging bands of a wealthy Caucasian
clan. My parents' handsome faces look at the camera lens with
perfect self possession and poise. My sister stands prettily
between them on a gilt chair draped with a bear skin, to
emphasise the scene of Mount Kazbegi on the backdrop. The
black and white image has been touched up with colour here
and there to bring out the costumes and animate the faces.
This was Givi and Vera's only photograph of Tiniko. It had
been taken on her fourth birthday, only a few months before
the polio got into her system. The pin must have just fallen
from the wall and, unknown to my parents, the photo with it.

The newspaper was spread out on the table ready for
mother to cut into toilet paper squares. I thought I would help
while she was busy hanging out washing, so I began to snip
away at the pages. The scissors did not work very well, and I
was not old enough to know how to handle them, but I
enjoyed the way the blades slid together, the small pieces of
newsprint falling away.

It was only when I moved the paper around that I saw the
photograph had been lying beneath and that I had snipped into
it without knowing. In a mood of childish experiment, I cut
further into the photograph. The blades sliced through the
furry drapery beneath my sister. I snipped again and she was
cut in two and then I began snipping all around her, believing
that if I could cut out the picture of my halved sister and leave
only my parents in place, I would somehow hide the damage

8

I had done. I worked on. I knew what I had done was very bad, and the scissors themselves were angry and were bending the photograph and marking its sheeny surface, and then all of a sudden they fell apart and I was left with my finger and thumb hooked into the handles with their blades swinging free.

I hid the cut up pieces of photograph beneath the wooden chopping board which mother always kept on the table. Then I saw the tiny screw that had worked loose from the joint of the scissor blades. It was very difficult to get the screw back in place but I persevered. I was so absorbed in my task that I had not noticed mother entering the kitchen. She laughed when she saw what I was doing. That screw's always falling out, she said, aren't you clever fixing it for me!

Later, I was playing on the balcony when I heard her terrible cry and I knew she had discovered the ruined photograph. Father taped it together and pinned it back on the wall and mother told me calmly not to touch it again. But I saw the look of anguish my parents exchanged, and in that instant the truth was revealed to me. Everything was broken. Nothing anyone did to mend things could ever really fix them. Even brand new things could not escape the process of destruction from the moment they were made.

This revelation included myself and mother and father and the glass in the window and the blue sky which I saw now was already so worn out that it would soon be gone forever. I had no words to describe the fear I felt. I accepted this truth as a child accepts the existence of ghosts and monsters. And what is more, I knew that seeing ghosts or monsters would be preferable to this pretence of permanence which I now saw in everything around me.

I clenched my fists at my sides. My parents were unaware of the danger we were in. I made a great effort to moisten my lips and try to think of something to say that would provoke some counter argument, some kind of grown-up trick to keep things glued together forever. My chest was tight. My throat felt sore. I opened my mouth hoping the right words would come. But the name who had chosen me because we sounded the same began chuckling in my lungs. And I had to turn away from mother and father and hold my hand over my mouth to contain his noisy splutterings.

My sister's pretty face was scarred and as the tape dried and curled, the extent of the damage I had done seemed even worse than at first. I kept watch on the scissors, frequently testing the blades for looseness, turning a kitchen knife in the groove before the screw could fall out. I kept watch on mother. I hurried to tighten the scissors before she got to the kitchen table where she used them to cut up bay leaves and cabbages, lumps of fat and the glowing sheets of pressed dried fruits which she dissolved into her winter soups.

*

The Khrushchev banners were roped to the cranes and diggers, fraying and bleaching as the builders worked in all weathers, cutting terraces into the rocky slopes around Tbilisi to organise the wild scrub lands into practical order. Nikita scattered grit and sand and his face was flushed with pinkly yellow stains thrown up from the sulphurous mud of the construction sites. The wind rarely managed to entice any sort of movement across his features. The tower blocks came straight out of the churned earth and stones. Complete suburbs were built in months. We were amongst the first to pass along the

wide straight road with its trolley bus tracks and plantations of
fir trees to secure the base of the disturbed hillsides. We were
the first chosen to stroll along such an avenue and peer into the
vast plate glass windows of collective food shops and dentists'
clinics. To pause and stare down into the great open trough
where the metro tunnel would begin. We had been selected to
live in a settlement of towers known as Nutzubidze Plateau,
named after the flat expanse of land topping the newly terraced hillside.

The lift had not yet been connected to the power supply
when we moved in so we had to climb the twenty storey staircase, stopping for breath now and then. We peered from the
narrow slits in the outer wall to views of other towers, pale and
flattened in the bright sunshine, and the radiant gaps between
them where nothing seemed to exist.

Our furniture had already been delivered to the apartment
and it stood about looking self-consciously old fashioned. The
apartment was filled with a light such as I had never seen
before. The light made me feel weightless and wide open as
the windows and the balcony door. I slid over the parquet
floor and ran from room to room. Then I helped father drag
things into place and held a chair while he fixed up the crystal chandelier. Mother was in the bathroom turning the tap on
and off to see the geyser flame up and die down.

I was certain it was no accident that we had been allocated
the top floor where there was only the one apartment, only our
door in the small square landing at the top of the long flight of
polished concrete steps. This separate floor occupied only by
my family was for me. It was for my security. This high up, we
were out of reach with only the sky pouring through the windows, only the birds flying below, only the wind filling my ears

with its meaningless sounds. I noticed how the television stand was wobbling on the parquet blocks so I folded a sheet of newspaper and tucked it beneath the shorter leg. I helped mother unpack the kitchen things. I took the scissors out to the balcony and tightened up the loose screw with my thumbnail.

From her first job of cleaning a public library floor, which would have shone with the ardour of her polishing, Vera had been promoted through the ranks from shelving books to becoming head librarian. The shelves of her small library were filled with dully coloured clothbound volumes whose contents were not in Georgian script but in closely typed cyrillic. I was not very interested in these books, although she encouraged me to read the volumes she brought home, many of them poetry. There was one in particular which she never remembered to return to its library shelf. She was at the kitchen table reading from it when she called me to her and with a serious face asked me to sit down and listen while she explained something important.

During the People's Revolution, she said, a group of young poets in Tbilisi decided to call themselves the Blue Horns. Everyone was naming and colouring themselves back then. It was to show how modern they were, how adventurous everything was going to be.

I fidgeted but she held me by both arms, looking into my face as she spoke. The Blue Horns wrote a personal, romantic, melancholy sort of poetry referring to Georgia as the original Eden with its peoples as keepers of their timeless Paradise. But despite their Revolutionary fervour the poets of Tbilisi had no interest in burdening their landscape with tractors or cement factories or smelting plants, said mother, nor in carving it up with canals and railroads and highways.

My gaze slipped through the window to where the towers stood firm against the racing sky. To my child's eye they seemed a true Paradise. Each tower contained more Edens than any line of mother's poems could encompass.

Death is coming ... Where is he bound, where has he been? Those are Paolo Iashvili's words, she said sighing and closing the Anthology. Sit still! I haven't finished yet. Paolo and his friend Titian Tabidze were the main force behind the Blue Horns. Boris Pasternak, who has only just died, mother said, stroking the cover of her book, came down from Moscow and fell in love with these funny, sad and dreamy poets with their beautiful wives and their clever children, and he also fell in love with our Tbilisi. They went on holidays together to the Black Sea. They paddled and laughed and made plans to visit Paris or New York for the jazz clubs, the modern art, the Ford cars, the latest fashions and a dance they called the jitterbug. And so they lived and wrote their letters and prose and poems as if there was nothing to fear. And yet a plague of fear fell across the land and terror's thorns poisoned all speech and all writing and all thought.

Are you listening? said mother, holding up the Anthology to keep my attention. In nineteen thirty-seven Paolo Iashvili was given the choice of denouncing his beloved friend Titian Tabidze or being taken and tortured by the secret police. Paolo took himself to the Writers Union headquarters, he took himself up the marble steps, his hand clutching something beneath his baggy jacket, his tie askew, his handsome face damp with tears. He took himself into the office where Stalin's portrait hung in pride of place. And there in front of his literary comrades Paolo took out the hunting rifle from under his jacket and shot himself dead.

A few months later the secret police came for Titian. They

dragged him away in front of his family. They tortured him until he confessed his anti-Soviet activities. My accomplice? Titian laughed in his interrogators' faces as he named a poet from the eighteenth century. His wife Nino held her stolen love in her heart and every day that passed she thought of him surviving in some distant gulag. Pasternak risked organising a petition to Beria pleading for clemency but the years turned in silence and even the explosions of the Great Patriotic War could not break through this silence.

I was by now caught up in mother's story. I could see that Stalin smiling down from the wall and I wanted to stop the man with the rifle and make him run back to his friend and plan their escape.

Why didn't they run away? I asked.

They just couldn't leave Tbilisi, she replied, and then when Titian was taken his family had to stay and wait in case he came back home. It's not so long since Stalin died, mother said in a low whisper, and it's only a few years ago that Nino got the news. She's an old lady now but everyone says it hit her very hard. Titian had been executed soon after he was taken. He was dead all those years she'd been waiting for him to come home.

I pulled away from her and stamped my foot. That's not fair! I cried.

No, it wasn't, said mother, but that time of terror is over now. I'm only telling you so you'll understand the power of words. They were poets! Now then Iosif, don't look so worried. Just be careful what you say. Understand? And now that you're a big boy I'll tell you a very nice secret. There's a baby on the way. What d'you think about us calling him Paolo if he's a boy?

Like that crying poet?

He was a hero.

She glanced out to the towers around the yard where the window panes were polished black. The dead poet lay bleeding on the floor, his shotgun still smoking in my mind. I shivered as I saw motionless faces behind some of those sun blackened windows. I had seen such faces engraved into gleaming black marble headstones. Their yearning eyes followed me as I passed the cemetery on the way to school.

*

The baby who came home with Vera was jaundiced and had no hair and his eyes looked too pale when they opened. He cried in his sleep. He cried as she walked him up and down the apartment. He cried when she fed him and cried as father bathed him in the evenings to give mother a rest. Without his swaddling he was a long thin baby with blue veins under his skin and visible ribs heaving in and out with his yells. I was the only one who could calm him. Perhaps I held him so tightly that he had no breath for crying. I always kept my mouth shut and I never spoke close to his face or made any sounds or singing, because the safety I had felt in our new apartment had proved false.

A few weeks after moving in father had come home with a mirror for the bathroom but he had forgotten that we did not possess a tool box or a supply of nails or screws. The all-in-one cupboard units, the sinks, the toilet on its plinth, the sky blue tiles on the bathroom and kitchen walls, the radiators, the hot water supply system and the State Radio speaker had come pre-fitted in the apartment and there had been no need to think of tools until now.

Father propped the mirror on the little sink and mother came to admire it but I could not bear to see it leaning so precariously behind the taps. I took a kitchen knife and unscrewed one of the screws in the wardrobe door in my bedroom. It was an old wardrobe and the hinges were loose and the screw came out easily and made no difference to the door. The plaster in the bathroom wall was soft enough for me to fix the screw into it with my knife blade. I hung the mirror up and stood back to see if it was straight. He smiled at me in the silver glass.

I kept very still but he did not go away. I understood now that he had never been away, he was living in the home of me and he liked it there. I reached out and tweaked the butterfly patterned plastic frame until it was hanging absolutely straight. And I nodded to him and promised I would keep him safe. I went out to the landing and waited for the lift mechanism to whirr and watched the guide pulley turn and the hoisting cable slip through its groove as the motor vibrated in the metal box hanging from the ceiling above the shaft. If I leant over the bannister rail and squinted down the narrow drop between the turns I could see the top of the head of whoever had been using the lift. These head tops became as known to me as the tops of our towers must have been to the eagles who passed over and out to the plains beyond in search of field voles.

One day my brother stopped crying and from then on he was a self-possessed baby, happy to sit propped in father's television chair gazing around from eyes as grey as the towers outside our windows. His hair grew blond, and mother and father looked at him with bewildered admiration. No-one was blond in either of their families. Very few Georgians are blond, except occasionally in some of the more remote tribes of the

High Caucasus. His blondness set him apart. The second thing that made my parents shake their heads and smile was that little Paolo responded only to the diminutive, Poliko. He simply hid his eyes behind his fists unless we said the name he wanted and would not remove them until we did.

Did he know what he was refusing? Could the baby have rejected the sorrow attached to that poet's name? Was this pale little being already attempting to change the course of his life? When my brother was born I had lived for seven years with a steel man alive inside me and the weight lay heavy in my chest. I wonder, if like my brother I had refused my given name during that brief period of my infancy, would our fates have been different? Would all the sorrow that was to overwhelm us not have been? Might I have lived like any other man, with only his private thoughts? I have never known such privacy. My house guest peeked into my mind. His shadow chilled my heart and fell over all who came near me.

*

Although Khrushchev was now General Secretary and Stalin was in the process of being discredited, his image was still taped to the dashboards of taxis. He was glued on the tin walled huts for road workers. He sweated above the controls in locomotive cabs and flight decks. He fluttered on the hot pipes of submarines and warships where the crew stood to attention on the sea-swept decks. His expression was benignly stern. He wore a peasant's tunic of bleached calico or a plain military jacket of khaki serge. If his hands were visible they would be gesturing towards some unseen achievement or one hand would be raised in acknowledgement of the unseen workers.

There were many larger than life bronze or stone Stalins set on plinths in public squares and gardens, but these three-dimensional Stalins meant little to me. Birds sat upon his head and left their droppings on his face. Dry leaves caught in the folds of his great-coat. Dust accumulated around his boots and when it rained he stood in muddy pools. When it snowed he wore a pointed white hat and white gloves and when it froze he wept icicles. The seasons made him clownish. And the statues had only the dull tones of their material, no avid strokes of pink to the cheeks, no touch of velvet brown to the eyes.

No, it was the framed Stalins that I worried about, for these painted or photographic portraits were mirrors and I had looked into mirrors and seen the mist of breath forming upon the glass.

At school we studied what our teachers called the unfortunate famines and the necessary purges, the over-subscribed labour camps and the mass migrations. We were taught how Revolutionary Necessity had forced Stalin and his cohorts to invent over-enthusiastic methods of dealing with an excess of mouths to feed. There were quotas of arrests to fulfil, and yes, it is true that tens of millions died. And after all the deaths and all the hard work we are still not safe, said our teachers.

Don't think you can relax dear little Pioneers, the teachers warned, for the Imperialist forces are out to destroy our great achievements. Missiles are at this very moment speeding towards the Motherland. It is only by the will of the masses that the nuclear warheads are deflected into outer space. The Capitalists possess limitless weapons. The night sky is not filled with stars but with spying lenses, pinpointing your home and following your route to school. Their bombs are aimed at you. It will happen in a flash. Get under the desk and put on this gas mask.

We live in an age of mutual cooperation. We are healthy and we follow the great plan. Divided into five-year segments of short but athletic leaps, the race to attain our glorious future shall be won. Each set of five years will bring greater yield as the roots of progress sink deeper into the Motherland's beneficial earth.

So they spoke, my teachers, while Stalin smiled behind fly-specked glass tilting at a vigilant angle from the wall. We stood to attention with our fake machine guns at our shoulders, our perished gas masks clamped to our faces and our red neckerchiefs knotted tight around our throats.

But I, an unheroic Pioneer, knew more than the wisest of our teachers, for I alone had felt the clicking of his fingers and the snorting of his breath as my same-named visitor scoffed at their fears of invasion from the West. I knew from my sighting of the cow's lungs how Iosif Dzhugashvili's blood ran always warm. The true enemy of progress lived on inside my chest. I heard him tapping at my ribs. Sneering at Nikita's homely building works.

*

Unlike most of the families in our tower my parents were not close to their relatives. Givi had lost two brothers in the Great Patriotic War and Vera was an only child. Both had come originally from Rustavi, an industrial town to the east of Tbilisi. Vera had inherited the tiny flat in the old quarter from an Aunt who had come to Tbilisi, found work as a hospital orderly and died of typhoid fever. When they were allocated the new apartment the old flat passed on to a distant relative from her Aunt's cousin's line. These inheritances were not formal as all property belonged to the State, but there were unspoken family codes that not even Communism could interfere with.

And perhaps my parents were haunted by the way Tiniko had died. Perhaps they blamed themselves for not staying in Rustavi where they could have lived in one of the new industrial workers' dwellings, the forerunners of settlements like ours, and perhaps that distance between them and their remaining families was something to do with this. They had come to the Capital to better themselves. Vera's work as head librarian and Givi's position of trolley bus timetable controller were far above their relatives' status, who worked in a meat processing plant specialising in spiced offal sausages.

The towers unified thousands of families who had been invited from the villages, from the old quarters of the city, from provincial towns. Different customs and quirks of speech were ironed out in the stacks of identical apartments. Productive days flew by in the new work places – the bakeries, the breweries, the plastic toy workshops, the piano factory and the cigarette packing plants. No-one here could be accused of being a Parasite On The State, as you would be branded if you did not work. The tenants had been awarded their modern apartments because they had achieved more than the required quota on a sun-parched collective farm. They had surpassed the planned harvest of lemons and oranges in the semi-tropical orchards. They had managed the smooth regulation of an ambitious schedule of pipe laying, had overseen a three-dimensional map set with tiny lights, had kept the tiny lights flashing, had proved that the five-year plan was going as planned. This is what I learned in school.

The builders had left heaps of rubble, half dismantled cranes, stacks of unused pre-formed concrete slabs which soon became playgrounds for the children of the settlement. And along with these wild places were areas with swings and roundabouts, walled in with mosaic scenes of children playing on similar structures. There were blue tiled paddling pools where the water was never allowed to become slimy. The steeply terraced hillside soon became marked with shortcut tracks. No-one going on foot used the damp tarmac road which zigzagged in long angles between the towers.

We dropped our rubbish into a chute on the landing below ours and never thought where it went or what happened to it. The toilet cistern flushed with a great gush of water which gurgled away down the twenty-storey drain pipe. We had a constant supply of hot water and gas central heating and bathed as often as we wanted.

It's all free of charge! Givi liked to repeat, as he turned up the heating even on warm days.

Little Poliko took a lot of my parents' attention and I liked nothing better than being out on the balcony alone. There I would stand gazing out at the ranks of towers rising on the terraces towards a yellowish haze emanating from the plateau. I checked the opposite windows for stranger's faces. I cocked an ear to the conversations on the balconies below, for I had not forgotten mother's warning about the power of words. I peered down from my bird's-eye view into the dusty vault where I observed my neighbours' comings and goings and more especially who they were with. And if the tang of that cigarette smoke drifting up to my nostrils was an American brand I made a mental note of the smoker's name. I was correct in every fibre of my young body. For if I were not, if I let slip my guard I knew that the overarching sky, which encased the Motherland like a protective glass dome, would be shattered by the high-pitched sound waves of my namesake's mocking giggles.

To work for the common good, to move forwards together, to be united in defending the Motherland, these were the binding rules which I imbibed and believed in from the bottom of my heart. This kind of Communism had swept us from the disease-ridden past into this hygienic present and I adored the twenty storeys of unbroken stairways, the smoothly operating lifts, the soft hissing from the overground hot water pipes, the low eternal hum from the electricity transformer that was hidden in a small walled compound near the foot of my tower.

*

Here is a bright summer's day. The surrounding blocks twinkle as the sunlight catches and reflects on the particles of mica in the cement facades, the windows shine with broken patterns of blue sky and the surrounding towers.

Poliko comes out and jumps to see over the railings so I pick him up and hold him tight. The wind knocks me back for a moment, dizzying in its force and intent. But I am used to it and it does not frighten me. I open my mouth and let the dry air come in. Look, I tell my little brother, pointing to a distant rectangle of gold beneath an aerial walkway bridging two of the farthest towers. The gold shivers. Then a cloud of dust obscures it and there comes a faint roar of engines and when the dust settles the gold has gone. Wheat harvest, I tell Poliko.

He wriggles free and runs back inside and I close my eyes and breathe in the smell of chaff and disturbed earth and cement dust. The balcony vibrates beneath my feet with each gust of wind.

I will be your guard, I whisper to the towers and I pull myself more upright and raise my chin.

A face watches at every window. Men stand on their balconies, wisps of cigarette smoke forming around their mouths and taken on the wind. Vertical strips of sky hang white between the blocks to the far reaches of the settlement.

Once more, in a flash, that little rectangle of wheaten gold appears beneath the aerial walkway. The combine harvester passes across the gold and is gone. The tannoys click and buzz from their posts in the yards below. The combine harvester appears again passing over the diminishing gold under the aerial walkway.

I hold tight to the balcony rails. My lips are burning because now the tannoys are ready and a song fills up my ears. I have been told I am tone deaf but I am singing a beautiful melody as the combine harvester passes back and forth with its fumes shimmering in a yellow haze below the aerial walkway.

I am a boy breathing wheat chaff and concrete dust. I hide a frightening name in my lungs. I have been warned that my voice is terrible. I know that my name is listening and does not approve. But I must open my mouth and let the songs of Georgia pour forth.

*

I do not know if my parents ever noticed the strain I lived under. How do you say that your ribs are the bars of a prison? How does a boy of nine explain the tapping at these bars? Or the curled up form of a disgraced hero snuggling under the red quilt of his lungs?

Givi was in charge of the trolley bus timetables for the lines running from our suburb into the city. He had taped up a sheet of paper in the tiny hallway of our apartment, and he spent hours poring over it, rubbing out the grids and rewriting his system of numerals and signs. The runners often fell from the overhead lines and the trolley would block the way until the driver re-fixed the long flashing prongs, so Givi was always in a state of dismay, his carefully worked out timetable always running late. Vera claimed that he secretly enjoyed this task. She used to call the hallway his office and would sometimes go to him there and peer over his shoulder with distracting suggestions. I do not recall my parents ever arguing. Now I see them there with the coat rack and the shoe cupboard crowding at their backs. A dim orange light from the plastic shade. They look as young as they had been in the photograph I had ruined. Vera has her black hair done up in a complicated knot. Givi has taken off his spectacles and turns to her.

Alright? he asks.

I was just remembering . . .

He holds her, his face buried in her neck, her head thrown back a little. They are both quite tall and slender, and they rock in a private rhythm which sends me tiptoeing away.

I went to the balcony to wait for father. It was a public holiday and he had promised to take me to his depot. I understood that he wanted me to be like him and this visit was to show me where to start. Military marches came thumping from the tannoys. The towers flickered with laundry and the glassy sheen of this white sky windy day. I did not often have the chance to be alone with father. I concentrated on the leaden music. But I could not hide the hope beating in my heart.

We came to the far side of the settlement, a flat expanse of concrete slabs grooved with tracks and overhung with cables. Blue-grey trolley buses with their runners pulled flat. Father wanted to show me the control room where he worked but the gate to the inner compound was locked for the holiday, so we stood in the yard with the trolleys and the damp wind carrying faint bars of marching from the distant tannoys. It began to rain.

Father tugged open the door to the driver's compartment in one of the trolleys. He let me sit at the controls while he perched on the box over the engine and lit up a cigarette. The wind rattled the door. Rain pounded the tin roof and smeared the windscreen. I gripped a shiny handle.

That's right son, that's the way to do it, he said.

Dad, I said quickly, there's something I've got to tell you about my . . .

It was then that I saw the Stalin pasted by the control panel. He was small and crinkled but not so much that I did not see his familiar smile and his hand raised in that encouraging salute. I screwed my eyes shut and opened them quickly to check I had not been mistaken, for there was something in his appearance which made my heart beat with fear. His hair and moustache were a lurid orange, his skin was lime green, his mouth and eyes were chalk white, and those spot-light eyes were aimed directly at me.

No, it's nothing, I muttered.

Alright my lad. One day when you're grown up you'll drive one of these around the city. How does that sound to you! Come on, let's get back home now.

In my boy's heart I hated those ugly trolley buses, their greasy seats, their draughty doors, the windswept yard, the oily puddles, the grooved tracks filled with dirty rain. We plodded home in silence.

He may be very small. He may be locked behind my ribs.

He may not have a voice to shout his disapproval. But he had the freedom of colours. And what was I if not a sponge of blood red and wheaten yellow and concrete grey? Now I understood that the hues of my region were not to be trusted. All outward appearance was saturated with inner intent. I had been warned what would happen to the look of me if I attempted to expose him again.

*

I do not remember crying. I believe I did not cry as a child. Poliko made up for my dry eyes. He gave vent to his feelings without restraint. Tears came easily and as often as his laughter. Despite his blondness and pale skin he always felt hot to the touch and he hated the sun. But the burning passion of his tears was nothing compared to the purity of his singing voice.

From an early age my brother was able to hold a line with perfect pitch. We learned our folk songs at nursery and school and at the Young Pioneers meetings we attended. I knew every one by heart. Each song was a place where I could forget who I was. I sang these songs until my throat hurt and mother would call me in from the balcony and sit me down in front of an Armenian cowboy film on television.

Why don't you invite a friend in to watch it with you? She'd suggest.

And I would slip out of the apartment and take the lift down to the yard and run to the electricity transformer where I leant against the wall and let the low humming fill my brain.

I do not know if Vera saw anything odd in me as a boy. My parents depended on me to look after Poliko if they had to work late shifts, so they must have trusted me. Yes, there was a time when they must have trusted me.

Now, as I sit alone, no longer a child, watching this reel of tape spin too quickly toward its end, I cannot tell if this humming in my ears is the sound of memory or the imperceptible note of my tape recorder motors. I would like to have interspersed this narrative with song, but I have only my own tone deaf voice to depend on and I do not think it worthy of wasting precious tape.

*

When Poliko discovered that he could wriggle into the mounds of builders' rubble I was the only one who could get him to come out. My parents were not aware he was playing this dangerous game. Children ran wild in the yards. Parents called down occasionally from the balconies and their children called back up and that was all that was required to keep some thread of contact.

He would not come out when the boys of his own age chanted for him, nor when the little girls sang for him to play with them. Everyone wanted to be with him, even when he was that stubborn seven-year-old child. They would plead with him to come out. They were afraid for him too, hiding under the unstable blocks of concrete, shards of metal and lumps of mud.

I sat on the edge of the mound and cleared my throat. The other kids scattered with calls of, Run, Iosif's going to sing! But I ignored them and began a long song I had just learned and had fallen in love with. Yes, I can say it was love I felt for those old songs. I had not got further than the second verse when I heard Poliko singing with me. He did not bother with the words but used his young vocal chords like a flute in counterpoint to my melody.

I knew that my voice was all wrong. But to my ears, especially when Poliko sang with me, I could hear nothing but the right notes and the correct intervals and which phrases to draw out or which to emphasise with a quavering in the back of the throat. We came to the end of the song and I lit up a cigarette and held it so that the smoke would drift in to Poliko. Sure enough he came crawling out. I gave him a drag and he grinned and I wiped the grime from his face.

Don't take any notice of them, I like your singing, he said putting his skinny arm around my shoulder as we sat on the rubble.

*

Our evening bath water rocked from the wind slapping at the walls of our tower. We slept in the same room and shared the creaking wardrobe. Our beds were so close that when Poliko was older we could reach across and light each other's cigarettes.

I had by now collected a few indispensable tools, among them a rusty saw I had found discarded amongst the builders' rubble in our settlement, a pair of pliers I had come across at the back of an empty drawer in the workshop of the Palace of Youth and an electrician's screwdriver I had bought in the State Department Store with the few kopecks I saved from doing odd jobs for our neighbours in the tower. Mostly I did these little tasks for nothing, mending a broken bell on a hallway door for example, without waiting to be asked.

I was using my screwdriver blade to scrape at the contacts in the slots of the tape recorders' batteries where an oxidised plaque had accumulated. The tape recorder came from the Palace of Youth, where Poliko and I attended music classes while other Pioneers studied martial arts, scientific experiment or traditional crafts and dance, before moving to the next step of Komsomol and the study of more advanced skills.

I had wanted to join the Pioneers' choir with Poliko but after my audition the choir master had chosen me to be in charge of recording the performances. He pressed the tape machine into my hands and directed me to sit at the back of the hall.

I do not recall the name of that comrade, but in giving me that tape recorder he gave me the tool I had been waiting for. It was a simple model meant for children's use without the refinements of the professional machine I have before me now as I record this testimony. Despite the basic operations of that Pioneer's recorder I was entranced by the slowly diminishing reel of tape and the equally expanding reel on the opposite spool. I loved the tiny perspex window over the panel where a red needle flickered with every nuance of sound. I could recall in perfect detail the diagram I had studied in the *Youthful* journal where frequencies and pressure waves spread across the page from an opened mouth to the inbuilt microphone of just such a tape recorder. When I depressed the record button I pictured the particles of magnetic iron oxide lining up to express each nuance of sound. Copper coil and magnetic iron. Electric motors and plastic tape. Oscillations and amplification. I knew these terms were fact. And yet at the same time I believed that the two spools were lungs and that I was meant to fill them up with song.

I sat clutching the whirring machine. Between me and the stage were rows of empty seats. General Secretary Brezhnev hung beneath the hammer and sickle, Khrushchev between the red flags. The Stalin hung alone, looking across the auditorium at his successors. Poliko stepped out from the choir and sang his solo part and the recording needle hovered perfectly still.

I am a Pioneer ready to be Komsomol. I know how to fix things that are broken. Our balcony has developed a crack in the concrete base which I have covered with a piece of linoleum. This makes my footsteps softer when I step out to guard the settlement. I have also wired a length of the same linoleum to the rails. It is parquet patterned but no matter, it keeps me out of sight when I crouch down. It is quite comfortable in that place in the corner of the balcony where the rails meet the wall of our apartment. From there I listen to the voices drifting upward on the breeze, from there I peep down to check the names belonging to conversations which need reporting.

My linoleum also serves as a wind break if the balcony door is open, and it gives some protection to mother's growing collection of cacti arranged along a small bookcase which she has placed on the balcony especially for this purpose. When I suggested to her that the bookcase would be ruined by rain, she replied that everything has two purposes, one is obvious but the other mysterious. She said that I should go and play with the boys in the yard. But I am too old for play now. I have work to do. I have my little brother to look after. He refuses to take anything seriously. Even these Saturdays at the Palace of Youth, where he has learned to dance and fight with a dagger and has the lead part in the choir, seem not to matter to him. I watch the red needle flicker and drop as Poliko's voice fades away to a hush that has fallen over his audience.

I slip from the concert hall as soon as the rehearsal is over and hurry up the grand staircase to the office where my Komsomol leader will be waiting for my report. The pressure in my chest as I walk the corridor. My throat drying so I can hardly swallow. The tightness in my stomach. My fingertips turning to ice. A special smile fixes on my lips. The air hisses from my nostrils. I knock on the door and enter and the Komsomol, who is not much older than me, beckons me forwards.

I had been walking from my tower block settlement in the suburbs to the end of Rustaveli Avenue where the Communist Party Headquarters were decked with Brezhnev banners. The workers were pollarding the plane trees and I paused for a moment to see the boughs falling.

I happened to glance across the road to where another line of trees was being cut. The church stood set back behind these trees, its doors open to a dim glow of yellow light. And it was then that I saw Vera walking in. I crossed the road, went to the church and peered inside to make sure. Figures moved about in the dark light. Candles hovered in molten clusters. I saw my mother bending her head and touching her fingers to an icon.

I made my report and the Komsomol wrote it in his ledger, congratulating me on my observations. There was more to tell, but I kept it to myself.

How could I explain that I had discovered that my mother not only went to church but had hidden God inside the tin cans where she grew her cacti? I was not inclined towards poetic imaginings. I had learned to live with an old man of steel inside my young chest and that had taught me to be practical and not give in to any hint of vagueness or to let down my guard in sentiment. So the dawning realisation that when mother touched her rusty cans and prodded at the stale earth she was communing with God, was hard for me to swallow.

31

I made a test. I secretly loosened the little wooden plugs that held the shelves of the bookcase on the balcony in place, so that the shelves were only balancing by the slightest amount. Sure enough the next time she went to tend her rows of tin cans, the shelves tipped and collapsed. I came hurrying out as if to see what had happened. I did not mean to be a bad son. I really did feel pity for her as she knelt amongst the grit and broken stubs of cacti. She murmured some soft words that I could not make out and then she crossed herself and began scooping the earth back into the cans. I asked if I could help, but she looked up at me with something strange in her eyes.

Go away Iosif, she said, I can manage.

I bit my lip. But he howled inside my lungs and his laughter came bubbling from my throat. I could never report the full story. And I could never, would never, report that Stalin was alive and happy in my chest. Vera brought her cacti inside after the collapse of her bookshelf.

*

A note on hospitality. The symbol of our national character, Mother Georgia stands looking out over Tbilisi on the rock-strewn ridge where ancient fortifications hang above the botanical gardens and the sulphur baths. Her voluptuous cast-aluminium form is of gigantic proportions. She holds a sword in one hand and a bowl of wine in the other, a being who will fight to the death to protect our homeland from all invaders, and yet who is also honour bound to offer sustenance and shelter to each and every passing stranger.

Within a few months of opening their doors to the lucky comrades who came to live in the towers, the apartments in our block were filled with extra family members who had not been on the official list. Nobody thought this wrong. Make-shift living arrangements are second nature to a Georgian. We will improvise any useable surface into a bed or a table or chair to accommodate visitors. Generations live together in harmony, building invisible walls around sleeping quarters, invisible doors between a young married couple and grandparents. My family were unusual in not having anyone else to live with us, but if anyone had turned up my parents would have welcomed them without a murmur. This is why my Georgian nature did not allow me to turn away my lodger. Even if I had been able, that is, to extricate him from the spongy mass of my lungs.

When I was young I did not question his right to stay or his constant presence. He was the man who never went out. The guest who sat around in the most comfortable armchair. I never forgot the nightmarish colours of that Stalin on the trolley bus control panel. I knew by now that the change of his hue had been caused by pigment degradation and that in time I too would be worn away by the vapours of his sighs. He would break through the look of me and one day I would awake with his barrel chest, his jowls, his droopy moustache, his crop of greying hair, his kindly crinkling eyes.

And there were the sparkling towers and the black ribbons of sky between, and hovering beyond the dark glass I saw my face with his smile perched comfortably upon my lips.

I dragged the chair to reach the wooden chandelier with its three arms missing. I had secured the ends of the loose wires with insulating tape. The remaining arm had a cracked light fitting and every now and then I pushed the bulb back into the socket.

*

The settlement divided into regions bounded along the over-ground snake of a water pipe, around the car parking posts, between ditches of running rain water, centred on a communal laundry block or the frontage of a collective produce shop. Each region was quickly occupied by the gangs of so-called legal criminals who sorted out neighbourly disputes, provided special cuts of meat for weddings, foreign shoes that would not fall apart, lycra tracksuits, toys and electric goods from West Germany, small arms, hunting rifles and drugs. No-one thought the worse of these gangs or their leaders. They mostly acted with good grace and were not usually themselves drug addicts or alcoholics.

This is the way of life. To be working. To be in forward motion for the five-year plan. To be united in fulfilling the required quota. We had arrived in an era of mutual cooperation where legal criminals worked in harmony with the police.

Alik looked after our region. I had known him since moving in to the towers. He was two years younger than me but was already a prize-winning wrestler, respected for his good manners and fairness. He favoured the weak, protected children who might otherwise fall victim to bullying, and he was always courteous to women and correct to the elders, driving them to market and carrying their bags of produce. Many a young comrade wanted to be in his gang, but he was choosy, inviting those who appeared indifferent. If anyone was in serious trouble they went to him before the police. He settled arguments. Handed out gifts of genuine Scotch whisky.

Alik had been a boy who always seemed to be a man. He had never teased me about my singing as the other children had. Had never yelled my name from a balcony so the entire settlement could hear and laugh at the incongruity of me, the short and round-faced boy with the famous steel man's name. But although I had nothing against Alik I did not want Poliko to get involved with him. I had other plans for my brother. His voice had become even more extraordinary as he reached adolescence.

*

The Voice of America leaks from the gap between the transistor radio and Poliko's ear. He is thirteen. Fourteen. Fifteen. He lies on his bed staring at the ceiling, mouthing the words to Western pop songs.

Poliko began to spend a lot of time with a lad called Victor who lived three floors below us. Victor was a couple of years younger than Poliko, he looked up to my brother, imitated his gestures and even tried to sing like him, although his voice did not have the same compelling timbre. Victor's family had done well. They had a new colour television and a VHS tape player. I knew very well what Poliko and Victor were up to in that apartment full of the latest equipment, while the parents were at work. Once, Poliko had invited me to join them. Victor fiddled with the VHS controls, slotted a tape cassette in and pressed play. I sat on the edge of the plush settee, torn between leaving and the desire to familiarise myself with this new technology. The television screen sprang into life but the picture quality was terrible. I made a few suggestions on how to tune the set, but Victor sniggered and said he had paid a lot for the tape and it would soon stabilise. Poliko was leaning intently toward the television, his face alight with anticipation. The wavering picture cleared somewhat. A Russian voice in nasal monotone began reciting the film title and the actors. *The Godfather. Marlon Brando.*

Switch it off! I demanded. Give me that tape. Poliko, you should know better.

But they shushed me and slouched back on the settee, intent on watching the black-market film. The disguised monotone of the dubbed voice was hypnotic. It insinuated the drama into my brain and I was compelled to sit there and allow the story to reel out before my eyes. But when at last the film came to its climactic end and Poliko and Victor applauded I set my face into an expression of scientific interest and asked if I could examine the VHS machine.

Wait, said Poliko. The best is still to come, there'll be a *pop-video* on the last part of the tape. Watch!

Now the screen flickered with brilliant colours. A pearly beach. Bright blue sky. Huge rolling waves gathering foam and roaring towards the sand, where groups of scantily clad youths stood holding long flat objects under their arms. The skin of these young men and woman was burnt orange and their hair so blond that it appeared to have no pigment. As they ran towards the sea carrying their shelf-like burdens a song came from nowhere and the running group began mouthing the words. In the background, with their feet dancing on the scorching sand, four long-haired men played guitars and grinned whist also singing the words to the song. I rose to leave.

Wait, don't go yet, said Poliko. Can't you imagine being there on that beach forever? No school. No work. No-one checking on you. No walls!

He turned up the volume and danced around me, imitating the gyrations of the boys on the screen. The waves exploded in spumes of white bubbles. A beautiful girl, her breasts half out of her swimsuit rolled and splashed in the turquoise water.

Figures stood on a distant wave and were swept towards the beach, their arms outspread as if flying. The boards beneath their feet lifting and swooping on the foam and carrying them onwards in a great arcing union with sun and water and beach. I had never seen such a vivid expression of energy. I could hardly contain the laughter that wanted to spill out and bubble like the foamy waves. I cleared my throat. Made my speech. Warned Victor that although I had sat with him and watched the film, I did not approve. He must know his parents could get into trouble if it were discovered that they had these illegal tapes in their apartment. Victor shrugged and said that his parents already knew and didn't mind. My mum loves Marlon Brando, he said. I tutted and shook my head. A small but persistent pain had begun to nag at the back of my eyes.

Poliko had re-wound the tape to the start of the extra footage. The brilliant white waves. The scorching beach. The beautiful youngsters. He was singing along with the jaunty song. Holding out his arms and flexing his knees in imitation of that speedy balancing act upon the ocean.

He is sixteen. Seventeen. Handsome, gangling, pale.

He did not have a regular girlfriend but was already experienced with sex. He had been all the way, he smirkingly confided, as though I too had done the same. But I had not yet touched a girl. I was busy with my work at the Institute of Ethnography where I now had a permanent research post as a musicologist.

I had impressed my professors with my commitment to collecting songs from Tbilisi rather than taking the option of travelling to the far-flung regions of the Motherland as did so many of my fellow students. My, perhaps narrow, but nevertheless important archive had been rewarded with a desk in a basement office which I shared with another musicologist, Natalya, who specialised in Tushetian tribal songs and the cross-currents with neighbouring Chechnya, and consequently was usually away in the field.

My aim was to archive as many renditions of a song as I could find. Each had its merit, each played its part in our musical vocabulary. My preference was for unaccompanied voice, being more dependent on the naked mood of the singer, but this was only one aspect of my passion and I would never turn a deaf ear to any song. My tapes wound around the reedy tones of a *duduki*, my red needle jumped to the jangle of a three-stringed *panduri*. I captured Oriental monologues with camel train and silk and the rumour of Celtic mystery running through the flat-fingered drum beat tapping like rain beyond the song.

Sound itself can only be written as waves or pressure bars skimming across the page. I knew how to transcribe the tunes into musical notation of course, and my notebooks were filled with jottings on the nuance of lyrical invention. But it was my recordings that I cherished most of all. The first hand evidence. The unadulterated immediacy captured on magnetic tape. My portable recorder was the latest lightweight model with a transparent hinged lid and a leather carrying strap. A neat compartment at the back housed the batteries. The controls were miniaturised and yet retained fine degrees of tuning. The high quality of the recording head and the tuning gauge allowed me to obtain a lifelike effect, indeed the microphone was so sensitive it could pick up the faintest breath.

I came to think of the reels of tape as mine, as I came to think of the recording machine as mine, although I knew that this was an unworthy thought, for my archive and equipment belonged to the State and my Institute had shown a perfect example of the generosity our Motherland showered upon us. Her only requirement was that I fulfil a certain quota of recordings which I soon overtook at the beginning of each academic session. I stored my reels of tapes in slim brown boxes, the spools and boxes numbered and dated with a code I had devised, cross referencing with other recordings of the many versions of the same song.

*

A note on methodology. Givi owned a Lada which he drove to the trolley bus compound even though it would have been quicker to take the short cut across the settlement. He could not understand when I did not want him to teach me to drive, and I could not explain my memory of being trapped at the trolley bus wheel where the multicoloured Stalin had smiled me to silence.

I never wanted to own a car. No matter if my neck ached with the strain of the tape recorder where the strap hung on my shoulder as I walked the lanes and avenues of Tbilisi. It is as natural as breathing for a Georgian to sing. And to sing in counterpoint with others is one of a Georgian's greatest joys. I only need walk with my ears tuned to the city, passing the restaurants, the open windows of apartments, the workers perched high on a scaffold as they took their break, the peasants standing at their stalls in the collective markets, the steps of the University and technical colleges, the parks, the railway station, the metro entrances and beneath the great bowl of the sports stadium, to find my material. Indeed, once the singer or singers noticed me drawing closer with my microphone at the ready, they would often redouble the passion of their voice, re-complicate the interweaving harmonies, singing on without pause as their eyes flicked towards me and then nonchalantly away. I walked everywhere, always with a supply of batteries, a spare reel of tape, because time runs more quickly when carried onwards by song.

My suit meant I was able to fit in anywhere. I had been to the cobbled quarter on the east bank of the Mtkvari where the tailors sit behind the plate glass windows of their co-operatives. I had no real idea of style or cloth so I simply asked for a suit that would be unremarkable.

The tailor looked up from his sewing machine, his fingers still working the cloth through the little pool of light over the foot where the needle raced up and down. He called for his apprentice to take the measurements. I pointed vaguely to a bolt of pale grey fabric. The suit was ready in a few days. I thought it very smart but Poliko said it made me look like a secret agent. Well, the suit served my purpose and gave me just the right air of authority without being showy.

It was fortunate that I knew how to use a needle and thread though, because it was not long before I noticed small breaks in the stitching. The thread did not seem to be linked in the correct way, and if pulled it would unravel. No matter, I sewed the little breaks together whenever they appeared. Vera said I should take it back to the tailor. But I could not forget the incident that had occurred when I gave my name for the order. The tailor had suddenly stood up, allowing his cloth and scissors to fall to the floor as he rushed out of sight into some dingy little back room. I could not falsify my name you see. It was printed on my identity card which I must carry all the time.

My pale grey suit enabled me to blend in to the aura of

construction that was going on all over the city, even with the rather icy sheen that soon developed on the cloth, and the occasional gap in the seams where the stitching was sneakily coming apart.

I was the first in either of my parents' families to study at University, but they did not really understand the serious nature of my chosen profession. Once I caught father idly fingering the controls of my tape recorder. I had left it on the good table in the sitting room and he was jabbing at the buttons as if they were the crude controls of a trolley. The spool was turning and the recording playing back. A snatch of conversation, voices joking about a load of concrete one of them had driven from the site to his neighbour's backyard in return for a carboy of wine. I switched it off and father tutted and shook his head.

Listen Iosif, he said, I can get you a good post at the trolley bus depot, something with responsibility behind a desk. Why not think about it?

Don't! I snapped because his hand was reaching out to touch my shoulder and the seam was in need of repair at just that place. I mean, I went on hastily, don't worry about me. I'm doing alright. I shall be promoted soon enough.

We don't seem to see much of you these days, he said. Got a girl have you? Your mother and I would be happy if you have. Why don't you bring her home and we'll get to know each other?

What's wrong with your glasses? They're lopsided. Let me look.

I worked on his spectacles, the hinges had come loose, needing the closest of attention. While I was carrying them to the window for the better light, father had his say.

41

Alright son. But you be careful with that recorder of yours. You go around as though you can do what you like. But mark my words. Just because you've studied, it won't necessarily keep you safe. Look at your brother, he's not bothering with his exams and such, but he's going to be alright. He fits in. He's got the right attitude.

I handed him back his glasses and watched as he put them on, checked they sat level on his nose, our eyes meeting and holding in the passing of the ordinary early evening sounds, the normal tone of the twilight giving way to lamps, the pedlar calling up that he had potatoes for sale, good fresh potatoes just pulled from the earth, the heat of our radiators convecting from the windows and the net curtains following the stream, their dull white veils breathing dust onto the table and my tape recorder, and father standing there as though, suddenly, he saw me and wondered who I was in all this usual life. But just as the airstream passed from the windows, so the moment wafted to nothing and he went and sat in his chair and reached to turn on the television. Perhaps it was my fault for letting it pass, the clarity of unknowing, but it went away with the potato seller's call, fresh from the mud, as he wandered round the corner of our block and I thought that if we, father and I, had gone and bought the sackful and carried it up together, we might have said not so usual things to each other, things that had never been said before, things that had no place in the regular pendulum of the tower as it swayed and righted under the command of the wind. I even found myself glancing at my hands as though there might be incriminating mud stains, the silent odour of wet fields, the thumb prints of this stranger who was supposed to be my father's son.

I gathered up my tape recorder. Took it to the bedroom. Poliko, as expected, was lounging on his bed with his transistor clamped to his ear.

How many times? I began.

He sang some line of song aloud, grinning, mouthing some tuneless lines of words I knew he did not really understand.

Why don't you listen to something normal for once? What is it about those foreign songs anyway? You know those stations are illegal. Do you want to get us all into trouble?

Calm down comrade mine. Here, have a listen. Put your ear right next to the speaker. Now then, tell me you can't hear them laughing at us.

Who?

Them. Keep the radio if you like. I'll get another. It'll be good for you. Turn the dial. Go on it won't explode. Turn it the slightest touch to the right and you'll get Radio Free Europe.

I don't want it thanks. And you ought to know better.

Lean out of the window. That's right. Now hold it slightly tilted. Hear them?

If he had commanded me to leap from the twentieth storey I would have. His manner was utterly persuasive and yet he did nothing special. It was simply impossible to argue with him. I felt the edge of the window sill at my ribs. The muzz of air-waves jiggling in my ear. The KGB blocking devices spluttering and fading, only to gain control once more and the illegal song seeming to come from a land where everyone was gasping for breath.

Look here, Poliko, I said tearing myself away from the admittedly compulsive rhythms of that music, it's time to think about the future. I've got a place lined up for you at technical college number seven. No questions asked. You're already on the admissions role.

No thanks.

But you haven't even thought about it.

No need. I'm going to find work. I'll do anything. Maybe road sweeping if I can get into a brigade. Alik says he has a friend whose uncle works on the roads.

But you've got such a talent, you need to meet the right people and if you were studying you'd have some status to start with. And then in the future when you're a little older I'll set you up with the Musicians' Union. Don't turn away. You'll have to stop listening to this western rubbish. You could be a big hit with that voice of yours. Don't you feel any responsibility to share it with the masses?

He groaned and fell onto his bed and pulled his pillow over his face. I looked away. Counted three minutes. Screwed my eyes shut. Counted two more minutes. I spun round. No sign of breathing and his hands hanging loose over the edge of the bed. Poliko!

And just as I leant to sweep away the pillow he flung it from his face, laughing like a three-year-old. I always fell for this trick of his. Always doubted. Always laughed along with him at my fearfulness. We shared a cigarette. He watched me through the smoke with half closed eyes.

I meant it, he said. Take the radio.

At that moment mother called out that Victor was at the door and then the lad came into our room. He was obviously upset, red faced and dishevelled and on the point of tears. He stood there blinking and clenching his fists. Poliko made no move so I peered at Victor in a manner communicating sympathy and said he could tell me everything and I would sort

44

the problem out. But he shook his head and drew a sobbing breath. Poliko stubbed out his cigarette, got up unhurriedly from the bed and in the same casual way slung one arm around Victor's shoulder and steered him out.

I waited at the window. They soon appeared in the yard. Poliko's arm still slung over Victor's shoulder. Alik coming toward them and shaking Poliko by the hand. I called down, What's up? But they walked away, the three of them side by side, no more than the idea of human shapes from this height, in the darkening air up here at the twentieth floor and the black caps of the mercury lights below, with the ground spreading an illuminated cloak around their shoulders.

Can I help? I called down to the empty yard. I heard the echo of my call return from a façade. Only the final fragment of the question in my voice. The question which haunts me to this day. The distance it must travel now before it finds my brother's ears, those ears he pressed so ardently against his beloved transistor radio, a grin lighting up his face at the forbidden pop songs. I do not know what happened to the radio. Perhaps I threw it out. I cannot remember. Now, as the tape spins onward and that question is lost amidst magnetic particles, I am besieged by the longing to erase all that I have said thus far. I do not know if I am fit to speak. I should record only the creaking wardrobe, the bedsprings, the slamming door, the swish of net curtains as the ghostly forms of those I love pass through our home.

I discovered that my fingers were flicking the dial of the transistor radio. Snatches of music blared out and were lost in the crowded forbidden airwaves, voices shouting fragments of vital importance only to be swept away in the oscillating maelstrom. Would that I had been free to sweep my visitor away as easily as these airwaves. I could not point my finger to my chest and say here is where the pain is. He was not so specific. He did not hurt me as an illness or an accident would. He was in me in the same way as the oxygen came into my blood. I was his iron lung. We were two metal men one inside the other.

I turned the dial carefully until I found the Georgian State Radio station and the evening programme of popular song and I whistled to the tunes, not singing, whistling. But in the closing dark the whistle did not sound quite right.

*

Thus it was that my brother went to work as a road sweeper. And it was soon after he brought home his first pay packet that I heard the dull throbbing of a motorbike engine in the yard below our block. I leant over the balcony rail. A localised cloud of dust obscured the scene. The engine roared from within this mud coloured aura. The sound of voices shouted in excited encouragement. The engine faltered and then kicked back into life and the bike came speeding from the dust, seeming to leap over the rubbish bins, the cat, the child as it zoomed away and out of sight. The sound of the engine roared from distant yards as I pictured the progress of the rider – some mad-cap risk-taker acting with no thought for his comrades' safety. The bike circled through the settlement and in a few minutes returned to our yard where the group of onlookers applauded and hooted. I sneezed. The exhaust fumes tasted sour in my mouth as the wind wafted them up to me as if for my inspection. Now the driver switched off the engine and the dust settled. I clutched the rails and let out a sigh. Why could my brother not act normal? Why must he always be the one to attract attention? Always do the very thing that could cause trouble? For he had been the driver. I saw his blond head and his skinny shadow on the ground as he stood with arms akimbo by the motorbike.

That evening I agreed to ride with him. My theory was that if I took an interest, even helped to maintain the old machine, which was a black-market trophy, a German DKW from the Great Patriotic War, I might gain some influence and temper Poliko's wilful refusal to acknowledge the danger to his and other comrades' lives in hurtling at high speed around the blind corners of our settlement.

I have said that I prefer to walk. I do not like moving at speed. I feel myself out of sync, slipping like a badly reeled tape when high speed motion distorts the pulse of my mind – which is far from perfect but which does at least attempt to be tidy. It was a warm summer's evening. The group of admirers, lads, girls, a few older men all stood around the military motorbike, touching its battered mud-guards, placing a tentative boot-toe on the kick start or stroking the worn saddle. They stood back when we appeared. I was on the point of changing my mind now that the ugly machine stood before me. Poliko greeted his friends and laughingly promised them all pillion rides the next day. He stood on the kick-start and jumped it into life. The noise was so great that I could not hear him but only saw his confident smile, his clear grey eyes, the jerk of his head as he gestured for me to jump on. I did my best to put on a nonchalant air. My suit trousers were a little tight. I felt the seam ripping at the back as I raised my leg and straddled the rack over the rear mudguard. Immediately propelled backwards, I grabbed Poliko around his waist, gritting my teeth against the rushing air.

I closed my eyes at first. But that only made me feel worse. So I crouched behind my brother's back, peeping over his shoulder as the brightly lit tower blocks flashed past on a speeded up conveyor. We climbed the zigzag road. He had not switched the headlight on. Out of the corner of my eyes I saw the oil-black tarmac streaming away beneath our wheels. Each hairpin bend brought a muted cry of terror to my lips. Poliko's shouts slipped past my ears as if they were drops of mercury shedding the dust which encased our passage. Now we had reached the plateau and the wide night sky. Stop! I yelled. But Poliko drove on and out across a tractor path. The bike bucked and skidded on the sun-baked ruts. He was singing now, his voice rising and falling like a theatrical wind machine. Stop! I cried as he let go of the handlebars and spread his arms wide.

I do not know why we did not crash. The bike careered through the wheat. The tall stalks thrashed aside, shedding barbed ears of corn, pelting us with ripe grains. A dun chaos – a place belonging to nothing but itself – a time that will never be harvested – the thoughts struck through my fear as I clung on to my brother's waist. His song had become entwined with the roaring engine. And I suddenly recognised the tune he was singing. It was that beach song. That song about flying on foaming breakers. That song about sun and sand and youngsters with nothing to do but dance. To my great relief he gripped the handlebars once more, and we swung out of the wheat and onto the tractor path at a slower speed. We came to a halt. But I was still hurtling through the night.

Alright? He called over his shoulder.

No! You could have got us killed.

Look at the sky!

I glanced up, afraid there might be a military helicopter tracking our terrible swathe through the wheat. The roar of the engine still rang in my ears. The stars were streaming away as if someone had opened a sluice in the dam of eternity.

That's where I'm going some day, said Poliko.

Up there? I asked queasily.

He laughed and said that he wanted to see exactly where the wheat came to an end. Maybe it never does, he said. Come on, we'll ride together. We'll just keep riding, you and me, and see how far we can get.

What about fuel? I countered. I think the tank's leaking. The fumes have given me a headache. I'm going to walk home.

I'm not ready for bedtime yet, he replied.

So I stumbled away from my brother on his motorbike in the wheat.

As for my plan of maintaining the wretched machine, the first time I knelt before it and touched the oil-covered nuts over the engine casing, I knew that I would not be able to continue. I took out my handkerchief and rubbed my fingers as clean as possible. I knelt for a few more moments trying to summon up the will to investigate the grimy wartime relic. Then a small scratched marking caught my eye. It was tucked away on the rear mudguard behind the saddle spring. I peered closer. Someone had cut a swastika into the paintwork. I took up a handful of grit and tried to scour the mark away. But it did not work. When I confronted Poliko with what I had seen, he shrugged it off, saying that he intended sandpapering it away.

Do it now! I demanded.

Calm down brother mine. What's the hurry? Anyway I might be on the enemy side for all you know.

49

That's a terrible thing to say. After what took place during the Great Patriotic …

But he raised his hands in mockery, as if I were a fairytale monster.

Sorry, sorry! He grinned and began humming.

The motorbike did not last long. It developed a fault and needed a part which Poliko could not find. He was not interested in the greasy world of maintenance. He kept the faulty machine chained to a ring he had driven into the side of the electricity transformer block. Children came to play on it. Courting couples perched on the saddle and flirted.

When I was out collecting material on the streets of Tbilisi, I often came across Poliko at work. Even in the dull khaki overalls of a street cleaner, he managed to look attractive. He had a wide leather belt buckled around the waist, the top buttons undone, the trouser legs tucked into his boots. He wore a red neckerchief of frayed cotton which I frequently offered to hem even though I knew he would refuse. None of his work-mates wore such a red rag around their throats. My pale grey suit, my technical equipment, my familiarity with this young worker was the signal for the brigade to take a break. I positioned myself upwind from the rubbish truck. My suit, being pale, showed any tiny mark. So I steered clear of their brooms and shovels, and the wind-strewn heaps of detritus. I set the tape. Pressed play. Gave the nod to Poliko.

Faces followed his voice from opened car windows. Pedestrians put down their packages or shopping bags and smoked meditative cigarettes. Traffic police waved lorries through red lights as they turned towards the compelling, unforced timbre of the outdoor tenor. I began to think my brother had been right in his decision to work in the open air.

I began to squirrel the greater part of my salary away for when he was eighteen.

I did not need much in the way of spending. Apart from the suit, the Institute provided all I needed for my professional life. At home mother cooked and cleaned and washed on her days off and would not have allowed us to help if we had tried. I often sorted through her cooking pots to tighten the Bakelite handles on the aluminium lids. I had pleased her by securing string around my pliers to clamp them permanently to the rod on the geyser controls which had broken one morning. Now we could easily turn the rod with no fear of the old knob coming off in our hands as it had used to do before it split in two.

Mother's cacti collection took up a large amount of floor space below the windows all along the outer wall of the living room. I turned a blind eye to her kneeling over them, her rotating the tin cans, her fingertips softly pressing the dull earth around the stubs. Not, of course, that I approved of her belief in God. But it seemed to me that her tin cans of cacti, father's timetables, even Poliko's transistor radio were part of our family, were, at the risk of straying into poetic fancy, the instruments which accompanied the harmony of our apartment and our habits of ordinary life within its windowed walls. These windows however gave me cause for concern when I discovered one in my parents' bedroom slamming to and fro in a high wind.

The windows all opened inwards, so it was not possible to fix any kind of stay. They were either closed or fully opened and I had arranged ties so that each latch could attach to the next in that position, thus preventing them swinging. The wind came up in moments, hurling itself at the towers and carrying newspapers and cigarette packs swirling into the sky. Women came out to collect their laundry from the lines strung from balcony to balcony. I reached to hold the banging window but the frame struck my head and at the same time the pulley wheels squealed and the lines began jerking with their shirt arms and trouser legs, stockings and underpants capering side by side over the void. Everything was imbued with the brilliance of bleach. A mere tug on the line and I would join that clean brigade steeped in chlorine and scrubbed to the fibre.

Son son, what are you doing?

I spun round. The wind caused Vera's hair to fly out of its grips and I smoothed the loose strands around her temples, my fingers trembling.

Do you remember? *Where is he bound, where has he been . . .?* You read it to me when I was young.

She reached behind me and pushed the window shut. No, she said, I don't remember. It was only a poem. Not real life. And I don't remember anyway.

But you must.

Why must I? So you can ruin it? I'm sorry, I didn't mean that my dear. Now come and drink some tea. Leave the window, it doesn't matter, it'll only come loose again at the next storm.

When she had gone to the kitchen I retied the strip of cloth which had come undone at the catches, a bit of cloth from a vest which we had both worn, my brother and I, until we had grown too big for it and I had cut it into these useful strips, the measurements of our young chests gone forever. Poliko had cried into this strip of rag when it was a vest. He had come to us wailing and had wept his way laughingly through his boyhood.

I did not know what it felt like to have my eyes brim over with tears. I despised the tendency to sentiment in my fellow musicologists with their watery-eyed sighs over favoured singers. I had been born to host a murderous name belonging to a well-known sentimentalist. I could not allow any hint of his nature to escape.

I never had liked the *Matrioshka* dolls that some children had played with at my childhood nursery. I did not like the bland sameness of their faces. Their tubby forms slotting so smoothly one into the other, the secretive rattle of their wooden skins each against the other's identical selves. I was not in need of psychiatric treatment. I was not irrational. His living existence within me was not an illusion, I was never in any doubt of that. I was able to stand back and see myself quite calmly, this outer shell of earnest young comrade with the riotous name lurching in his chest. There had been moments recently when his rat-a-tat-tat at my ribs was so insistent that I had been forced to bend over and fold my arms around myself and hold my breath.

*

I had been running though my tapes one quiet afternoon in my office when my colleague Natalya burst in followed by two strangers. We spoke native Georgian at home and amongst friends, but Russian was our official language. Natalya and her guests were speaking in Russian but it only took me a few moments to realise that the strangers were from England. They had slipped away from their Intourist guide, much to their glee it seemed, and had met Natalya in order to look through the Institute's archives. They too were specialists in traditional song. They soon made themselves at home, setting out their Scotch and offering around their loose tobacco and thin packs of paper.

It was pleasing to see how impressed these visitors from the West were with our facilities, the free reign we had in our choice of subjects, the ease of travelling to distant regions and the care taken in our archiving even the smallest fragments of song. I played through some of my best recordings from the farthest tower blocks where the wind whistled in perfect harmony with the song and where bursts of tannoy broadcast were overlaid and mingled with the singer's voice.

The whisky was almost finished when the two guests began to wonder aloud how we managed to keep up such a happy front when we must surely be suffering inside. I stood up rather unsteadily. It would not, of course, be correct to insult these guests directly. I began packing away my tapes.

Do we look as though we're suffering? I asked. Do you not have suffering in your country? I've heard about your miners losing their jobs and then being beaten by the police. Our Soviet Union provides everyone with a permanent job, free housing and free health care. We can travel for practically nothing over vast distances. I could fly to Moscow tomorrow morning, lunch on the finest caviar and be back home the same night, or I could catch a train to Mongolia, sleep all the way in clean sheets and shave with hot water at dawn, just to see the eastern sunrise. Can you say the same of your government's care?

I do not know what they answered. I saw only the knowing looks of disbelief on their pasty faces and my comrade frowning behind them as I made a little bow, closed the lid of my recorder, slung the strap on my shoulder and left.

But my thoughts did not dwell on those misinformed visitors, for something far more important had occurred to me whilst playing my recording from the tower blocks. In my mind I heard the lines from a poem in mother's Anthology. It was by that crying poet, Paulo Iashvili. She had often read it aloud to me I was young. *The sound of bells in the wind, Bells in the wind . . . Nau nau nani nau nani nana . . .*

I walked until the light faded. I smoked a pack of cigarettes. My excitement did not dwindle.

When I took my report of Natalya's illegal meeting with the English visitors to the Rector he sat back in his chair, rubbing his knuckles into his eyes as if clearing away a headache. He wrote down a few notes, slipped the paper into his desk drawer and locked it. Then he sat back again and looked long and hard at me. I took the opportunity to impress him with a few words about my growing archive. I must admit I became quite animated. But the Rector began shuffling through a heap of documents on his desk, then he flicked on the intercom and spoke to his secretary on quite another subject. I left without him appearing to notice.

The Rector's office was on an upper landing where the parquet creaked beneath my feet. As I passed back down the marble staircase I noticed, for the first time, the little objects lying in the shadow of niches set into the wall. I saw the marks where someone had chipped away at the cutting edge of a flint arrow head, the hand-shaped curve of a bronze hasp, the crack in the rim of a wooden bowl and the thumbprint in the fragment of an amphora. I had the most peculiar desire to take one of these dusty and forgotten exhibits. But I went on down to the entrance hall, the doorman sitting sleeping on his three-legged stool, the narrow steps to my basement office where to my satisfaction I would work alone from now on.

*

It was not possible to hold a conversation with the other Iosif Dzhugashvili. The only sounds he made were the shufflings and tappings from within my rib cage. He conveyed his meaning in mime with his smile, his crinkly eyes, his warning frown or his companionable wink. I could not go on living as a constant host to this tight-lipped guest. My throat was always sore. I had tried holding a small amount of propolis in my mouth, but the beeswax guardian of the gate had no effect other than a temporary numbing which only made the return of feeling more difficult to swallow. So it was imperative that I find some kind of occasional release from my duties.

Part of my linoleum balcony barrier had torn away in the wind. The remaining section had become brittle and needed replacing so I went out on the balcony to see to it. The towers were brightly lit in the purple gloom of evening. I heard the sizzling fat as mother fried her spiced rissoles. I heard the faint jangle of Poliko's radio and father's snores as he snoozed in his television chair. I pulled the balcony door closed, stood facing into the conflicting airstreams born from the angular landscape of the settlement, the irresponsible eddies which circulated the non-stop yapping of the dogs and swapped the ownership of voices calling greetings up and down the towers.

Parquet pattern crumbled in my fingers. I brushed flecks of linoleum from my suit. I wanted nothing out of place. The wind was trying at my hair, but no matter, I had organised this aspect of myself to suit all possible occasions. It serves me well to this day. I am dark and my hair is thick but I have some clippers which work well enough if I keep them oiled, and I am in the habit of shearing my head, for I am afraid a black fleece would grow over my skull if I allowed it. Enough about my hair. The wind could not spoil it.

For a moment I wondered if it was a mistake not to have my tape recorder with me. But I did not want to contaminate the experiment with any extraneous device. I thought again of my sudden realisation, *the sound of bells in the wind, bells in the wind*, and the voices of song riding over the background clamour of the city.

I went over the instructions that had come to me through the absent sound of bells. Point 1: There are no bells any more. Not ringing that is. They hang silent. Point 2: The human ear longs for reverberations calling over and above the hubbub of life. Point 3: Without the bells our singing supplies the need for a sound which has no purpose other than to remind one of being alive. Point 4: But a bell can both call and recall, both signal a beginning and an end. In other words a bell is more like the workings of a key where a voice in song is akin to the door of the dwelling of life.

I had not quite understood it all yet. But the conviction that a bell was a vital component of my experiment remained unaltered. I could have had recourse to a cow bell or a door bell. But they did not have quite the right sort of gravitas for this occasion. I took up a nonchalant posture and did my best to picture myself as the bell in question. A little tricky I had to admit, but the wind was eager to help and I allowed it to rock me back and forth on my heels as I closed my eyes and opened my mouth for the chime.

Nothing happened so I thought I would have a cigarette and rethink my plan. But when I opened my eyes the world was not the same any more. He was on the other side of my skin. I reached out to touch, but he was too quick and he stepped lightly backwards, raised his chin, flicked his fingers over his moustache and let rip with a jaunty ditty. His peasant's tunic fluoresced in the utter darkness surrounding us. He stood looking outward towards a small glittering rectangle of snow on the distant plateau. I could not say if I knew this song or not. It had many verses. They rushed past my ears and some words were familiar and others were utterly strange, and yet they were all of a song, all adhering to the rules of music and rhythm and repetition. Now he sped up the tempo and began to pirouette with his arms held high, his head thrown back, his teeth flashing beneath his moustache. Dust came swirling around his patent leather boots as he pattered round and round, and each glimpse of his face showed him winking and his hands whisking to encourage me to join him in his dance. I took a tentative step or two but I knew I must not take my eyes from him. His boots had already worn a grey patch on the parquet pattern where it lay thin over the ridged concrete.

Nau nani nau nau nana nau nau, I chimed, fearing he would pirouette a hole right through the balcony. *Nau nani nau nau nana nau nau . . .*

But the air went out from my lungs as something struck me on the chest. I staggered back and found myself sitting on the linoleum with Poliko staring into my face. Behind my brother stood – I did not dare to name him – leaning casually against the balcony rail. Poliko held my arm and would not let me loose and I watched helplessly as he – how to name him to my brother? – flickered his fingers in farewell and leapt over the rails.

Let me get up! I pleaded.

You stay where you are. Here, take my cigarette. Calm down.

I am calm. I have to see where . . .

Poliko allowed me to stand, but would not let go of my arm. He was taller than me, wiry but strong, and he had that way of blocking any argument with a good-natured shrug. I peered over the balcony rail. Nothing but the far down pools of concrete under the vaporous lamplight.

You alright? he asked.

Of course I am. I was practising a song, very unusual, not sure of its origins, a hybrid perhaps, very intriguing, was just going over the words.

My brother's grey eyes were extremely penetrating when he wanted them to be. He nodded to the balcony rails. You wouldn't ever think of . . .?

Who me?

Alright then, because I'm going away for a while and you'll have to look after yourself.

I was very distracted of course. My attempt to chime a little break, to offer him a few steps in the fresh air, to gain a brief absence where I might tidy up his quarters had failed in the worst imaginable way. He was on the loose and who knew what he might attempt after so long being stuck inside the lungs of a man who could not even hold a line in tune. And yet, and yet it had been wonderful to see him in the flesh after all these years. He must have noticed that I was no longer that innocent child of his first choosing. Yes, now that I thought about it I was rather pleased with what had occurred. No matter that he had run away, he would not forsake the comfort of my lodging house. It was not a failure after all. We had come to an arrangement. I would continue to carry him around tucked up in my chest, and I would give the nod or the refusal, let him have a bit of slack, but only when I chimed the bell as it were.

So the notion of me having to look after myself when it was everyone else who had to be looked after by me, including my brother, because I am the older and have always guarded him, the notion made me laugh aloud.

Going away where? I spluttered.

The draft. My papers have come.

Ah, of course, you're eighteen. Well well, who'd have thought it eh? But it's alright, I've been putting something aside. Leave it to me. I'll just need your documents.

Poliko smiled and shook his head.

You haven't lost them already?

No, I've got them here.

Let me see!

And I'm going to report tomorrow.

But you can't want to submit to the draft. You've got no qualifications, you'll be the lowest of the low in some freezing camp on the edge of nowhere, it'll be worse than brutal, that grin of yours won't help.

Listen to the great believer!

No, you listen to me. I can't allow you to waste two years in the lowest level of the military. It's time you took yourself more seriously. I've got important connections in the Ministry of Culture, I'll get you set up as a stage performer, you'll be paid well, you could go right to the top with your singing voice. Now give me those documents.

Sorry, no doing comrade. You try to keep steady while I'm away. I'll ask Alik to watch out for you.

Let's discuss this properly in the morning, I said, glancing over the rails, because I thought I had seen the flick of a white tunic disappearing around the corner of the opposite block.

I went down to the yards and wandered around, smoked a cigarette, watched the dogs trotting through the lamplight. I thought I would feel at least some relaxation from my duties but no, he was my inner doll, and it was worse because now in what felt like the empty bucket of me the same-named host, he banged uncomfortably against my uninhabited ribs. My lungs were a sponge gone dry and the wind bowled me along, knocked me against low concrete walls dividing scrubby patch from scrubby patch, swept me down steps towards more steps going up to the same place I had just been blown from.

Fallen leaves scuttled with me on my search. Plums and apples dropped from the dark. Autumn, and not a whiff of snow in the air. I came to the unrealised cable-car, the first pillar standing with arms outstretched, a narrow ladder bolted to the side and the gear mechanism rusting on the ground. I whisked up the rungs to the top of the pillar, embraced the shuttered grain of a concrete tree, craned my neck to see the far reaches of the settlement. The towers stencilled onto the plain of wheat. All colourless under the colourless moon. The ladder trembled. I glanced down.

He came nipping up the rungs, the top of his head merging into my shoes, my suit trousers enveloping his shoulders, my shirt ruffling as he squeezed through my abdomen, the pressure pushing out my breath as he reached my chest. I clung on for a few more minutes to allow him to settle back in.

And what if I had not gripped those rusting rungs and had allowed my fingers to slip and my body to tumble backwards through the night air? He would not have had time to adjust. His quarters would have been smashed as with a demolition ball. Our blood would have seeped away into the cracked concrete, sinking forever into the alkaline depths of true death. My lungs expanded and relaxed as he gave a small contented sigh, easing his tired limbs into a more comfortable position. He would sleep after his excursion. I too would go home and sleep. The experiment was completed, the method and result recorded in my nerves. The conclusion was drawn. A bell and a lullaby were the age-old emollients for the dread of being the last alive in any type of world. I would not repeat the experiment. In the morning I would go and talk to the right people about Poliko's draft. There were comrades who I need only murmur appropriate hints to. Comrades like myself whose hearts were cast in the shape of the red star. As I strolled home I saw the row of windows on the topmost floor of our block where Vera, Givi and Poliko were preparing for bed. How desirable that innocent scene seems now. A family at bed time.

*

My brother treated his draft as if it was going to be a holiday and he infected Vera and Givi with this idea, even though they both knew the reality. Plenty of families in the towers had sons who had been drafted. He would be set to work on some construction project and because he had no qualifications or family contacts in the military he would be given the most dirty, the most dangerous tasks. For the first year he would be bullied. In the second year he would be expected to bully the new recruits. This was the way it was. We would not know where he would be posted and he would not be allowed to tell us when he got there, even if he knew where he was, which was unlikely given the vast reaches of the Motherland and the similarity and secrecy of the military posts. I could have bought him out but he refused my offer. I had done it for myself and felt no guilt. I believed in patriotic duty, but there were sometimes more efficient ways to fulfil that duty. I had not been able to allow myself to miss two years' worth of song.

As I have said I felt a strong personal bond with my tape

recorder and I had worked out how to remove the casing, setting out the screws for repositioning and using a fine sable brush to remove all traces of dust from the three motors, those being the driver for the supply reel, the take-up reel and the main drive itself. I was in the process of such a cleaning on the morning of Poliko's departure.

Vera lifted a hand to wave goodbye to the space where he had stood just moments before with his knapsack slung over his shoulder. Givi got up from his TV chair and went to watch for him at the window and she joined him there.

See you soon! Poliko shouted from the yard.

Goodbye son! They called.

Vera sighed, They'll cut his lovely hair.

He'll be alright, said Givi.

I screwed the upper section of the tape recorder casing back into place and remarked that it was a good job I had glued down the soles of Poliko's work boots not so long ago. They turned to look at me and seemed rather glum, so I smiled. But Poliko had left us with his laughter and by comparison my smile was a mere copy. I made a sweeping gesture to demonstrate the width and breadth of the Motherland's bounty as I reminded my parents that none of this would be possible without sacrificing personal feelings for the greater good.

That's right son, said Givi.

But I could not help thinking that the quick look he gave Vera did not match his words. The last trace of Poliko's laughter had faded away. My smile had no nice sound to replace it with, only my breath whistling in and out of my nostrils as I gathered up my tapes and recorder and set out for the Institute.

*

There were places at the far reaches of the settlement where courting couples could be private in the back seat of a car or beneath the pomegranate and lilac bushes that grew on the shale. The land had been prepared for building but the project was never started and the scrubby terraced cuts were home to stray dogs, feral cats, small rodents and the white eagles and falcons that came to hunt them. Where the land flattened above the scrub there was a greasy lake surrounded by reeds and a stretch of pebbled shore scattered with used cartridges where lads took their black market pistols or their father's hunting rifles for target practice. Draining the last drop of their vodka they would stand the empty bottle on a plank and push it out onto the rain-bowed water. The sound of gunshots and cracking glass was as normal as the swish of falcons' wings or the muffled sighs of lovers. Like the legal criminals, these places for secretive sex and target practice were tolerated so long as they remained unspoken.

There was always the lad who owned a pistol. The one who took it seriously. The one who handed out the cartridges and allowed his friends to shoot so long as they brought along the vodka. But it was never Poliko. Owning a firearm would have been too serious for his taste. For him a pistol was just an excuse for a game with one eye shut, the windswept water rocking the plank where an empty bottle stood waiting. My brother's face lit up with humour as he imitated the musical ping of the bullet if it struck home, and the pathetic little splash when the bottle fell off the board. He never cared if he hit the target or not. He could not be bothered to take aim properly. There were never any accidents at the lake target ground. Never any drunken tomfoolery ending in tragedy. The pop pop of gunshots was akin to the sound of amusement park rifles. For Poliko a gun meant nothing more than having fun. This is a fact which shines as clear as those vodka bottles before they sank. But now, as I think of those luminous glass shards weaving through the oily water, I feel my fact drowning with them and I cannot swim down and rescue it.

I did not find a willing girl for the shale banks. I could not risk such an intimate encounter. The trysting place was too much a part of the tower blocks, and I had my duty of guardianship, and my other name to look after. Even to imagine what it would be like to lie with a girl beneath the lilac caused my ribs to hurt. Let me make it clear that I and he were two quite separate beings. It was not that he could control me, quite the opposite. But he was a constant companion. And he would scoff at me. So I had no desire to allow him access to my fumblings with a girl on the shale.

After Poliko's departure I concentrated entirely on building up my archive. I would soon be invited to my Union headquarters and offered something worthy of my ambition. I was all set for a post in the Ministry of Culture. There were times when I was even glad of the outward sound of my name. It was a signal which I could send before me to convey my willingness to serve the Motherland.

I had become quite a well-known figure in the restaurants. The night-time tables were rich with melody as song passed from table to table with the jugs of wine or the presentation of a bottle of champagne. I recall the first time I walked, slightly the worse for wear, from a cellar full of diners to the humid night air and continued walking with no intention of returning to the towers.

I mean to tell the facts as best I recall. All that I say is as it was – as far as I could perceive it through the green glass bricks dividing me from my comrades who did not struggle to share their breath with an intruder. I have learned the language of half-truths and of one thing meaning another. Sometimes a lie is necessary to outwit a harmful truth. I mean to unreel my life thus far and reveal the things I have done and seen others do. A hope occurs. I hardly dare speak it aloud. He. My chubby pal. Not partial to hard facts. Prefers grandiloquent fictions. I think of a tower block made from facts. I think of a prison of facts. A tower of facts. I shall trap him in facts. I shall build them up around him. But this is dangerous talk. He stirs. He has developed the habit of pinching the inside of my skin. Most uncomfortable. In the armpits.

I crossed the river and strolled alongside the white walls of the central heating supply factory with its tall thin chimneys emitting luminous clouds into the night. A woman came towards me. I went with her to the lane between the high white walls. She was not surprised when I requested a special favour. I offered more than she asked.

Now sing, I said.

Anything?

Anything.

I pressed record and the spools turned to my dismal voice joining with her song, my intermittent groans as she worked on me.

Other nights I walked further afield finding the places where highways became rubble tracks. Where anonymous statues looked away to the dim lights of distant collective farm sheds. I skirted the perimeters of tower block regions I had not known existed and which I never found a second time. The women never refused to sing but I would never have forced it on them. The voice was often damaged. A song half remembered which I encouraged by singing along. And the sexual act was never more than her handling and satisfying me. This was the most I could allow. I would not couple, not with him looking on. I felt affection for these kerbside comrades. They cared nothing for me or my work and never asked my name. Of course it was necessary to keep this part of my collection to myself.

There are no excuses. No pointing the finger to my houseguest. I did this myself. I thought of the night tapes as any ethnographic worker would. They were not pornographic to me, they were pure, unfettered human endeavour.

So while Poliko was away I learned, in a limited way, about sex. Limitations also have great space within them though. Inside my not very muscular chest were many chambers, one within the other, the cells of my tissues were his private rooms where he lolled around, bored and annoyed that the baby he had chosen had turned out to be the unentertaining comrade of me.

*

My brother's laughter sounded in the accidental slamming of a door or the chatter of the sparrows on the flat roof of the tower or from an exclamation in the wind, gently incredulous, brushing away any doubt or melancholy.

A few months after Poliko's draft, Soviet troops moved into Afghanistan. Father began looking out for him on the television broadcasts of conscripts building schools and clinics at the side of mud-made villages. Once he cried out and pointed at the screen, certain he had seen Poliko in a squad of grinning sunburned lads wielding shovels and pickaxes. Although we had no contact with him, Poliko did not feel completely gone from us. If he was in Afghanistan he was doing his patriotic duty, and I re-thought my former opposition and became proud of my brother's part in guiding our sand-storm blighted comrades towards the modern world.

And the two-year span was always shortening. We had his homecoming to look forward to. Vera had already begun pickling cucumbers and peppers ready for his return. Storing our love for Poliko in pickle jars or as tiny dates inscribed on timetables or on the long sleek magnetic spools of his songs, none of us thought too deeply about the separation. He was just like any other conscript and it was our duty to be proud of him.

One incident stood out in the routine of tower life. A funeral was taking place. The family concerned lived on the ninth floor and the door to their apartment was open as is the custom during a wake. I though it odd that the coffin lid was not standing in the corner of the communal hallway as is usual before the procession with the open casket to the cemetery.

I did not know this family all that well, but it was customary to call in and say a few words of condolence so I entered the apartment expecting to find the deceased lying in a coffined bed of satin set on a strong table while the women sat on chairs around the walls of the room. But the coffin was hardly recognisable as such, it was the dull grey metal of water tanks with crudely welded seams binding it tightly closed. But worse than this industrial looking casket were the scuffling women centred around a black-clad mother who was stabbing at the zinc with a bread knife and crying that she must get it open to believe it was her son inside. The other women were trying to restrain her but they were also fingering the zinc seams as if they might find a way to unfold them, and they elbowed away the men who sometimes entered the tormented fray with loud voices and reddened faces.

I backed out and found a neighbour on the stairwell landing who said that the dead son had been sent back from Afghanistan in this sealed zinc coffin, that the parents were forbidden to open it and had been warned not to spread unpatriotic rumours.

Maybe he had some kind of plague, the neighbour speculated.

I did not speak of this to mother and father, who had been at work during the funeral. The television news gave good reports of Soviet troops digging irrigation channels and wells, laying roads, building schools and hospitals, and the few American-aided fighters in the mountains, who would rather have their people submit to the ignorance of religion, were easily dealt with and did not prevent our conscripts working to raise up the living standards of our Afghan comrades.

I pictured my brother driving a jeep through a parched village, children running alongside as he threw them sweets and cigarettes. I saw him raise a pickaxe and strike it into the loose red earth of an irrigation ditch. I doubt him too much, I admonished myself. Admit it, I told myself, he has a better instinct for the masses than you do. Go on, say it – Poliko is a natural Soviet for all his love of those illegal radio stations.

*

There are many planned spaces for relaxation in the settlement. There are pitches laid for ball games, tennis courts, little parks with tubular steel seats in the shade of pine trees, small concrete tables with chess boards cast in black and white cement.

But there are also many unplanned spots with earthen fireplaces, one-legged benches and two-legged tables nailed to the trunks of trees at the edges of the terraces. These accidental table tops are the favoured boards on which to set our clay wine jugs, crystal glasses, stone baked bread, salty cheese and pickled peppers.

On the higher slopes of Nutzubidze Plateau self-seeded trees have flourished into large specimens of walnut or acacia. Their canopies hide the settlement, the air is sweet with sap and leaf, the improvised tables bear molten candle stumps, the tree-supported benches are customised with broken chair seats or plastic covered cushions.

I pushed on towards where the aerial walkway joined two of the final towers. I was in nostalgic mood, recalling my childish sentry post and my little moving picture of the wheat harvest beneath the walkway. But now as I peered upwards I saw that the walkway could never have functioned. The concrete span stretched between two blank facades. Its tin roofing was gone but for one rusted section which creaked in the wind. The handrails hung askew and bright specks of light showed through the span. The shadows of the last towers stretched away on the undulating wheat. A plank laid across two stacks of worn-out tyres served as a resting place where I smoked a cigarette, looked out over the shushing grain and fell into a reverie.

The songs of Tbilisi are coins passing from hand to hand and acquiring a patina that does not diminish the value. The songs may warp with the emotion of the singer but will remain essentially unchanged. They are our currency of identity, minted from the life of our streets and stamped with the singer's mark of unconditional love for our ancient city.

All of a sudden my thoughts were shattered by a grinding racket as combine harvesters advanced side by side, each emitting a black plume of exhaust and surrounded by quivering fumes. I had never seen so many at work together. Within minutes the harvesters had cut through to the edge of the plain and their yellow headlights swept over me and all was smoke and smouldering earth. I could see no operators on the machines as they turned and roared away into the storm. My ears rang from the clatter of engines. I was blinded. Exhaust fumes and chaff choked my throat. In a daze I fumbled for my handkerchief, dabbed my eyes and wiped the dust from my tape recorder. How efficiently the machines had stripped the plain bare. How brightly the sun burned down upon this productive earth.

Someone began singing from one of the towers behind me. A female voice with an uncouth edge, a fast tempo, a simple tune repeating after only four bars, as if the singer was working as she sang and the turn of the round was encouraging her hands to complete the actions of her task. The voice was so strong that it carried far beyond me out across the plain, straddling the distance, muscular, athletic, as if in competition with the retreating roar of the combine harvesters.

I stood at the base of the tower but it was impossible to tell which floor the singer was on. Laundry fluttered on lines strung from balcony to balcony obscuring most of the view upwards. I could not help noticing that these outer towers were not of the same quality as the rest. The entrance doors were missing from the hallway and peering in to the gloom I saw that the stairwell was too narrow to fit a lift in the shaft. I stepped back and shouted out a hello towards the upper balconies. A man called down with a name but I called back, No, that's not me. And a woman called out, Who are you then? And as is the custom, calling our names up and down the blocks, I replied with my name in full.

Then you'd better come up if that's who you are! laughed the woman. Floor fifteen, second door.

Was it you singing just now? I called.

But there was no reply so I went in and toiled up the fifteen floors. My face was burning, not from the climb but from the way the woman had laughed at my name. And when she opened the door and stood there with that glint of amusement in her eyes I would have turned on my heel had it not been for her hair. One side hung long and wavy but the other side was cut up to her jaw. Her face was rather elongated and hollow-cheeked and her eyes had flecks of amber in the brown. But it was the darkly unbalanced waves of her hair that really held me there as she smirked like a schoolgirl with a private joke.

Was it you singing? I asked.

Who wants to know?

I could not take my eyes from her hair. One side so luxurious and the other cut so short, and the way it moved in this draughty landing, the way the waves complimented the sharply defined planes of her face.

I'm an ethnomusicologist and I'd like to record you, I said as I tugged the strap from my shoulder and held out my tape machine in a ploy that never usually failed to get agreement.

That's impossible, she laughed.

I'm sorry, I thought it was you singing just now from your balcony.

Oh it was.

But then will you allow me to tape you for posterity?

Posterity!

For the archive of our mutual endeavours.

Oh, is that what it means? Sounds important.

It is.

Well you can come in comrade Iosif Dzhugashvili. I might let you send me to posterity, but first you must do something for me.

She led me through an apartment much the same as many others I had been invited into to make my recordings, the usual polished parquet floor, the crystal chandelier, the standard furniture with glossy walnut veneer. On the wall behind a couch bed hung a satiny cloth with a scene embroidered in silver and black thread. A group of antique people dipped their urns into the rush of a tumbling stream while fallow deer and pheasants stood calmly watching, and beyond was a vista of silver mountains picked out against a pure black sky. A factory-made panel such as this was common, I had been in many apartments whose walls were decorated with similar hangings, but for some reason I found this particular tapestry so compelling that I wanted to stand in front of it and look longer into the scene. But my songstress went out to the balcony so I followed after her.

I had never before experienced vertigo on a high balcony, but now, with the vacant air before me and the bright hot wind beating in from the plain, I stood clutching my tape recorder while my insides twisted with fear. She told me to put the recorder on the table. I stepped stiff-legged to the little worn-out table and with mechanical actions brushed away the flecks of rotted veneer, set down the player, opened the lid, placed my finger over the controls and keeping my eyes locked to this little island of stability I waited for her to begin. But she made no sound and I suddenly became convinced she had left me alone out here on the perilous balcony. Then something flashed before my eyes. Something cool and familiar came to my free hand.

You can finish the cut, she said.

The scissors were blunt, I knew this from the way the blades came together as I flexed my fingers and thumb. The faintest click where they did not meet as smoothly as they should. I thought I should take my recorder and leave. I had never cut another person's hair in my life. The balcony was narrow and the white bed linen flapped and snapped on the line above. Half of her neck was hidden behind the long wavy tresses, but the other half was pale above her sun-tanned back and the scoop of the green dress she wore.

Now she began to sing with quite another texture from the sound that had captivated me on the plateau. I reached out towards her neck. Her voice sank to a low cunning sort of melody which made me think of marshlands and silent fish weaving amongst the reeds. I cut a strand. The scissors were even more blunt than I had thought. I cut the next strand. It hung warm and damp in my fingers and I let it fall and saw it tease apart in the wind and sweep away in countless curling threads. Her dark melody became visible as more of her neck was exposed and the sharp nodules of her spine vibrated against my fingers. In a daze I continued snipping the tiniest amounts trying to make the dull blades do a better job than they could. Her ear lobe peeked from beneath the hair as I lifted it away strand by strand. And then I came round to face her and without thinking I raised her chin a little so that I could measure my side with the one already cut. A few more snips and I was satisfied. I stood back to admire my work. Her eyes were closed. Her singing finished. I had never felt so happy in all my life.

Does it look nice? she asked, opening her eyes wide and giving me a coy smile.

I think so.

Not very decisive for a man of steel are you?

Would you let me record that song?

Come inside and I'll think about it.

I stood staring at the tapestry while she got the wine from the kitchen. My mind was in turmoil. I was certain she had bewitched me and was mocking me. She came back with a jug of cloudy white wine and an uncut coil of cigarette which she told me quite openly she stole from the Astra packing plant where she worked. She nipped off two cigarette-sized lengths and I poured the wine.

To victory, especially for you. I made the formal toast and drank in one.

And then I set out my recorder and it was necessary to pick some long hairs from the spools and to re-dust the casing with a clean handkerchief which I always carried for that purpose.

Now I saw that this young comrade was not so beautiful after all. She stood there with her Astra hanging from her lips, allowing it to flick up and down in a most unfeminine manner as she said, Why bother recording anything? It's a waste of time. Look at the birdies, they don't need to be saved for posterity. And anyway I never remember my songs. They don't mean anything. There's no point to them. I might as well tell you right now comrade ethnomusicologist, I'm nothing special. Here today, gone tomorrow. Just like the wheat! Poof!

We both turned automatically to look from the window where the ploughs were working over the stubble and other vehicles came behind with spouts and sprayers leaving a nitrate haze in their wake. I closed the lid of my recorder, bowed and thanked her for the hospitality and let myself out. I could not recall the notes of her balcony song any more and with each step I took on the long draughty stair I lost more and more sense of those warm damp strands of her hair until when I at last came to the litter-swept exit I could only think that I had encountered an extremely unbalanced young comrade and I was fortunate to have escaped her wiles.

Stepping out into dazzling light, the dust clouds swirling over the plain. A piercing whistle coming from above.

Hey, comrade Stalin, you didn't ask but I'll tell you anyway, my name is Maia Dolidze, she called down.

*

I am not in the habit of taking things that do not belong to me. The only things I need are the intangible sounds of song. And these I carry away as magnetised particles. My reels of tape are the colour of dried blood. The colour of spilt blood. This telling is of the same colour. But other colours seep in as I see Maia in my mind's eye. Her pale green dress against her sun-tanned back. The earthen colour of her voice as she sang her way into my family's hearts. The unripe plums we picked together, their green matching her dress, their blind flesh matching my inability to see the true meaning of her questions. The colour of veils, of lovers lost in cloud.

I found that I had accidentally carried away her scissors in my suit jacket pocket. Their plastic covered handles were cracked and the blades were loose on an unscrewable central rivet. I tried to sharpen them on my whetstone. But the metal alloy was soft and my efforts only wore away the almost non-existent edge. It did occur to me that with all the steel we produce it ought to be possible to manufacture a decent pair of scissors. But doubtless those in charge of directing the steel quotas had greater things to think about than humble kitchen scissors. I bought a brand new pair of the same type I had bought for Vera, with a nut and tightenable grooved bolt at the joint.

Bear with a brief interruption while I take the chance to clarify allusions to my other name whilst he sleeps. If I sometimes do not speak of my guest it is not because I have forgotten him but because he is wide awake and pacing. And who would speak openly about the bad habits of a guest in their hearing? Or of that guest's petty sulks at the bright rapping at the door of a lovely girl who acts as though the well-worn armchair has been placed at the heart of the home purely for her pleasure? And now I am struck with the despairing thought that the purpose of this narrative is not some heroic declamation of my guilt but only to present him with the bill and an account of expenses, worn-out rugs, frayed nerves, shattered windows, stained handkerchiefs, blocked drains, broken chairs.

I wrapped the new scissors in vine leaves and tied the stems in the same way as the peasants package cheeses in the collective market. Perhaps I should have bought Maia a fresh cheese instead, but I had an idea that she would appreciate the humour in my packaging. I do not think I had ever made a joke of a gift before. I wanted to erase my behaviour with her which I saw now had been full of my own wounded pride. I smiled to myself as I prepared the package and imagined Maia's laugh when the scissors fell out. This was all I allowed myself to imagine. She was not my type, even if I had been free to find my type, she was not for the life of privilege that lay ahead of me.

One day in the not too distant future I would leave my beloved towers for ever. It was a necessary sacrifice. I would guide others on my path, and my place of dwelling would have to represent the goal they too could achieve. As my parents had risen from the tumble-down confusion of the old city to these hygienic apartment blocks then I must also rise – although not, you understand, in the vertical sense – to one of the leafy regions of nineteenth century salons with a doorman at the entrance hall.

In a mood of inexplicable nervousness I trudged up the tracks to Maia's tower. I regretted bringing my tape recorder with me now. And I could not help noticing that my vine leaf wrapping on the new scissors was wilting by the second. I dabbed my face dry with my folded handkerchief.

The urgent voice of the public broadcast reverberated from the facades at the heart of the settlement, but here on the perimeter there were no overhead cables and no tannoys, the blocks faced the plain alone, bleached to the colour of bone as they stood brave and watchful over the wheat. The next crop had sprouted green on the turned earth.

I had seen her slip out to the balcony when I came in to the apartment. Her parents Dato and Eliso were at home and received me as though I had come to woo their daughter. Eliso took the little package from my hands, discarded the vine leaves without a glance and began snipping the thin air with the scissors with a forced gaiety.

What sort of girl would allow a stranger to cut her hair?

Don't be embarrassed, I got it out of her. She always tells her mother everything in the end, she said casting a grim look toward the balcony.

I wanted to leave immediately but Dato brought a jug of the cloudy wine and manners forbade me leaving until we had drunk it all and made the correct toasts along the way. He had me sit opposite him with his chair drawn close to mine, but even in this proximity he beckoned me to lean closer. I thought he must be hard of hearing so I raised my voice as I explained about my work, even opening the lid of the tape recorder to demonstrate the controls. But to my astonishment Dato took the liberty of closing the lid back down, and he flapped his hand as if to shush me and slid his eyes toward the kitchen where Eliso had gone. As if to explain his stilted manner of speech he told me that he worked in the telegraph department of the post office.

My attention kept slipping to the tapestry on the wall behind his chair. You recall the harmonious scene of man and beast, of water and rock? But now the figures bending at the stream were barely discernible, the creatures were virtually lost in a haze of loose threads. It was as if someone had dragged a grater over the silver and black weave. I did not think the damage was irretrievable though, for the tapestry could be repaired with a bodkin and a careful hand to re-weave the threads back into the correct formation. I drank down another glass.

Victory for your beautiful daughter! I toasted.

Now Eliso came with a plate of meringue and perched on the arm of my chair, blocking my view of the balcony where I had become convinced that Maia was smirking at my discomfort.

To your victory, Eliso! I toasted.

But the ritual of toasting and the sequence of subjects is not what I mean to speak of now. Enough to say that I drank and did not feel the alcohol and that is one of the purposes of speaking formally with wine, the sequence of toasts channels the effect of the alcohol, focuses and burns off the inebriation. This is the age-old way with wine for a Georgian.

The vine leaves lay shrivelled in the ashtray when I took my leave at last. Eliso clung to my arm as she walked me to the door. She was a fine-looking woman with the same narrow face as her daughter, but there was something too intimate in the way she spoke. She stood between me and the door.

Believe me comrade Iosif, she said in a low voice, I know what I'm talking about. Maia needs a firm hand. In my line of work I deal with all sorts of *mental* deviation. Not that there's anything like *that* in our blood, but it can appear out of the blue, you have to keep alert. Maia has always been difficult. I tell you this because I can see you're the sort who won't take any nonsense.

It's been a pleasure to find how well we understand each other, I smiled and bowed my farewell.

I smoked a cigarette as I sat on the plank bench collecting my thoughts. It was nothing to me if I had seen Maia or not. Yes it was unfortunate that my little joke had fallen flat, but such is the fate of someone like me who was not born to make others laugh. I am not given to self pity. I have no room for maudlin thoughts.

My accommodation is rather cramped. We have to live cheek by jowl. My inmate grows bitter while I maintain order. He has developed the habit of plucking the hairs from his moustache. They catch in my throat. His fingernails scratch in my wind-pipe. A breath of air. A breath of air. But wishing he had not chosen me is as futile as wishing I had been born blond instead of with the stubbornly black Caucasian pelt.

I see my brother speeding towards me over the young wheat. His hair is the colour of ripe grain. His laughter overpowers my cry at the damage he is doing to the crop. A vision in the heat haze. But soon, soon he will be with us in the flesh. His conscript experience will have grown him into manhood. When he returns I will try once again to set him up in the Musicians' Union. I had not realised how much my heart aches to see him again. But just then my musing was interrupted by Maia who had crept up without a sound, sat astride the plank and punched me lightly on the arm in a very unfeminine manner.

Hello, she said as if we were old friends.

She had a length of uncut Astra which she deftly nipped in two, offering me one part. Before I could reach for my matches she lit one of hers, so I bent to the flame, even though I felt most uncomfortable allowing a woman to hold a match for me.

Sorry about my mother, she said. Eliso thinks everyone's interested in her mentals, she's in charge of keeping them docile, she'd as soon give you a shot of tranquilliser as feed you meringues. Actually that was her on her best behaviour to impress you, she does that with all my boyfriends, not that I have one now, she's made sure of that. Do you still want me to sing?

I thought you didn't believe in recording songs.

Oh I don't, but I owe you something for cutting my hair, which you did well by the way – have you ever thought of a change of career? It's not my own song. I'll tell you about it

after. I chose it specially for you. I had an idea you might . . .
but never mind. Ready?

She turned towards the plain. I depressed record and the
needle wavered as she drew in a breath. The blades of wheat
glittered from green to white in the sunny wind. I knew this
song but I had never heard it performed with such vehemence.
The melody has the quality of a snake charmer's pipe while the
singer tells how she gave up her beloved son to be buried alive
in the walls of Surami Fortress. *I had no choice, I gave you so that
Georgia would be free for ever from invaders. My darling child, I laid
you on the stones and watched the wall grow high around you.*

I held up my hand to record a moment's silence when the
song was over.

Are you always so serious? she laughed when I let my hand
fall.

Would you like to hear it play back?

Not really. Did you like it?

Oh yes, yes . . . The best rendition I've heard and I've heard
this song performed many times before. The Legend of Surami
Fortress goes back to the nineteenth century, a ballad invented
to record a much earlier historical victory against the odds and
like most folk songs it's based on real life, you might even say
that folk lore and cultural memory are so entwined in our
embattled history that it becomes . . .

She put a finger over my mouth. The breeze moved her
hair around her face – the kind of pensive ascetic face found
on icons, except that her eyes were full of mischief as she said,
Alright comrade musicologist-what-did-you-say-your-name-
was. Do you want to hear my little part in the real life of the
legend?

It was my grandmother who taught me The Legend of

Surami Fortress. She was very stern but I adored her and I loved going to stay at her village house in the summer. When I'd done my chores I used to climb up to the fortress mound where I spent hours searching for the boy's bones in the ruins. Grandmother made a bed for me beneath her walnut tree so the oil vapours would breathe good fortune into my sleep. She always slaughtered a hen for my first meal. And she always told the same story while we plucked the feathers.

It was the time of the Great Patriotic War and she had prepared herself to lose her husband Jaba. The war came to an end and she had no news of him, and there were rumours of soldiers returning from German prison camps only to be transported to the gulags as traitors. So it was like a dream when Jaba walked in the door and took her into his arms and she thought she'd never stop laughing with joy. My father was a little boy and didn't understand the tears Jaba cried when he gave him the spoon he'd carved and carried through the fighting for this very moment.

Jaba was a trained draughtsman but he was put to work in the collective, starting at the bottom in the chicken sheds. There were too many men working in the shed so they always held a few jobs back for the times when the collective boss came to inspect them. The boss was never satisfied, he blamed the hens for deliberately holding back their egg quota. He'd bend over their cages and bellow neck-wringing threats at them.

One day Jaba sketched a little cartoon on the back of a quota sheet to amuse his comrades. He was going to scribble over it but at that moment a contingent of regional collective chiefs arrived for a surprise inspection. In the flurry of making themselves look busy the cartoon was forgotten. The boss came strutting in with his superiors, he presented them with the quota sheet and spoke loudly of the record quantity of eggs he had personally produced. But for some reason his superiors were smirking behind their hands and he did not get the accolade he was due for. It wasn't until they had left that the boss found the cartoon on the back of the quota sheet – a strutting cockerel whose head was an unmistakeable portrait of himself.

Jaba was taken away the next day. The next week Grandmother was notified that her husband had been shot for counter-Communist activities.

*

Maia gave me her telephone number but I did not call her. The pressure of her finger on my mouth remained like a scar and even when it eventually faded my lips still remembered the shock of her touch. And the tragic absurdity of her story with the waste of a good man's life also remained with me, and like her finger it had touched on something too intimate. The time when any casual word or action could lead to execution was not so very long ago. Reviving the memory of an individual who had been victim of a monstrously warped ideology was to release an infestation into the healthy body of our modern Motherland, and she had passed this sickness on with her finger at my lips. I wonder now, was that the moment when our fates were sealed? Her finger on my lips. A shared contamination which would pass through me to my mother and father and brother.

I archived the reel containing her song on a shelf apart from my main collection. And for reasons that were unclear to me, and were against my principles of detailed annotation, I made no notes, and I left the label and the side of the tape box blank.

A plan of my office would show a long narrow room with a small window let into the wall near the ceiling. I am underground and the complicated bulk of the Institute bears down upon the ceiling and the window, which looks onto the pavement and is too grimy for any real daylight to enter. My desk and the desk I have commandeered from my misguided comrade stand against one of the longer walls, while the opposite wall is covered in shelves. These shelves lie on brackets which tend to pull away from the plaster if I do not keep up a regular programme of tapping them back into place.

I have rewired the light fitting to accommodate the 500-watt bulb which hangs like a sun over my desk. This enormous bulb whines as it lights but I am used to the high-pitched emission, and I do not think my mind would settle to my work without this single, on the edge of hearing note. The bulb has one drawback of giving out a great deal of heat, and, as in all buildings, the central heating pipes are permanently on. But the illumination is crucial for my peace of mind, for there are no hidey-holes, and the intensity of the light is such that there are no shadows on the walls or ceiling. On my desk are two red polka-dotted cups filled with pencils. My sharpener. My eraser. My notepads. A typewriter. My current tapes and the tape recorder.

Thus I set out my time beneath the brilliant lamp, and this light enters my orifices. It burns into my lungs. It, at least temporarily, pins my other name on its beam, and he becomes a mote, a speck, a nothing. There are drawbacks. After such treatment my house-guest is not at all happy. But I digress. The original Iosif Dzhugashvili and the sly ways with which he managed to express his unhappiness are not a very sympathetic subject, I fear.

*

Poliko was due home. We did not know exactly when but Vera said she could feel him getting closer. She had become very fond of a particular cacti even though it seemed no better or worse than the rest in her collection, none of which ever grew larger or did anything in the way of flowering. Since receiving that first warning on the unpatriotic distractions of entering a church, after the report I had made during my Pioneer days, Vera's religious tendencies found their outlet solely in these tin can gardens. Perhaps, for Vera, there was something saintly in the way the cacti endured their privations. She starved them of water. Even this favoured one, which was covered in downy prickles and stood no taller than her thumb, was set in stuff that looked more like concrete than earth. She used this tin can to lean her Blue Horns Anthology against, like a cookery book on the kitchen table. In the midst of cooking she liked to peek at a poem, stirring the lines into her beans and crushed walnut or her lamb and aubergine stew.

When Poliko came in unannounced one evening I stood back to allow mother and father to embrace him first. Father rushed out for wine and fresh bread. Then I wrapped my arms around him as I had been longing to do. But I found that he was trembling and he felt very cold. He pulled away and let out a thin laugh and said he was very tired.

Has it been a long journey? I asked.

Hitched from Tashkent, he muttered giving another thin sort of laugh.

He reached for a cigarette from a pack on the kitchen table but then seemed to forget he was holding it. His fingers were shaking. His hair was shorn army fashion. He was tanned but the skin around his eyes looked bruised and his lips were cracked. He wore a dirty T-shirt, stained blue lycra tracksuit pants and ruined plimsolls on his bare feet. He needed a shave and a bath, familiar food and a night's sleep and I was not going to push him to communicate right now.

Despite mother's gentle attempts to persuade him, Poliko would not change his clothes for the home-coming meal at the best table. Father stood for the first toast. But Poliko clenched his fists and began beating the table in tight little thumps and the dishes and glasses rattled and his face was suddenly wet with soundless tears. Givi proceeded with the toast, the first words in honour of Vera, but before he had gone very far he faltered and set his glass down and the wine slopped as Poliko pounded the table in the silence that had befallen us. I placed my hands over his. The skin was icy cold and there was an unnatural force in him as he struck the table top, which I feared to try to stop. Vera had risen and was on the verge of tears and I shook my head at her and she said that she would go and make tea with cherry jam. But although this was Poliko's special favourite he made no sign of having heard her.

Now come on son, Givi said, you'll find everything will be alright after a good night's sleep. I've been saving a surprise for you. Got a nice little job lined up for you in the depot. You'll be trained as a trolley bus driver. I was going to tell you tomorrow, but seeing how you are . . . You'll come to the depot with me in the morning and meet your new work crew, a batch of fine fellows, real comrades . . .

But the tears came streaming down Poliko's expressionless face and I had the horrible feeling that my brother had been destroyed, and the only thing left of him was this water streaming from his reddened eyes. He allowed me to lead him to our bedroom and he fell onto his bed like a tree falls to the axe. When I tried to help him undress he clenched his arms around himself and so I left him alone. And worse, he gritted his teeth together and would not utter a word. And all that evening my brother fell deeper into his abyss. He had got himself home in order to fall, I realised. But why and what had caused his despair was a mystery.

I spoke softly with mother and father late into the night. Givi recounted his own confusion on returning from the Great Patriotic War. But Poliko had been building not destroying. Yes there was the bullying common to conscripts, but they all suffered the same and they all had their chance for revenge in the second year and that did not seem to us the kind of thing that would damage Poliko. He was so easy going and good humoured and would have sung the boots off any Sergeant's petty game. Mother wondered if he had met a girl who had broken his heart.

In that case, she said, he'll get over it soon enough. We must find someone else for him. A new love will heal him, you see if I'm not right.

I lay on Poliko's bed with the quilt pulled over us. I had not undressed but I felt his coldness seeping into my bones. He made no sound and lay stiffly on his back but all night I felt his tears dampening the pillow in the dark. I did not sleep. I thought of how close we had been as children and how we had drifted apart in recent years. Did I know my brother any more? And what did he know of me? The little living dead man lay inside my lungs, aligned with my fear like the micro particles of magnetic iron lie on the plastic tape of my recordings. He was eyeing Poliko through his blood veil, was staring him out, was waiting for him to crack apart and spill the beans. So I held my place on the bed that night, guarding my brother who had nothing to admit to but these soundless tears.

I rose at dawn, lit a cigarette, allowed the smoke to drift over Poliko's face. His sore eyes followed the trace of the smoke in the twilight but he did not reach for the cigarette. The sparrows chittered on the roof. The wind came up with the daybreak and the net curtains ghosted at the windows. I switched the transistor on, tuned to the Voice of America. Night-time in the West. Luckily a broadcast of the shouting pop music he liked best. Hey! I said, shaking him gently. Listen to this! He sat up, frail against the wall. He would not remove that filthy T-shirt, the electric blue lycra pants. He allowed me to wipe his face with a warm wet cloth. I rubbed the cloth over his hair, the grain-coloured fuzz on his skull. My brother had come home wrapped in his handsome young form but inside he was old and barren. This I was certain of as I tended him, shaving him, gradually getting him to the appearance of normal but for his clothing. He was not crying any more but this absolute indifference was worse, this mechanical copy of my brother.

I watched the news to check on events in Afghanistan. But it was all positive. And even discounting the usual excessively optimistic statements, the super-structure of well-being which was as familiar as the concrete blocks around us – the scenes of Soviet soldiers side by side with smiling villagers, the newly built roads and clinics, the occasional footage of an impervious Soviet tank or a jubilant raiding party, hardly seemed cause to turn my buoyant brother into this husk.

Two, three, four days and Poliko did not improve. He ate without looking at his food, swallowing without chewing. He drank his cherry tea and smoked his cigarettes like a robot turned to the fastest speed. Givi and Vera could not take time from work so I stayed home with him. I played my tapes of him singing on the city streets. I turned up the volume on the Voice of America when they broadcast the jangly songs he liked. I sat by him and talked and did not ask him questions.

What did I talk about? I hardly knew myself. I am not an easy talker and at first I struggled to find subjects of interest. I found myself speaking of Maia. Of her unusual singing voice and her rendition of The Legend of Surami Fortress. I even found that I made a fair mimic, found myself purring like Eliso, clipping my sentences like Dato. And do you know what your fool of a brother took her as a gift? I spluttered, because I had become quite caught up in my story.

I swallowed down a terrible urge to tell him my secret. I found myself becoming furious with Poliko. Sitting there so clamped up when it is me who has lived a life of holding my mouth shut. Me who has to be on constant guard lest my visitor force his way out. For recently he had been tinkering with the lock. I felt his fingers jiggling at the mechanism. I understand locks all too well. They frequently malfunction. Have I not mended almost every door-lock in this tower?

In the evenings when Vera and Givi came home I shook my head to their eager looks and we sat in the kitchen with the door closed. Father still thought that Poliko would soon snap out of it but mother took a more pessimistic view. She wanted to bring a doctor.

You see, there was no-one to ask about what had happened to him. Once the two years are over a conscript is simply let go at the gates of his camp. From there he must find his own way home and return to civilian life and work or be branded a Parasite On The State. This is the rule. I forbade mother from bringing in a doctor. I hoped Poliko would come through with our help and would not be marked with an official medical pronouncement which would go on his Party record and might affect his future chances.

On the fourth day both Vera and Givi were off work and so I took the chance to slip away to my Institute for a short time. I had been due to make my annual presentation to the board of Professors and this was the last day they would sit. I had only to play my quota of songs, read a brief analysis from my notes, deliver a copy of the tape to the Institute Archive.

I hurried through the tape, skipping and fast forwarding in a manner I would not normally permit myself. The Professors seemed not unduly concerned though. The large curved desk behind which they sat was set on a dais and I could only see a row of academic heads resting on their hands as if they were enormously heavy.

And so, I concluded, I submit to my comrade Professors that I have discovered an entirely new subset of song, a form which includes the ambient sound, the singer and the surrounding world material become one voice . . .

The Professor in charge of the presentations waved his hand to silence me, stamped my annual quota and called for the next. I refused to look at the Stalin as I bowed and made my way out, even though the sun was winking at me from his protective glass. The painted one, with his vivid red lips and his velvet brown eyes, would only make the live one struggle to see how fine he had once looked. For I did not think I looked so fine on his behalf. I had not slept since Poliko's return.

Mother and father were sitting at the kitchen table and I saw at once that something was wrong.

Is he worse? I asked.

Don't be upset, said father.

We did it for the best, said mother.

He's with experts now, said father.

What have you done!

The doctor said Poliko needed removing from disturbing influences. She gave him a shot and took him away, whispered mother.

All the last days of anxiety, the sleepless nights, the strain of trying to keep everything seeming normal in front of Poliko came tightening around my skull and I let out a loud oath and slammed my fist on the table top. The cactus tin fell over and rolled off the edge. The earth spilled out and the cactus caught on the hem of Vera's dress and scraped against her bare leg as it fell. The floor covered in grit. The cactus uprooted. This I saw in the blink of an eye. My fist at the table. My shriek of fury.

Where is he? I screamed.

We don't know, mother whispered from whitened lips.

She touched her leg where the cactus had grazed. Givi bowed his head and cringed. I could not bear to be near them. I slammed into the sitting room, a crazy hope that Poliko would be there in the television chair. A sickly laugh came from my throbbing throat. It ran with me, a cackling comrade, spinning on the turning rail, running his hands along the lift shaft grilles, the greasy dust, the ancient oil, the scabs of rust, blood-iron on the fingers.

I went to the electricity sub-station and pressed my back against the cinder wall which conveyed static when wet, and it was always drawing up the wet being in the path of the broken outflow of a laundry house, and my spine flicked its little lamps on and off and my chest swelled and the transformer sounded its drone from within my lungs and after a while my mind cleared. When Alik came along I hailed him and told him what had happened.

I wish I'd known he was in such bad shape, he said, passing me a cigarette. Listen Iosif, there's only one place they take veterans with problems and that's the asylum. They won't let you in to see him. I've tried myself on behalf of one of my lads whose mother's been in there for years. It's a lock-down worse than jail. If he's in the testing category he'll be safe for a while. It's when they get him to the observation wards he'll be in trouble. He'll be pumped full of pills and left to dream his life away. Sorry to be realistic Iosif. Such is the Motherland's loving care, eh? By the way I've come across some mislaid Levi's if you're interested. It'd make a change from that suit of yours, comrade.

He strolled away. I smoked the cigarette. The dusk heavy with the scent of the too-early cherry blossom. The trees never learn. The blossom comes out pink and sweet and then the sky turns grey and the snow falls and the fragile clusters thicken to a blobby sham.

I set off to the opposite slope of this one-time forested valley. There I passed between unrendered walls marking off narrow vacant plots, and irregular walls of thick cast slabs set wide apart so that the plants beyond, the printing press, the

Melodia record production plant, the piano factory, the Astra
packing works seemed provisionally set down on a provisional
landscape. All was quiet. No workers. No sound of machine
or press. I lost my way and doubled back between the upright
slabs, and each false turn made me more determined to find
my brother. Upwards until the ground levelled and there were
no more boundary walls. It had become dark as I walked
between the columns of black Cyprus trees to a mown park
and the rustle of unseen poplars. The rustling grew louder as
I approached a brightly lit building, and it seemed that it was
coming from the neon lit windows, this furtive whispering of
a vast company of fragile leaves.

I was not alone as I stood gazing up at the blank windows.
A woman called out a name. But there was no reply. These
comrades, bathed in the spill of neon, did not speak amongst
themselves. I realised that they were used to being here in the
night and that I would also have to become used to being here
in the night. I called out for Poliko but did not expect a reply.
I walked three times around the outer walls. One more lone
figure thinking of a loved one inside the Institute of Mental
Wellness.

*

I returned the next day. Snow threatening on the wind. I tried
to gain access but the guard at the door required documents
and proof that I was the medical Professor I claimed to be. I
turned away and walked around the walls. The sweetly irregular tones of a cow bell came ringing from the grassland
beyond the park.

Now I passed the Astra plant with its massive enamelled
cigarette puffing a twist of enamelled smoke. Wrought iron

tobacco leaves on the gateway. The gates swung open and a shift of female workers came streaming out in their headscarves and tunics, chatting and laughing as they flowed around me. I could have come another way down the hill. I did not have to linger here. Nor peer so hard at the girls going past. I cannot say that I had a plan. I was virtually without thought. No sleep and worry about Poliko and feeling bad at my rage with mother and father, and my lock-picker hard at work in his den. I could not blame him for making the den. The rest of me was scrubbed bare of comfort. So he had a right to make a cosy place in my lungs. But the tinkering of his fingertips was a great distraction.

The girls brushed by me, cheery-faced and reeking of tobacco. There she is! I pushed my way towards her and called her name. Her friends looked me up and down and giggled and propelled her towards me. I stood there blinking and frowning. She was much more beautiful than I remembered.

Maia took my hand and led me through the crowd of work-ers, and we sat in a canteen and she ordered two beers. She took off her headscarf and ran her fingers through her hair. The canteen was noisy, the tannoys broadcasting up-beat jazz piano of the style that goes nowhere with a great deal of haste. She glanced around at the empty tables near ours.

Wait, she murmured as the waitress came and slammed down the beers.

She accepted a cigarette. I lit it for her and then lit mine and we smoked and sipped our beer.

You look terrible, she said.

It's my brother, Poliko. He's been taken to the asylum.

That's bad, she said.

I stared at a ring of beer on the plastic cloth.

I wondered if your mother might help me. Am I right in thinking she works in the Institute of Mental Wellness?

Maia put down her beer, leant toward me and hissed, Whose side are you really on?

I looked up at that and she slid her eyes around in a mock paranoid scan.

I'll pay for the beers, I said as I rose to go.

But then she held my arm and I did not wish to make a scene. Already some of the workers had glanced over at us. And I was unshaved and the seam of my suit jacket had come unpicked again at the elbows.

I sat down with a sigh and said, I don't know what to do.

Sorry, she said, let's start again. But if you want to rescue your brother you mustn't go to Eliso for help.

*

We had waited until Eliso was on night shift. I was in luck because she worked on the admissions ward. Maia told me with a grim laugh that it was this that had given her mother expertise in applying tranquilliser drips to the inmates who were not yet used to being away from home.

I walked directly across the echoey hall to the night guard's desk and rapped it so that he woke with a start. Standing so that he would not see Maia slip in behind me, I held my identity card in front of his eyes, spoke my name loudly, tapped my tape recorder and announced that I was here to collect the annual quota uptake on fragments of song from the Mental Sleep Department.

These songs, I continued with professional solemnity, can only be heard late at night whilst the Institute is at its quietest, for the singers' voices are very small.

I frowned down at the guard.

But small does not mean they are of no value. I will find my own way up, I said as I turned smartly on my heel.

I fully expected the guard to race after me and demand more proof of my quest, but I reached the staircase and went up and there was only silence behind me. My speech had excited me. My ears tuned in to the slightest sigh or moan, and as I climbed higher through the darkened levels there were sounds I could not name but which had compelling melody within them.

But now I had arrived at the corridor to the admissions ward where Eliso sat reading at a desk by lamplight. I crept close and softly cleared my throat. She looked up. I put my finger over my mouth and hissed, Shhh!

I had not rehearsed my part but found myself acting a figure of authority without difficulty. I flashed my identity card in front of her eyes and stood sternly as if awaiting a report of her duties. She had been reading a journal of the sort filled with romance on tractors and heroic deeds on factory conveyor lines. She closed it hastily and pulled some files to hide it. I nodded just that tiny bit and allowed myself the smallest of smiles. Her expression, at first alarmed, became conspiratorial.

My dear comrade Eliso, I murmured, what a piece of luck to find you here on this of all nights. I've been allocated the mental-night-songs quota, what a bore, but duty duty . . . You understand . . .

Comrade Iosif, she replied, how can I be of service?

We're quite alone, no? The truth is that when I was given this assignment I knew in my heart I'd find you here. In my profession we learn to recognise a singing voice even though it may be hidden by natural comradely bashfulness. But a woman like you must be heard. I know you'll do me the honour of allowing me to record you.

I had by now positioned myself between Eliso and the doors to the ward and I had set the tape recorder on her desk and opened the lid and was fondling the spool in a way that I hoped would keep her attention. Every now and then there came a distant howling and I could not say if it was dog or human. The little lamp flickered with uneven oscillation and the air was intolerably stuffy and hot. The narcotic sleep of the mentals suffused the night. I struggled to hold my thoughts steady lest they give way to my twin name who was hollering to be part of this plot.

Eliso eyed the tape recorder and sighed, If only I was free to sing for you. But I have my patients to think of, I might disturb their slumbers, my voice is very strong, I might have been an opera singer had I not chosen to serve my poor damaged comrades instead. But let me think. There's a room down the corridor where we could be private . . .

I could not believe my luck. I had to get her away from her station outside the ward and she was offering the solution. She led me down the darkened corridor, switched on her torch and shone it into a small storeroom. The narrow beam fell on stacks of linen. Eliso closed the door while I set about making space for my recorder on a shelf.

Had it not been for the muffling linen those sagging shelves would surely have cracked with the piercing intensity of her soprano. Eliso, Maia's mother, the night warden of mentals, with her tautened lips, her dramatic eyes, her tongue trembling in her opened mouth, her throat rippling and chording, flashed her torch at her face and then into my eyes. The bed linen might be privy to the aches of limbs that had stumbled into doubt but this aria of Eliso's was madness itself. Panic dried my mouth as part of my brain began calculating how long it would take until she used up the air in the cupboard. But on the other hand I could not help but shake my head in wonder and appreciation. It mattered not that my back hurt where it pressed against the shelving, nor that I could no longer recall the start number on my tape recorder counter. I could not recognise the composer, something classical perhaps and yet also too melodramatic to be serious opera. The words were lost in the acrobatics of her vocals. Perhaps there were no words. It might have been that she was simply performing arpeggios, each rising a semitone above the preceding in an exquisite climb over broken glass. And now, shut in this enclosed cabin within the vast shipwreck of the lunatics, I too began to lose my hold on sanity. So when at last she fell silent, and although she was obviously expecting it, I was the one to make the first move.

How can a man who has never kissed before say that he did not enjoy kissing a female warden with a streak of cruelty in her? I could blame it on my twin-bed-guest but you will know I would be lying. I do not know how long we kissed and fondled. The torch had fallen to the floor. I pulled away to catch my breath and in that instant I heard the flick flick of the end of the tape running around the spool. I cannot say it was easy to extricate myself from Eliso's embrace. But I felt behind me for the door handle. If I had brought the correct sized screw driver I could have opened its casing and adjusted the release mechanism on the spring, but as it was I rattled at it until it turned. Ah yes, my tape recorder too. The torch light skimming across the corridor floor. Silence out here. But for that distant howling.

I turned back to Eliso, returned the torch to her, adopted a posture of authority, raised my chin, spoke sternly.

I have my quota to fulfil. I shall proceed to the next floor comrade warden Dolidze. And let me say that I have never heard a finer operatic voice than yours. You are wasted. Wasted my dear!

I marched down the corridor towards another staircase and descended to the basement and a dark kitchen where cockroaches whispered on every surface. I found the kitchen workers' door and as Maia had promised, it opened outwards.

No sign of them. I stood frozen in the mercury light through the bare-branched poplars. Night wind hissing across the manicured grass. Each passing minute confirmed my failure. Maia was discovered. I had made everything a thousand times worse for Poliko. And Maia would rightly despise me for failing her. Now the memory of what I had done with Eliso crowded in and I felt sick and ashamed. I would go now to the night guard's desk and smooth it out for Maia, who I would say was my assistant. I would make a big fuss about having somehow lost her in the levels of sleeping mentals. But to my dismay I discovered that the kitchen worker's door had clicked shut and I could not open it to get back inside. Then I heard footsteps on gravel. A muffled giggle.

Iosif, Maia whispered, come and help me wake this sleeping beauty.

We walked Poliko between us to where we had ordered the taxi to wait at the entrance to the park. He might have been drunk, the way he half stumbled, half dragged, mumbling and drooling. He was wearing a hospital gown that came down to his ankles and I draped my suit jacket over his shoulders. We got him in the back and sat on either side of him. I handed a lot more roubles to the taxi driver and we sped away. Neither Maia nor I said a word but sat looking ahead with a sleeping

Poliko wedged between us. I had not felt this happy for I do not know how long.

Maia leant to the driver and said, Take us to the sulphur baths.

They'll be closed at this hour, I said.

Don't worry. Use your name. And a bottle of vodka, she replied.

I had brought new Levi's from Alik and a clean shirt and with some difficulty we managed to ease Poliko into them on the back seat. But it was like dressing a tailor's dummy and my stomach twisted with sorrow and fear as I handled my brother's slender passive body. Maia cradled his face between her cupped hands and told him that he was going to get better. I bought the vodka from a night kiosk near the bath houses.

We waited while the taxi drove away. The old city creaked and groaned in its sleep. The bats and rats followed their ways through air and cellar, their black shapes peeling from flaking walls and crumbling stone like little bits of memory, fragments of life, patched up history coming apart. The low, brick-domed baths emitted a sulphurous breath and even the stars above seemed struck alight with this earth-bound fire. Poliko slumped between us. I took most of his weight. The banners flapped and heaved on the Communist Party Headquarters a few streets away.

Hey, comrade Stalin, whispered Maia, let's get this dissident inside before they catch us!

I wished she had not said that. I was taking this huge risk for Poliko but somehow she had commandeered it and it all seemed like a big joke to her. I chose the best bath where the Party Chiefs like to loll. It was not difficult to wake the night guard and bribe him to open up. We passed in, two drunken comrades, one of high rank, with a female night worker to share.

But now that we were in the enclosed and damply hot atmosphere of the bath, Maia became serious and perhaps even a little shy. After all, we were going to undress my brother and immerse him in the water and we too would take off some clothes. She went away to find towels and I took Poliko into the changing room and sat him on the slatted bench. He seemed to be less sleepy now, at least he held up his head and his eyes flickered half open.

We're going to have a bath, I told him. Then you're coming home and you're going to get well. I won't leave you until you do. So if you want to get rid of me you'd better hurry up and get better.

Then I tugged off his clothes and pulled him up and led him over the wet tiles to the next room where the hot spring water dripped and swilled from every surface. I had taken off my shoes and socks and suit jacket but I was immediately soaked in perspiration. The damp air was soft to the touch. The sulphur fumes invaded every pore. I manoeuvred Poliko into the straight walled bath and lay him with his head propped on the edge. The room echoed with drips and swishing water. I leant close to Poliko and asked if he was alright. To my delight he nodded his head the slightest bit. Maia came in with a stack of towels. She had taken off her coat and dress and wore only a thin slip. I looked away.

How is he? she asked.

He's waking up.

Rub his skin, she said.

So I washed and rubbed my brother in the bath.

You're all wet, she said, I'll do it while you take off that shirt.

We changed places and I peeled off the wet shirt. She glanced at me and grinned.

You look better out of that suit, she said.

I felt very awkward. Her slip was so revealing. Now she turned her attention to Poliko and she rubbed his limbs under the water and stroked his forehead and massaged his scalp.

Blondy, she murmured.

I kept my eyes on Poliko, his pale torso and his tanned arms and legs and face, his sinewy length and his covering of wiry blond hair, and beneath the water that is not so cloudy to hide him, his sexual part floating curled on its nest of denser, browner hair. She is humming under her breath as she moves his scalp and his cropped hair under her hypnotic fingers. I dare not look at her bending over the bath. The water a constant blood heat temperature. The room lit only by a single bulb. Sizzling wet wiring. The cold shower drips and dribbles. The leaking stream runs to the grid at the centre of the brown tiled floor, disappears into the drain. She flicks back her damp wavy hair. Visible beneath her slip, her long spine and her hips and her buttocks as she kneels at the bath side. She turns her head, catches me staring at her.

Take over now. Keep massaging him. I'll be back in a minute, she said.

She wrapped a towel around herself and went from the room.

Hey brother, I said as I massaged his feet, I hope you're enjoying all this attention.

He twitched his lips and I laughed aloud because that was definitely a grin in his mind.

Maia returned with three bottles of beer and I flicked the lids off on the shower pipe. We sat on the bath edge and I held the beer for Poliko to drink, but he raised his arm from the water and took it himself and he was shaky but he knew what he was doing.

Is it alright with all the tranquilliser in him? I asked.

Maia shrugged and said, Maybe not, but he seems to be enjoying it.

He peered up from his watery bed and his gaze stayed on Maia.

Shall we stay here all night? she asked him.

His eyes flicked toward me. He took another shaky swig of his beer.

If you'll come in with me, he slurred.

She did not get into the bath with Poliko and he became sleepy again soon after. But as Maia and I hauled him from the water he felt supple and warm and my heart lifted with hope.

It was all so natural. We Georgians often share our sulphur baths, and anyway Maia was not the easily embarrassed type and I was so relieved and thankful for her help that I would have condoned anything she ordered. But she was also not the ordering type. She did things with confidence but was not bossy.

Now that we had succeeded and our plot was accomplished, and, so far as I could tell about Poliko's health, he was better than I could have imagined in such a few hours, I began to recall my part with Eliso. As we dressed Poliko I asked Maia if she thought her mother might have raised the alarm.

No, she replied, before I went into the ward I managed to stamp a release document on her desk. And anyway no-one ever tells when things go wrong. No-one admits to failure because failure's been obliterated! Don't worry, your brother probably won't even be missed. It was lucky we found him while he was still in the first ward though. You did well to get Eliso away from her post. How did you manage it?

I took her to sing in a cupboard, I said.

Maia burst out laughing. If your brother is as crazy as you are God help the State! she said.

After the humid atmosphere of the sulphur bath the early morning air felt chilly. Poliko had draped his arm over Maia's shoulders and she guided him with her arm around his waist. I left them for a moment while I went to look for a taxi and when I returned they were sitting on the edge of the low domed roof of the bath house. I saw them before they saw me. In the monochrome light of dawn they looked like a couple posed for an old-fashioned studio portrait. Blessed with the beauty and grace of a distant era. I gazed at this apparition for a second and then I pulled myself together. My brother was still half-drugged and not safe yet. I had to get him home. I had no time to dwell on the way they sat so close together. Nor did I comprehend the chemistry that bound them in that silvered unreal light. I had forgotten the lesson learned in childhood when my scissors had cut my sister in two and the world was shown up for the broken thing it is. I did not see that Poliko and Maia were toying with appearances and had each found in the other the cracked mirror of their dreams.

Since my furious outburst, mother and father had been subdued. I had not told them what I was planning with Maia, partly in case it went wrong but also because I could not trust them not to interfere. But there is a part of a Georgian's mind which does not belong to known scientific laws and which, like the sulphur springs, overflows and infiltrates, a part which radiates the heat of thought and the sensation of imagined action. Therefore it is impossible for us to be truly secret, because always a portion of the thought will seep through the skull and swim the air and sink directly into the mind of another Georgian. It may or may not arrive at an appropriate time. It may or may not even be noticed, so used are we to receiving these moist mind messages. This is a fact.

And so when I came home with Poliko that early morning I found Givi waiting in the yard by the entrance hall to our tower. He had the lift door jammed open with a stick.

Well done son, he said with his finger on the door button as we juddered upwards.

*

Now I must return to the cactus tumbling from the dry earth in the rusty tin can, grazing the front of Vera's leg with its furry hooked spines.

I had never liked her cacti collection. The suspicious intervention of God suffused their dull grey stubs. The illusory power of icons lurked within the metallic gleam and the oxidised bronze of the tins. Perhaps I was even glad to see at least one of them destroyed as it was trampled on the kitchen floor in that flashpoint of my anger.

Since the accident Vera's leg had become inflamed but she made light of it. We had been distracted thinking about Poliko, me most of all with the rescue plot afoot, and as I said, Givi had received my thoughts and unknown to himself was busy preparing the way home, had jumped to the very morning of our return and had already jammed the lift and had asked Vera to keep the curtains drawn and brew up tea with cherry jam. So Vera's leg was bottom of the heap of our thoughts.

I had once caught her trying to pluck out the spines with some tweezers which did not meet properly. I took them from her and set about realigning the flat ends with the pliers which I removed from the geyser for the job, re-stringing them back to the geyser tap rod when I had got the tweezers perfect. I asked if she would like me to help as I could see the fine haze of bristles where the skin had become red. But mother wanted to do it herself and I thought perhaps this intense concentration was better than sitting and flicking through the pages of her Anthology and biting her lip.

And then when I came home with Poliko, and he was so much better, I believe Vera forgot about the soreness in her joy at having him back.

The issue of my parents having Poliko taken away was never talked about again. Vera and Givi went to work and I stayed at home to watch over my brother as he slept a natural sleep. He woke and ate and then slept again. Each hour brought him closer to normality but I could see that this was hard on him. The slip-stream of wherever he had been in his mind was still dragging and he had to conserve all his energy to stand firm.

After about a week of this Poliko was well enough to go out on the balcony where I joined him for a cigarette. I tugged on the worn patch of linoleum and said I would look out for something brighter to replace it. Poliko narrowed his eyes and regarded me through his cigarette smoke.

I know what you've done, he said, and thanks for getting me back on my feet. But you won't ask me to talk about it will you? I just want to forget. And it's best you don't know anything. Don't let mum and dad try to make me explain will you?

I saw that his fingers were trembling and I quickly reassured him that I would do whatever he wanted.

107

You're a good comrade, brother mine, he said. But there's one thing I don't want to forget. When I was in the sulphur bath I had a dream about a masseur with singing fingers. I can't stop thinking about her.

That was no dream, that was Maia. I couldn't have got you home without her. Actually I promised to call her as soon as you felt up to meeting her. And yes she was in the bath house and yes she saw everything.

He grinned at me and flicked away his cigarette stub. Alik happened to walk across the yard. He looked up, saw Poliko and let out a loud cheer.

Congratulations! he called, how did you do it!

Naturally I did not say a thing and Alik just stood with his bullish head tilted back, grinning up at us. Then I had an idea and I called down to ask if he had any new jackets.

Plenty, he shouted.

At that moment a woman's head popped out from a window on the opposite block. Any white nylon zippers? she called down.

Large, medium and small, he replied loudly.

Another voice from somewhere out of sight called out, Any denims?

Ready-faded with silver stars on the back, Alek shouted.

But Poliko was wearing the leather jacket that he had used before his draft. He was adamant that he did not need a new one. The leather was cracked and grey with wear. Poliko had come home from school one day proudly wearing the thing, it had been too big for him then but now, despite its dilapidated state, it was a perfect fit. I kept my dislike of the worn-out jacket to myself. If this return to an item from his youth was going to help keep my brother well, then I would not argue. I determined to repair the pockets which hung in tatters where the old fleece lining had perished.

*

Maia soon became part of our family. I cannot say it was easy for me at first. I had harboured thoughts about her which I only realised when I saw her together with Poliko. But they fitted each other so well with their clowny mannerisms and light-hearted banter. If I was jealous I know I did not show it.

And strange, but for the first time in my life I was glad of my permanent visitor. I reminded myself that with him on constant look-out it would have been a tarnishing of Maia's brightness to have allowed myself to become intimate with her. She had turned her light on Poliko, and I had never really been anything to her other than a musicologist with a tape recorder. So my unrelenting room-mate made sure I did not slip up and betray any futile emotions, and I found myself feeling grateful for his unerring eye.

Vera treated Maia like a daughter. In the evenings they often sat at the kitchen table companionably shelling and pounding walnuts or peeling garlic to pickle. Mother read from her Blue Horns Anthology and sometimes Maia sang one of the poems that had been set to music. If Poliko came to the kitchen mother put her work aside and left them together. She shut the door on them, and if father went to go in she whisked her hands at him and shook her head.

You can wait for your tea, she whispered. There's a pair of love birds not to be disturbed. You see what I said! she beamed at me.

Her sore leg had still not cleared up. Givi and I tried to

persuade her to go to the doctor but she said she wanted nothing more to do with doctors and covered her leg with her hand or her dressing gown and pretended that she did not need to hobble across the room.

No-one can force another to sing. Poliko had not sung a note since his return. I laid traps. I played tapes filled with mysterious maidens half seen in the sulphurous steam of a bath house, with a warrior returned to seek his wife only to spy her in the arms of a stranger on a vine-draped balcony, with ghosts wandering the ancient alleys in search of their missing lover. Shamelessly sentimental songs of despair and loss, age and regret. Tear-jerking songs of Tbilisi as a mistress of fading beauty, guilt-laden songs of the River Mtkvari as a lithesome girl seducing the mountains from their guardianship over the city.

My mellifluous caravanserai of Occident and Orient snaked through our overheated apartment and out of the open windows, the *duduki* pipe and the three-stringed *panduri*, the finger drum, the old-fashioned voices, until even Vera and Givi were crooning along and neighbours in the surrounding blocks were leaning from their windows like flowers attracted to the sun.

It was now about three weeks since Poliko had recovered. Maia had found him work at the Astra plant where he could be invisible, although no-one had called about him going missing from the Mental Wellness Institute. She said that Eliso had not mentioned it either.

Such action as I undertook to rescue my brother did not taint my pride in the Motherland's benevolence, even if her care was a little over-enthusiastic at times, and her sight a little dimmed to the mutual back-scratching of her children. I had to admit though, it was lucky for us that questions had been done away with.

I lounged on my bed while Poliko lay back on his and Maia straddled him ready for play fighting. We were comfortable with this arrangement. The notion of privacy in the sense of having an inviolable personal sleeping place does not exist for us Georgians. Even if, like Maia, there were no brothers or sisters to share a room with, our readiness for a visitor remains on high alert. Of course I frequently left them alone. I had my notes to type up at the office and my night acquaintances to pursue.

Maia suddenly leans over to the bedside table and without a by-your-leave she switches my tape recorder off. I jerk myself upright and glare at her but she drapes herself over Poliko with her head turned from me and her ear pressed to his chest. I get up and close the lid of my recorder. I want to reprimand her but at the same time I am too annoyed to speak. I am about to stalk out but then she starts singing a silly song meant for children which repeats the same phrase and adds one name or action each time it goes round.

I step over to the window and hold the net curtain away. There, my smiling face hovering amongst the towers. The many lighted windows and the blackly starlit ribbons of sky. The tick-tock of my guest's pocket-watch which he has taken to re-setting every few minutes, clicking the glass open and turning the hands and clicking the glass closed and winding the mechanism so tight that my ribs ache with the tension of the spring, and the sprockets and cogs grinding as they race to undo themselves.

Behind my back, suddenly, two voices singing this nonsense song. Poliko lightly and Maia louder, with undeniable humour in the combination of masculine-tentative and feminine-certain.

But now Poliko takes the lead, his voice rises high and I had forgotten how this tenor affects my nerves and causes these shivers to break out all over my skin.

My ears are not clean enough to properly receive such beauty. He makes up the most ridiculous lyrics, the most far-fetched names and impossible actions, and Maia has the game now and she tops his inventions, their voices overlapping and confusing in the joke of their competition. But all of a sudden their song unites and the craziness is mutual, the names and the actions improvised from a single mind, the simple circular two-part melody taking on a sophistication of tonal grades and phrasing far beyond anything predictable.

They have passed into the river of minds and have met at a musical confluence. My fingers fumble at the tape recorder lid. And yet I am too leaden to move.

I did not turn from the window. The glass divided us, my strained smile was safe out there. Oh, but I did not want to always return to my name's misfortune. This duet was remarkable. I began planning Poliko and Maia's future as stage performers.

*

Since singing that nursery song Poliko and Maia had found a form to be in love with and they delighted in showing it off. Many evenings the television was blank and the State Radio knob turned to silent as they entertained Givi, Vera and me with their twists on the songs we all knew so well. Even when they found the haunting dissonant harmonies which seemed to have been lying dormant in the melody until their vocalisation, they always kept it light and with some peculiar funny alteration to the lyrics.

I think my parents were bemused by this rearranging of tradition. But neither spoke against it and Vera even began copying down fragments of their new lyrics and saying shyly that she thought she might make poems from them. Givi was content so long as Poliko went to work and continued not to cry any more. I do not think my father had really recovered from seeing his son so destroyed, and now he watched Poliko warily, as if he might at any moment shrink back into the swaddles of a wailing baby.

They were both hugely attractive, warm, careless, with a covert humour in their eyes and always seeming to be taking part in a practical joke. This is how I want to picture them. Kind. Generous. Witty. But I must dirty my hands with another block of fact. It is heavy with pain. Repellent as a block of human ash.

Alik had managed to source the part needed for Poliko's motorbike. He even got one of his lads who knew about such things to fix it in. Alik did not ever ride the bike, nor would he accept a spin on the pillion. But he approved of its black-market history and perhaps he had hoped that in rejuvenating the bike he would help Poliko get back to his old self. Whatever the motivations, he had taken it upon himself to mend the bike while Poliko had been in his state of mental collapse. At first Poliko had not seemed to care about the machine in the way he once had. Maia took up a lot of his attention. But then they began riding it together. Sometimes she would be the driver and he would be perched on the rear rack, clinging to her slender waist, waving as people gaped at this unorthodox arrangement.

Although I did not like to see them on the foul machine, and I still recalled that awful mark scribed below the saddle, I did not interfere with their joy in making such a show of riding around the blocks. Maia was a good driver although she had had no training. Neither had Poliko. They showed no fear of speed. They wore no special garments on the bike. The wind tousled their hair and reddened their cheekbones and when they came back to the apartment they brought with them the reek of grease and engine oil.

It was a particularly cold winter. The yards and lanes around the settlement were frozen. Ridges of sparkling mud and ice-covered puddles made getting around hazardous. That evening as we all gathered in the apartment after work, a heavy snow began to fall. I had spent the day snugly ensconced in my office sorting through an early set of recordings. Poliko looked tired after being out all day in this harsh weather. His face was raw and his hands seemed to be giving him pain. Maia was pacing up and down by the windows, clicking her fingers to a tune she was humming. Every now and then she paused and leant her forehead on the window pane and puffed out a sigh. Dinner was almost ready. Givi was sitting close to the television as usual. I had laid out the removable parts of my recorder to give it a good clean.

Let's go! said Poliko out of the blue.

Now? said Maia spinning round from her place at the window.

Why not? he replied.

Because it's too snowy, I advised, understanding his meaning.

He came over to the table where I was working on my tape recorder. Then he leant over me and hissed into my ear, Keep out of it. It's none of your business what I do.

I had never heard him use that cold tone of voice before. I

did not know where to look. I was actually afraid of returning his gaze, which was drilling into the top of my head – I could feel it in my skull. I tried to carry on with the intricate part of disassembling I had arrived at. He leant over me, waiting for me to respond. Then he jogged my arm so the little screw in my fingers was jolted away and fell to the floor.

What are you doing! Be careful! I muttered.

Be careful, he mimicked.

I looked over to Maia for help. She would surely smooth out Poliko's bad mood. But she was watching with a neutral expression. Then he span away from me, grabbed her by the hand and they rushed out, not even taking their coats. I followed after them in alarm. They had taken the lift so I used the stairs. By the time I got down to the exit they were already outside, holding their faces up to the falling snow flakes.

Come back in, I called. You'll catch your death.

Then the terrible fact of Poliko striding over to the doorway where I hovered with their coats. Pushing me in the chest. Hissing, Get out of my life. I hate you and everything you stand for.

My blood ran cold. I could not recognise this staring man. His skin was taut and white, his lips were thin lines and his eyes were blood-shot. I took a step backwards in shock. He stared me out for what seemed an age, then he gave a small shudder and his face returned to something like normal.

Want a ride? he asked.

You shouldn't . . .

That's true.

He walked toward Maia but she peered around him to where I stood in the doorway. The snow was falling thickly now, the flakes clung to her face and she blinked them away from her eyes. She called, Sorry. Or perhaps I imagined she did. They were lost in the falling snow. I heard the bike start up, the flooding roar of its engine. I heard it skid and grip and skid again. I peered into the night. A glimpse of foamy waves as the bike scythed through the white-out. I stood for a long time, numb and dazed in the freezing hallway. That sudden fury. That hatred on his face. Maia in the background, pitying me. Yes, that was the look she had given me.

I could not help laying the blame on the motorbike. It was a bad influence. And that symbol of inhumanity hidden beneath the seat. I do not believe in black magic or any sort of voodoo. But my stomach turned at the thought of a swastika speeding along beneath their coupled forms.

The next day I took a file and scoured the mudguard to the bare metal behind the saddle spring. If Poliko noticed what I had done he did not mention it, but I believe that he had truly forgotten about the fascist symbol. He had never spent time examining the bike or poring over its intricate parts. It was only the speed of the old warhorse that he wanted.

He never aimed his anger at mother or father, at least they never spoke of it with me. I never witnessed him being angry with Maia either. I had no doubt that I was the only victim of my brother's sudden outbursts. If Maia seemed more with-drawn than usual, I put it down to the long winter. They continued to go riding in icy conditions. They wore the least possible clothing and came home shivering and elated. There were times when I was on the balcony, a coat draped over my head, my cigarette warming my hands, when I caught snatches of their voices as they raced the tarmac road. They were singing. I could not make out the lyrics. But they were singing in perfect harmony even though they would not have been able to hear their own voices over the din of the engine.

I went to Alik. He told me that the local police would not apprehend them speeding around his territory.

It's so dangerous. They could crash. I wish they'd stop, I said.

In that case I might have to give the bike an overhaul.

You'll do that? I asked.

I don't like to see a woman acting like a man. It's not right for Poliko to be seen with her like that.

Thanks.

Think nothing.

With the end of winter came the end of Poliko's motorbike. When he found it would not start he simply left it where it was and never spoke of it again. It was not even chained up. In time someone wheeled it away and it was gone from the yard and from our lives. I once asked Maia if she missed the rides, but she shrugged and replied that nothing lasts forever. Her answer reminded me of our first conversation, I'm just like the wheat, she had said. Poof. Gone.

*

It is possible for magnetic tape to carry up to four parallel tracks, although my preference is for the single track, the straightforward gathering of live sound in all its rough edged totality. I wish that I had been able to hold a recording device to this story as it unfolded moment to moment, around and within me. No doubt there are portions of this narration, my final recording venture, which do not always relay the accurate facts I seek. I am trying to recapture erased actions and sights. I am trying to unpeel the magnetised layers of emotions and dreams. I must make the effort or else fall back under the charm of everything that caused my brother to turn from me. So much has gone forever. My reels wind tight on the spindle of truth. It is the central core which can never be heard.

Things occurred without my knowledge. People I loved said things that I would never hear. Our national genetic weakness in the skull, that factor which enables thought to leak mistily through the cranium and condense in another Georgian mind, does not occur at the flick of a switch but, as in the process of distillation, needs flame, needs emotional heat. In the every day, my family's thoughts were a mystery to me.

I have always known I had an anti-talent for singing, a voice that would compel my comrades to flee from the source of me. I only ever wanted to collect the actual evidence of my ears and eyes. My imagination had other business to attend to. My mind was a depot where my honoured visitor spent many an hour idling amongst exotica. It has been imperative to keep the conveyor moving, to deposit vast quantities of material for his consumption. For my guest has an appetite which I can never satisfy. Unused to such limited quarters as he is, he demands entrance to the no-go zones in the depths of my soul, where my brain-waves wriggle and jiggle for his pleasure. I do not know if I am capable of outwitting him. But this store of facts lies apart from my soul. It is sited on the arid plain of loss. I shall continue to build it up in the hope that he will not wish to amble into this parched place.

Tbilisi is scattered with semi-sunk pipelines, with the cast shells of hollow archways where secret spiral stairs are said to lead down to the warren of tunnels connecting all regions of the Motherland, with perspex-clad frontages of almost finished

State department stores, with underground caverns where the shapes of fountains, concrete benches, Aeroflot ticket booths, collective shops and restaurants reflect on the waterlogged marble paving slabs. Tin advertisements of State factory goods hang askew on hoisting ropes. A Lada, a bottle of Sovetskaia champagne, on the way up to be screwed to the skyline.

And against these modern visions the old quarters hook their wonky balconies, prop their feeble walls and lean their slipping roofs. Occasional earth tremors make sure the city foundations are never permanently settled. Nor are her walls ever completely light-tight. The air is always sharp with builder's lime and rubble dust. The city grows in a long narrow valley with the River Mtkvari as the hunch-backed spine. Traffic fumes cling to the water and the lower slopes of the escarpments, and the fug of late-night banquets and the sulphurous exhalations of the earth are for us Tbilisians as oxygen is to others. This is the medium on which I shade in the ghosts of my family, from which I inhale, all at once, a muddle of interlinking events, gathering pace as the reel comes near its end, trailing behind all that went before like the verses of a song, sung and gone, but each verse vital to the tale.

*

I was meeting a comrade in the Ministry of Culture. I had once done him the favour of securing admission to my Institute for his niece, and I happened to know that the Musicians' Union were under pressure to extend their quota of new talent.

The spacious office was empty but for the desk and our chairs. I could not help but picture myself behind that desk, leaning back in the same relaxed posture as this comrade who had not needed to be reminded of our little agreement but had poured two glasses of good brandy and pushed the box of Cuban cigars toward me. He flipped off the intercom. Posters of stage performers and dance troupes peeled from the walls. The portraits of former Heads of State hung behind the desk. The Stalin glass was so dusty that he was all but invisible. His gilt frame was chipped along the moulded foliage where the revealed plaster had turned grey. No matter, when I sat in that chair I would not have to look at him. I set up my tape recorder and played the recording I had made of Poliko and Maia in duet.

To my relief, despite their acting like a pair of star-struck love-birds as I had recorded them singing, they had agreed to my proposal. Poliko's hair had grown down to his jaw-line and it fell over his forehead in a lazy yellow wing. Maia had cut hers even shorter. The waves had become tight curls and the stunning effect was of a swarm of buzzing black bees clustering around the pale length of her face. No, she had not asked me to cut it this time.

I do not think my comrade in the Ministry of Culture (whose name I am unable to reveal) was all that impressed by the songs on my recording, and I have to admit that here in the important air of the Ministry, Poliko and Maia's variations did sound a bit odd. But he shoved the ledger over the desk and I signed the contract for a new double act to fulfil a quota of fifty-two stage performances in one year. In return they would receive a regular payment, would be allowed to give up working at the Astra packing plant, and if they proved popular with the masses the following year's contract would bring them the privilege of an apartment of their own.

Oh, I have not yet mentioned the fact of Poliko and Maia's engagement to be married. So, there it was.

A few words about the Beatles and counter-culture. The *Fab Four*, as we know they like to be called, are immensely popular in Georgia and as examples of working-class boys are not frowned upon by the Communist Party. In Tbilisi we have an official Beatles fan club and a Beatles band who play fair imitations of the Liverpool sound. Pop songs are not supposed to be upsetting or disturbing. The masses want love and pretty tunes, swaying rhythm and a drum beat that grandparents can dance to.

Other breeds of pop music have sneaked over the borders as illegal albums hiding in Melodia record sleeves. They are recorded on spools, passed around and re-copied until the original sound is all but destroyed. The Voice of America. Radio Free Europe. The BBC World Service. Radio Monte Carlo. These are the other conduits for the noises they call heavy metal and punk, the siren call of chaos from the West. There are secret short-lived venues where youths imitate the musical death-throes of their self mutilated heroes, until the KGB arrive to put a stop to it.

I had forgotten to come up with a name for my new double act. So when it came to filling out the contract, perhaps my penning the initial B, without even quite knowing what would come next, had something to do with the popularity of that quartet from Liverpool. However that may be, I wrote The Bells as my double act's name.

I did not really hold the genre of pop song in very high esteem. And I had some qualms about how Poliko and Maia would fit in to the category of popular stage performers, which is a more visible league than traditional stage performers, Classical stage performers, jazz stage performers, or the sub-set category of peasants who have their village Culture Hall stages and who perform anything with unforced naturalness at the drop of a hat. But my Ministry comrade needed to up his popular quota, and if The Bells were going to reap the rewards of the system, popular they would have to be.

*

Vera rests her leg on the kitchen chair while Maia holds a cold flannel on the swollen shin.

Maia looks up at me and says, We should try a phage treatment. Would you have time to get some?

Yes dear, says Vera, I'll take the phage, they're not doctors' medicine. D'you think the French Cottage still exists? Put a light under the pan of beans would you and pass me the corn meal.

And while she kneads the meal with water and oil and presses out the *chadi*, Vera conjures the 1930s, describing a time when Giorgi Eliava and his Parisian pal Felix d'Herelle strolled around Tbilisi talking incessantly about their beloved bacteriophage.

But it all came to a sad end, she murmurs glancing at me.

Why must I feel responsible? My guest arrived in my lungs with blood on his hands. I had not ordered the amiable phage researcher to be slain.

It was Beria who did it, I mutter.

That's right, Vera says, Beria took against Eliava because he had a beautiful wife who was an opera singer and who refused his advances.

She, my mother, frowns at my grey jacket.

Eliava always wore beautifully tailored suits. Put some oil in the frying pan will you dear, she says.

I blink to clear the mist in front of my eyes. The *chadis* lie like baby fists on the scratched formica table top. I scrape off the dried dough with the back of a blunt knife blade and scoop up the mess and drop it into the plastic bucket whose handle I have removed to saw into door wedges to stop them slamming in the wind.

I'll get the phage, I say.

*

I turned into a steep street leading from Rustaveli Avenue toward the Mtkvari embankment. Here, half hidden behind stone walls and rows of Cyprus, was the bacteriophage laboratory complex. I continued down the street towards the outpatients' clinic and joined the queue of comrades waiting to be seen. As I stood in line my thoughts circled around a dark hour of night when I had walked this very street to the river embankment.

The lone woman knew a secret way where fig trees overhung the wall, hiding a breach into the grounds of the bacteriophage complex. There we did what I paid her for and she sang well enough for me to want to listen to the tape that same night. The night watchman at my Institute was used to me keeping my own hours and he hardly raised his head as he snoozed on his three-legged stool.

I am meticulously careful to keep my recorder in mint condition. I know the controls better than my own hands. And so when the spool played through I was certain I had not made any mistakes. The silence on the tape was a true recording. The woman's singing, my grunts and groans, the usual hooting of an owl or scurry of a rodent had been obliterated, not by my depressing the erase switch but by some kind of over-riding pressure in the air. I leant my ear to the speaker, intent on searching for the slightest sound, but not even the soft hum of the three motors had been picked up on the tape. It was then that I realised he had slipped out of me. This soundless recording and the vacant rooms of my residence, this spinning plastic ribbon and the revolving doors of my throat, my plush red quilts, my two-way mirrors, my simple board and lodging, they were not secure, they did not delineate his form any more, they did not represent a man-shaped hidey-hole, were no longer a home from home with the familiar name-board swinging over the entrance.

So I got down on my knees and crawled beneath my desk. I crawled across the floor and checked in all the corners. I dragged my chair out and stood on it to see up beyond the light. The light burned my face. The filament rang, rang. I pitched my voice to match it. Thin and high, *nau nani nau nau nani nana nau*. His burly silhouette loomed upon the shelves, folding into the slots and undulating over my spool boxes. I jumped from the chair and pressed the off switch on the tape recorder. I ripped the spool away and shook it so that the tape unfurled and then I struck a match and set fire to the pool of tape on the floor and my basement filled with foul smoke. I struggled on tiptoe to open the window but it would not budge. With my arm over my face, only my eyes peering around, I sought him out. Calling in the manner of a bell, if a little muffled behind my jacket sleeve. For I felt pity for him you see. He had no other home to take him in. Living as he was, he could not be left to undulate shadow-like over closed walls. I held my arms wide to gather up his tubby self as he shuffled rather shamefaced toward me. The smoke had cleared now and so I lit a cigarette and perched on the edge of my desk to savour the slightly plastic flavour of the tobacco. Meanwhile I felt him sinking back into his cushions and, yes, chortling softly at the turn he had given me.

So I had an uncomfortable association with this place, I did not want a repeat of that albeit unsuccessful outing of his, and I could not wait to get the phage treatment and be gone. When at last my turn came I bent to the low hatch in the outer wall. All I could see of the clinician was a portion of her white lab coat.

I need a phage for a leg that's been stung by a cactus, I said.

Is it your leg?

Of course it is, I replied, thinking to hurry things up.

Then you'd better come in and let me examine it, she said.

I limped through a small waiting room to the treatment clinic where the air was stifling and noisy with the hum of refrigerator engines. The clinician was busy behind the opened door of one of these. I thought about leaving while I could, but my leg was throbbing and my blood pounding in my temples.

Take off your trousers, she said as she tended to something in the fridge.

I'm sorry, I mumbled, I made a mistake, the phage is for my mother, she's too poorly to come herself.

The clinician finished what she was doing in the fridge and closed the door. I flexed my leg as if to show her it was better now. She was looking at me with an expression that seemed to say she had seen many cases like me. She was, I saw through my embarrassment, very attractive, which only made me feel worse.

Shall we begin again comrade? she asked wearily.

My mother's leg has been stung by God, I mean, a cactus. That is, there's a tin can with old earth and God in the roots. Stung her leg badly. Won't heal up.

I felt my face flush with my idiotic words.

Your name? she asked.

Iosif Dzhugashvili.

Her pen hovered for the briefest moment before she wrote in the records ledger.

I'll need a sample of the wound. Take this swab and rub it on the worst area. Bring it back tomorrow. Come later in the day when I've finished with my other patients, she said looking me straight in the eye.

I returned to the bacteriophage clinic the next day as the workers were making their way homewards. The clinician took the swab and smeared it on a slide and then sat peering into a microscope.

Staphylococcus, but which strain? she murmured.

Her white lab coat rode up above her knees as she perched on the high lab stool. I smoked a cigarette. Set my tape recorder on one of the steel topped benches. I now believed that the clinician was deliberately ignoring me. I coughed and yawned but still she sat with her back to me. A long thick black plait fell over her shoulder. I pushed away a sudden urge to take hold of that plait and . . . At that moment, still peering down the lens, she beckoned me closer, whispering, Do you want to take a look before I destroy them?

Why did she have to whisper? She eased from the stool and I took her place. But although I saw a bright moon-ish disc and a far-away squiggling mass I could not really make anything out. I grunted as though I were impressed, and looked up only to find that she had her head stuck in a fridge.

We'll try this one, she said coming out with a tube of liquid. Can you sing? I asked.

But she did not reply. She was busy with a pipette, her lips on the glass tube, sucking up the milky broth and dropping some onto the slide where mother's bad leg was smeared. I shuddered and began to feel sick. Now she stooped over the microscope once more. If it had not been for Vera waiting for the treatment I might have left this white-coated clinician right then. Again, I return to the cactus, the tin-can icon, the saint in concrete. I blame it. I lay all blame at its wispy feet. I pour a libation of blame over its grey stub. I scorch its prickles off with blame. I freeze blame into its water-filled flesh. But it alters nothing. I was already falling in love with the white-coated clinician.

Focus! she said as I peered once more, at her command, down the microscope lens. Reluctantly I twiddled the focus until all came sharp and bright. Now, I heard her say from afar, watch out for the moment of lysis.

The yellow full moon contained a mass of ghostly creatures with box-shaped heads, rigid tails and tangled spidery legs. Now they swarmed towards a globe which hung on the outer rim of the luminous moon like a world in reverse. One of the box-headed creatures clung to the surface of the globe and pricked it with its tail and emptied itself into the quivering interior. The globe by comparison to this invader was a planet to a grain of sand. The bright yellow moon juddered as I gasped and recoiled and then pressed my eyes closer to the lens in fascination. For now the globe-world's interior was steadily filling with neat ranks of replicated boxy heads from which sprang rows of stiff little tails and tangles of spidery legs. More and more of these twins manufactured themselves from

127

themselves, and the speed of their work and the perfection of their reproduction far exceeded any human quota ambition. The globe-world was filled to capacity and yet more of these tiny soldiers squeezed into place. Then without warning the globe burst apart and the squads fled in all directions and the yellow moon was infested with box-headed ghosts. I could not take any more.

Did you see lysis? she was asking excitedly.

I nodded and stood up shakily.

Got a cigarette? I asked, quite forgetting my manners.

The phage are everywhere. Inside you. Inside me. Here take one of these.

She offered a pack of Turkish cigarettes. I hesitated and she said, Family contacts.

No it's not that. Those *things*. Are they what I've got to give my mother?

You saw how they ate the bacterium. The little dears are always hungry!

I took one her cigarettes and lit hers first and tried to regain my composure as I sucked in the perfumed smoke. The fluorescent light strips, the row of tall refrigerators, the steel-topped surfaces, the grey tiled walls and floor, the neat stacks of petri dishes and empty glass flasks, the silvery incubator in one corner, the sink with its tall tap and bottles of disinfectant, the odour of hygiene above a low note of diseased flesh, all spoke of order. But I had just seen a world exploded by order, and once again I was the young Pioneer who did not know how to warn his parents that everything was breaking.

I should go, I said.

But I haven't prepared your mother's treatment, she said.

We were standing over the microscope. I had only to turn

to look at her. To find her watching me. To take the cigarette from her fingers and stub it out under my shoe and do the same with mine. She raised one eyebrow. A small smile curved her lips. I put my hand on the back of her neck where the plait hung and my fingers went beneath the plait to her warm skin. She looked me in the eyes.

What's this? she said.

The moment of lysis, I replied.

She laughed aloud. I pulled her towards me and quietened that laugh.

Enough for now to say that it was always going to happen thus. She had invited me to her clinic after hours. I went to her with that kiss already completed in my mind. I do not know if that disgusting scene at the end of the microscope lens had acted as an aphrodisiac. But my senses were aroused and I was ready to invade her, if I may speak so lewdly. I soon discovered that Tamoona was no passive globe, nor was I such a militant conqueror.

Even though, or perhaps because, we had just met, desire dragged us to the floor. I had not been with a woman in this way before. But I discovered that I only need follow her cue, and she seemed to like what I was doing. And for me, the touch of her voluptuous body beneath the lab coat was unbearably erotic and finding her ready to take me fully and being gentle because I was not sure of myself, but learning by the millisecond the unspeakable strangeness of joining with another and hearing their cries of pleasure. I thought, for the briefest of moments, that I had heard her speak my name at the height of our passion. But I swept the thought aside. I was not going to allow him to spoil this. And for another micro-moment I suddenly wondered if it was all a big mistake and I had been wasting my life in pointless worry. This too I swept away. These were nothing to the emotions sweeping through me, this lovely woman in my arms, this surprising calm, as we lay smiling on the tiles.

In general Tamoona Kabakidze was not given to impetuous actions. She was a stern commander in the domain of her laboratory, she was meticulously correct with her series of tests, her incubation periods, her smears of agar jelly, her jars of filthy river water, her swabs of pus and phlegm. Each of the ten refrigerators contained rows of different phage cultures, which she grew from sewage enriched with chosen bacteria as others grow yeast or yoghurt strains. As I loved my tower blocks so did she love her invisible settlements of viruses and bacterium. As I archived my songs so did Tamoona archive her phage. I carried the treatment home that night. Mother swabbed her leg with it and by morning the redness was subsiding.

I sat at my desk all that day staring at the high narrow window and the feet tramping past. No-one interrupted my day dreams. Could it be this simple? Love had brought Poliko back to life. Could love also have ushered my badly mannered guest out for ever?

I bought a huge bunch of golden chrysanthemums. A bottle of deep red *saparavi*. Walnut and honey cakes. I waited as we had agreed until after dark when she would have finished her lab work. She let me in at my tapping on the hatch in the outside wall. Her lab coat smelled of starch. I had been planning what to say all day.

I followed her through the darkened waiting room into the whitely lit clinic. My gaze fell upon the covering of one of the fluorescent tubes. She took my flowers and set them in a large glass flask. The covering only needed pushing back into its clips. I quickly clambered onto the work bench. Dust fluttered from the plastic sheath as I jiggled it into the clips. A cold light. Pink when you got close to it. I leapt down and rubbed the dust from my hands. I had dumped my bag with the wine and cake on the floor and now I set them out with a flourish. My heart was beating faster than usual. You look lovely, I told her as I pressed my thumb into the cork until it sank down the bottle neck. She looked bemused, but she busied herself finding something to drink from, two small graduated beakers which I hoped had been sterilised. I poured the wine. Raised mine for the toast.

To your victory!

She wore plum-red lipstick. Her hair was tied back in that long plait, her face was a beautiful mask, the prominently curved Georgian nose, the black eyes and full lips, the unblemished porcelain of her skin. She sipped her wine and I held my glass high to extend the spirit of my toast for a moment longer. It was then that I saw the Stalin. She followed my gaze.

Surprise! she said. I brought it in from the waiting room. It needed a dusting but it polished up fine. It's for you. I can see the likeness now I've put you together.

But I'm not related. Not in any way.

No? Well there must be some old genetic link. You've got the same smile. I missed you today. Did you miss me?

Yes, I missed you, I muttered.

Do you always jump up on strange tables and fix things?

What? Oh, no, only for you. I love you.

The words came tumbling out not at all in the way I had been planning them all day.

She raised one brow and sipped her wine. Iosif Dzhugashvili, she said, if we're going to have a future together there are rules. First, no more jumping on my work tops. Second, don't bring that tape recorder here again.

He winked from behind his freshly cleaned glass as I stood blinking and clutching my recorder. Oh yes, it had been slung across my shoulders all the time.

Well, I have my rules too, I countered, pulling myself taller, staring him out and reminding myself that it was only a portrait. And they are, they are . . .

But I never found out what my rules were going to be. She simply removed the strap from my shoulders, slipped her arms around my neck and breathed, Let's not argue before we've even started.

Tamoona's distrust of recording equipment stemmed from her ancestral business. The Kabakidze clan had long been indistinguishable from the secret police, the NKVD, the KGB. It was how things worked, clans rising through the ranks, bloodlines passing from post to post, favoured nephews and nieces jumping the rungs of the Party ladder to the top. I had understood her background as soon as I learned her family name at our first meeting.

When we parted on that second night we lingered on the street while she waited for her car to collect her and take her home. From over the wall around the phage laboratory complex came a blurred light and the sound of raised voices and laughter.

The French Cottage, she murmured. When I was a child I was allowed to roam the phage laboratories while my family held their parties over there. I decided early that I'd rather heal than torture. Don't misunderstand me though, I respect what the KGB do. It's necessary to keep a tight rein. We can't allow the West to succeed in destroying us. But you understand, don't you, my sweet Stalin!

If you don't mind I'd rather you didn't . . .

At that moment a Volga purred along the kerb, a black-clad driver opened the door and she slipped in, kissed her hand to me and was gone. I stood for a moment looking at the haze of light beyond the stone wall over the street.

The kindly well dressed Eliava had built the French Cottage to accommodate his friend d'Herelle while they developed miraculous phage treatments to protect the diseased workers of the world. I tugged my suit jacket straight. I lay no claim to heroism nor natty dressing. Eliava was shot for his bourgeois tendencies. D'Herelle returned to Paris. The KGB commandeered the French Cottage. But the dedicated researchers in Tbilisi continued with their work and over the years they founded a great library of bacteriophage, of which on Tamoona's shelves were the agents of death for putrescent wounds, septic burns, boils, furuncles, diabetic abscesses.

Like humans with likes and dislikes at table, these phage viruses also have preferences when it comes to devouring bacterium. Gorging and multiplying they attain the moment of lysis when the host bursts apart and the newborn phage run amok still wearing their boxy party hats. The drunken voices subsided and one man spoke alone in a toast.

Victory to Yuri Andropov, our exalted chief!

Victory, roared back the voices.

I strolled away. The night was calm and overcast. The lights of my towers twinkling in the suburbs. The banners bearing Brezhnev's face hung silent and still on the offices of State. Bacchus and wing-faced cherubs leered from the Classical facades of a deserted Rustaveli Avenue. The plane trees held their limbs against the round of seasons and the first dry leaves fluttered to the ground. I was not over the shock of what she had done for me. I felt around inside my ribs. A hollow scoop where something lay curled. I tentatively warbled the first bars of a song, *I will not see you for many years to come . . .* The shape rose from the scoop and slunk away. I walked on. The paving was covered in the finest of dusts and the kerbs seemed made of cardboard. *And when I return you will not know me . . .*

*

Leonid Brezhnev died and Yuri Andropov took his place as General Secretary of the Central Committee. We all knew that Andropov was dying from incurably diseased kidneys. But so long as no-one spoke of it he continued to live in the best of health. Andropov had been with the Committee for State Security for most of his political life. He had become the chief face of the KGB. So long as we did not look that face directly in the eye his paranoid gaze would pass over us.

Poliko and Maia had taken to stage performing like the naturals they were. Poliko and I did not spend much time together now that The Bells were out all evening until late. I could not prevent the satisfaction glowing in my mind. I had been the cause of my brother's new-found stability. He did not hate me any more. I had not suffered any more of those ugly outbursts. I could hardly bear to think about the things he had said to me in those awful spasms of his fury. But I was his older brother and had always guarded him, when as a child he had raged and sobbed with feverish intensity, when he had laughed and played with the same commitment.

I do not think that Vera and Givi ever witnessed Poliko's

adult rage. It was like the beam of an experimental weapon aimed only at me, a beam able to penetrate my heart and slice bits off and weld them back in place in the wrong order. Such pain, as I recall the way he sought me out on the balcony when I had just finished mending his jacket pockets for the fourth time. He came out wearing it. Fished in the pockets for his cigarettes. He must have felt that the pockets were now secure. He stood there with both hands dug into the pockets. He stared beyond me to the sky between the blocks. He seemed frozen to the spot. I asked him to close the balcony door as it was banging in the wind. He did not move. Then his eyes slid from the distant view to me. I saw the way they moved, his eyes, mechanical and such a grey as if cast from concrete. You know he is taller than me, my younger brother. He came at me with his eyes wide. Before I could get out of the way he had me with my back to the railings. I felt the full force of his weight. His heaving chest. His panting breath. His words through clenched teeth. Don't tell me what to do. He leant against me in a trapped hands-in-pockets posture. I strained to keep my balance with my back bending at the rails. Stop! I gasped. He pushed me with his chest, his skinny ribs, his flat stomach, his hips. We might both fall if I did not hold the rails behind me and plant my feet as firmly as I could. Who are you to give me orders? he hissed. His furious stare fixed on me, distorted by his close proximity. My pulse was racing. My mind emptied of all but the unfairness of this onslaught. I did not want to fight him but all my instinct was compelling me to punch and struggle with him. Get off! I sobbed with the last ounce of my composure. He broke away with a thin laugh. Shook his head as if to free it from some tangled net. He stared at his fingers protruding from the torn jacket pockets. Not worth fixing up, let him bleed, he muttered. Then he turned abruptly and went inside and I heard Vera call from the kitchen if he would like some tea and his reply in a normal tone of voice.

If I did not confront him with these episodes in calmer moments it was because I was afraid to do so. I prepared little speeches about it. But I could not bring myself to show him his warped behaviour when he was so happy in everyday life. Nor could I bring myself to speak to Maia about it, to divide her from the Poliko she adored, to set up some sort of secret code between us, watching for any sign of mental illness. No, I would not entertain that. And then, as The Bells rocketed to the heights of popularity, Poliko's dark moods fell away.

I shall not recount any more of those dark memories. I shall let my brother stand in the sun of his good character. Our lives at that time were in tip top condition. Love. Marriage. Success. Happiness. These were the slogans we lived by during that change-over from the broad sweep of Brezhnev's five-year plans to Andropov's daily announcements on the ever present threat of dissident subversion. But that was all far away in Moscow, far on the other side of the snow-peaked Caucasus. Here in the Soviet Republic of Georgia our regional Communist Party Chiefs settled their affairs with gracious hospitality around groaning table tops.

My only disappointment was my lack of promotion. But that it would come and that I would reap the benefits of my dedication I had no doubt. Meanwhile I settled into the routine of a new set of recordings of old favourite songs.

I arranged it so that my singer stood as close to an Andropov as possible. His banners were larger than ever before and were immensely ponderous in their movements over the marble walls of State. I may, perhaps, have been somewhat officious in my insistence of waiting on the spot for suitable gusty weather conditions. But no matter, my material, or rather my singer, rarely complained. And if a certain weariness crept in to the vocals when at last I let fall my hand and pressed record, it only gave a more human texture to the accompanying slapping, wheezing and worrying of the flaccid expanse of Andropov's face.

*

A vision of The Bells performing in a busy restaurant. Chrome and perspex chandeliers modernise the candlelit tables. Tan leather chairs comfort the backsides of Party apparatchiks. The atmosphere is charged with expectation. A roar of approval goes up as they stroll on stage, dressed in matching black and silver sequinned jumpsuits. Maia's brunette curls and Poliko's smooth blond hair have become their signature motif. They appear on posters pasted to the circular stands around the city, their faces close together, long red sunbeams emanating from behind their heads, as if the dark and light of their hair is a meeting of night and day. But here they do not need sunbeams. They spread their own woozy warmth as they croon above the electronic keyboard and the snare.

In Poliko's mouth the Russian pop songs conjure up an exotic breed of woman, a compliant bedmate, teasing and ultimately fatal. Maia acts the part, accusing her lover of unfaithfulness, sobs then flaunts her beauty as she catches the admiring glances of another man. They do such a thorough job of hamming up the corny songs that people in the audience begin to weep or smile with nostalgia for some lost dream. Then the two voices, hers of earth, his of open sky lead the audience away from all they know. They are taken to another country inhabited only by these two voices. These two voices depending on each other for life, and each note in harmony with another and giving birth to that new life. People throw kopecks at the stage. Girls advance shyly to try to get an autograph from Poliko. Young men send champagne over for Maia.

I often took Tamoona to dine when The Bells were performing. After their set they would join us at the table. Radiant. Laughing at some private joke. Poliko and I lounged back in our booth while Maia and Tamoona leant close, chatting about female interests I supposed. We were a typical Georgian table. We were typical ambitious Soviet couples. I even dared to think that I might not be so bad looking after all – at least in the company of Poliko, Maia and Tamoona, under the dazzle of the chandeliers and behind the glare of candles. The only set-back to my new-found confidence was that Tamoona had developed a penchant for uttering my name while we made love. I had left it too late to ask her not to.

Our only serious disagreement had been when I took the Stalin down. She accused me of being disloyal. She said I would never fit in with her family. She sobbed and would not allow me to comfort her. So I hung the Stalin back on the wall, telling myself that I did not have to look at it.

You see, my namesake was still missing from his cosy quarters in my lungs. And I was emboldened enough to forsake the codes of hospitality. I was willing to do anything she wanted to keep him out. We met at her clinic after hours. We never spent the whole night together. Vera and Givi turned a blind eye to Poliko and Maia sleeping in our apartment bedroom as if they were already married. But Tamoona and I played a less homely game of steel surfaces and tiled floors.

She asked me to accompany her to the Mtkvari embankment where she let down a bucket and drew it up filled with sewage-tainted water. I took the bucket from her and put it down and slid my hand beneath the cleavage of her lab coat. She looked at me without expression as I fondled her. It was dark and no-one around and the traffic sped past too quickly for anyone to notice us.

Afterwards, she said.

I picked up the bucket, carried it to the clinic and sat watching her as she warmed a meat broth and mixed a portion of it in a glass tube with a scoop of the fouled water. Then she delved into a refrigerator. Proteas or Streptococcus? she asked herself as she came out with a phial of clear phage liquid to top up her tube of soup. She had forgotten my existence.

I lit a cigarette and paced around the small areas between the steel-topped benches and the refrigerators. I tightened the lids on jars of agar jelly, straightened the rolls of lint, rearranged the stacks of petri dishes. From the corner of my eye I observed her drop liquid phage from her pipette onto the bed of bacterium laden agar. Perhaps, I mused, her phage have invaded the tissues of my lungs though the agent of her kisses, and they have devoured the remains of my bad-mannered guest.

*

Givi had finally come to terms with the flailing trolley runners and had found a way to build the faults and hold-ups into his timetables. He stood at his sheet of paper on the hallway wall, tapping his pencil against his teeth and humming to himself. Vera came home and found him there and they embraced, just as I had seen them embrace when I was a boy, mother's head flung back and father's face nestling in her throat. Now, mother's dark hair has a streak of grey running from her forehead into the knot, her hips have filled out, her throat is not smooth any more. Father's hair is white but still thick, his face deeply grooved, and he is stocky and slightly shorter than Vera. But here in the orange-lit hallway the signs of age disappear and I see them as they were when I was a little boy.

Alright Vera? Givi asks.

Never better, Vera replies.

She holds him away from her and touches his cheek.

Maia is pregnant, she says.

Oh-ho, our little Poliko's been busy!

Yes, a baby on the way, a grandchild for us to love!

And they clasp each other and laugh with excitement.

My feet make no sound on the parquet. The balcony door opens smoothly without a squeak. The new linoleum covering is already cracking over the concrete ledge where I stand and hold the rail and stare out to the farthest towers and the small rectangle of wheat beneath the aerial walkway. Odd, but I am overcome with nostalgia for my troublesome guest.

I lean out and peer down the vault. A funeral procession passing in silence across the yard. Another sealed zinc coffin. There have been quite a few in recent months. No-one talks too much about them. The families have lost their sons but no-one knows who really lies inside the welded grey caskets.

Most nights I sleep on the couch. Impossible not to overhear Poliko and Maia in the bedroom. A row of prickled shadows stand sentinel by moonlight. The net curtains billow into the room and drape the television and fall away to billow once again. The heating ticks. A distant gurgle sounds in the bathroom drainpipe. I am tired but cannot sleep. Tamoona had already known about Maia's pregnancy when I told her. I wonder if it will happen with us. We take no pre-cautions. If it does we will marry. Anyway we will marry. No-one will think the worse of Poliko and Maia for jumping the gun.

Although the official quota only required one performance a week, they were now constantly engaged. They could not refuse. The Bells were the darlings of the Musicians' Union. As soon as they had fulfilled the contract for this year they would move up the ladder, be given an apartment of their own, a car with driver. Perhaps my only misgiving in this climate of hap-piness was about the moustache.

Tamoona had wanted me to grow it so in a mood of exper-iment I agreed. I felt quite wild as the dark shadow grew rapidly into bristles, stacking up into a thick brush which I must clip every day and groom so that it swept to either side of my mouth. I asked Maia what she thought about my new look but she bit her lip and frowned and did not seem to know what to reply. Poliko said it looked like an unfortunate leech lost on my face.

D'you think so? I replied, because Tamoona says it makes me look distinguished.

At this Poliko narrowed his eyes and considered me. You're really serious about her aren't you, he said at last.

They came home late at night. They came reeling to the bedroom and dropping giggling onto the bed. I slipped away and lay down on the couch. The bedroom door was thin and I could not help overhearing them while they whispered in the dark. They were making up stories about the diners who had applauded them that night. Comrade so-and-so was jealous about his neighbours getting a new tv so he crept in and stuck a fork in the works one night. A huge electrical flash lights the room. By this flash can be seen a naked backside humped over two upright legs. The jealous comrade flees. The next day the neighbour knocks on his door and says he has a fork for him. Very tasty too. Your wife's fork. Very tasty. Haha. Haha.

I had learned to un-listen to their childish jokes. But there were nights when I lay staring into darkness as they told stories about life on a sunlit beach. They lived in a bamboo hut. There were other bamboo huts with other couples, some with children. Their own child spent its days playing in the surf. We'll be working on our new songs for the band. No school for child-to-be? No school. You catch fish and I cook it for dinner. And you sew our clothes from that flowery printed fabric. I can't sew. Yes you can! Alright. Hawaiian. That's it. When we've made the record album we get a boat. That's it! And we sail off. No, we moor it in the big surf and everyone comes for our farewell party. Whisky. Gin and tonic. Then we sail off. Yes, then we sail as far as the eye can see. How far's that? Forever. I have a harpoon gun. What's that? To catch big fish. Okay. So we never have to stop. Moor. What? It's called moor with a boat. So we never have to moor. Never. Ever.

I reached for my tape recorder. My fingers found the switch in the dark. The soft hiss as the reel span. Before they slept they would sing an old-fashioned ballad to cleanse away the cheap thrill of pop songs. I had to be ready. The tape must be running while they whispered to the end of their story. Many nights this was my sleeping pill. This soft hiss of tape. The mild burr of the motors. Their whispered stories. Two voices singing in my dream.

*

I was typing up some notes when my office door swung open and a tall, florid-faced man stepped in without knocking.

Iosif Dzhugashvili, he said, ethnomusicologist, thirty years old, apartment forty-two twenty, block eleven, Nutzubidze Plateau.

I hardly had time to rise from my seat when he flapped his hand stiffly to tell me to sit back down. My pulse quickened as thoughts of my imminent promotion raced through my mind. I half rose again intending to offer him my seat, I had no other in the office, but once more he gestured me to sit. He rolled his eyes upwards to the out-sized lamp. I made a hasty attempt to organise the clutter on my desk.

Excellent, he murmured to the lamp.

How can I help you sir? I asked, feeling some discomfort at being seated while my important visitor stood with his face raised to that enormously bright light.

He wore a wide shouldered dark grey suit. His silver hair receded from a domed forehead. A large hooked nose presented two silver-haired nostrils flanked by red veined jowls. A heavy gold ring on the finger of the hand he had used to make me sit down, in a gesture, I now realised, that was accustomed to being obeyed. It was some moments before he looked away from the light and turned to my shelves and began examining the labelled tape boxes. I sat quietly picturing the office in the Ministry of Culture, the larger, finer desk,

143

the red leather swivel chair, the Stalin at my back. I had no Stalin in my lowly basement. Feet came plodding past the narrow window. The tall visitor shed no shadow where he stood directly beneath the light.

As a Young Pioneer you carried out various surveillance activities. In your Komsomol years you made several useful observations. You recently reported a comrade for her anti-Soviet associations with Western tourists, said my visitor without turning from the shelves.

I've always tried to do my Patriotic duty, I murmured, trying not to sound too proud.

Indeed, indeed, he said clasping his hands behind his back and bending to peer more closely at a tape box.

Would you permit me to play some examples of my material? I have a brand new set of recordings ready for this year's quota.

Not necessary, he interrupted and swung round to scrutinise me. We know all about your – ramblings, shall we call them?

Now he stepped to the desk and placed his hands upon it and leant toward me. Quite an expert with the tape recorder aren't you?

All in the service of Soviet achievement, I replied with a self-effacing smile.

My visitor slapped his hands on the desk and gave a loud barking laugh which he cut off just as suddenly. As I have said before, my low-ceilinged office tended to overheat. Beads of perspiration broke out on my face. I felt for my pocket handkerchief and then decided against it. I looked up into the hair-filled nostrils and attempted to appear composed.

But the interesting question is, what, or more exactly *who* else you're servicing, he said with a leer that was quite repellent in its implications.

I have no idea what . . .

I'm Tamoona's uncle, he interrupted.

His handshake barely touched my fingers.

All I need from you, he continued, is an assurance that you're not going to let her down. Tamoona's always been my favourite. What a fine figure of a girl eh! But you know all about her after-hours treatment don't you!

I drew myself up as much as I was able in my seated position. He had picked up a reel from my desk and was idly allowing the tape to unfurl. And suddenly an inspired thought came to me. I need say nothing on the subject of my honour. I need only act as any comrade should act at this level of subtle signals.

Allow me to present you with an example of my work, I said. Let me just box it for you.

And so saying I snatched the reel from his hands, slipped it into a box and gave it back to him with a half-bow, as formally, that is, as I could manage it from my seat. I passed my fingers in opposite directions over my moustache, neatening the twin streams of growth. One must always be prepared. Promotion can strike from any quarter.

Excellent, excellent, murmured Tamoona's uncle as he rolled his eyes once more to my 500-watt bulb.

When he was gone I sat bolt upright for several minutes going over and over what had been said. I could find nothing wrong. That I had been logged was not a big surprise and may even do me favours in the future. I could not say that I was particularly fond of the KGB of my era, it was normal to distrust them. But then nor could I find any personal reason to be anxious. The French Cottage gave out a baleful glow at the back of my mind. But the haunted years of terror and midnight arrests were long over. I smoked a cigarette. Rolled a fresh sheet of paper into my typewriter.

It was my habit to replay the current tape as I wrote up my notes on the songs it contained but I had just given that particular tape to Tamoona's uncle. I leant back idly in my chair, allowing myself to bask in this feeling of satisfaction that now engulfed me as I took in the implications of the visit. I had managed myself correctly and had even taken the position of strength by presenting the gift – not that I would dream of trying to outwit a comrade in such a position as my visitor – and yet there had been a heroic element to that tape which would not harm if it rubbed some of its ardour off on me. The songs had been collected on a particularly gusty day when the scaffolder and I had been clinging to the in-progress scaffold and the wooden beams were groaning like a ship at sea.

Above us hung an Andropov, slapping at the topmost scaffold where other workers were toiling. My singer stood tall at the outer edge of the planking, not taking hold of anything and rocking on his heels as he began to sing in a fine bass. Soon his work mates swung down to our level and all stood without taking hold on the edge of the planking. I cannot say I felt very steady up there on that loosely nailed web of splinters, even though I was crouching down over my equipment. The Andropov set up a counter rhythm as it slapped at the structure and the scaffolders worked this off-beat into the harmonies they sang against the solo bass. And now as I recalled that quivering creaking scaffold, the arrhythmic Andropov and the wind carrying the worker's melancholy song in gusts to my microphone I almost regretted giving the tape away.

But tapes, tapes, I had so many others and must settle down to organising this unlabelled chaos that had somehow accrued on my desk of late. I gazed at the mess and let out a rueful sigh. This is what comes of so much happiness. This is how love marks you with invisible ink, with its orders only for the heart, its lists of things to do with another's body, its regime of slipshod accounts and wool gathering.

I reached for another tape to play through as I worked but to my surprise it held the very singing scaffolders I thought I had just presented to Tamoona's uncle. Then as I began to play another tape my mouth became dry with apprehension. I need only listen to the first few seconds of a reel to discard it and reach for the next. And all the time my brain was telling me what it knew. But I could not agree with it, not until I had played each tape and all were present and correct but for one. For let me make it clear that I was not so mazed by love that I could not recall with exact detail the whens and wheres, the how manys and the who of my unlabelled archive.

I had just given Tamoona's uncle my latest recording of Poliko and Maia in bed at night. I had lain on the couch with the reel slipping round, sleep slipping through my brain, their whispers slipping with my dream. I had not yet listened to the complete tape. But now my mind was filled with uneasy images.

I have spoken before of the Georgian talent for mind-reading and the sodden route such thoughts have to travel before evaporating in the hot climate of a distant brain. And of how we take little notice of such transferences, accepting the gift as our native right. It would be easy to say, with the hindsight I can now apply to those uneasy images, that I had been forewarned of the horror to come. That even before I came to know the contents of the tape I understood its impossible dream. But I do not know if that is true. Outlandish vignettes flashed up in my mind like scenes cut from a film. Impossible to piece them together. And the jumbled pictures faded as quickly as they had appeared. I would never be able to recall them. They left only a sickly dizziness in my skull. A sensation of something intolerably wrong.

In a flush of self disgust I swept the tapes from my desk and they clattered to the floor. Even more disgusted at this wanton act of chaos I had just performed I knelt down to gather the scattered tapes, hurriedly reeling the ribbons back, and some became twisted and creased beneath my fingers and others were reeled too tightly on the spool. I noticed a wad of dust beneath my desk and puffed it away. The little window darkened and something thudded to the ground out there. Potatoes up from the earth ... potatoes up from the earth ... The pedlar had leant his sack on the glass. The lumpen weight of it was in his mouth, stuffed with clay, the voice struggling to emerge.

I got myself up, brushed off my knees, went and rapped at the little pane. The peasant, who no doubt felt shifty at his private sales enterprise, dragged the sack upwards and shambled from view. I rapped once more on the filthy glass. Then I tore the front cover from an out-of-date journal, crumpled it and wiped the inside of the window clean. It did not help it very much. The glass was little more than an extension of the paving on the other side. I smoothed the soiled journal cover. It had a picture of a muddy plain where uprooted potatoes were stacked mountainous against the skyline.

I finished collecting the spools. Put them in their boxes. Inspected my thoughts and found myself quite calm now, even allowing for the remaining frisson of excitement caused by comrade Kabakidze's attention. He had come to inspect me and had found me just as I am. There was no harm in having given him that tape. Poliko and Maia were The Bells. They were on the right track. Everything was as it should be.

Who can understand the images conjured from the depths of the mind? Things appear within the skull which we can never have seen. Three dimensional portraits of unknown people form from the coils of the wakeful brain. Who are these strangers walking on the curves of our open eyes? Who owns those voices chattering in the inner ear? Where is that landscape never before seen? And if you think it odd that I pose these conundrums whilst speaking so adamantly of the one who stalks through my body as if it were his own, then you do not comprehend his familiarity. He is not a stranger. He is famous! He, as other parasites, needs only a single host on which to thrive. But I digress.

Through the rest of that day the arc of my unshaded lamp welded my thoughts firmly to that state of calm. Steady progress saw my notes completed, the spools boxed and coded and slotted on the shelf, and the shelving pushed back onto its brackets. The words of an ancient lullaby came for me to warble as I worked.

Let the wind rock your dreams, let the river sing you a tree, let your shawl be woven with gold, let the mountains be your book. You'll be free to fly with the ravens, you'll be free to swim with the stars . . .

*

Vera's leg had healed up nicely. She was full of praise for what she said were the Mysterious Workings of the Universe, smiling at my reply that perhaps the logic of science had something to do with her cure. Mother was without any vices. Or no, there was one but it was specific, non-transferable and located only in early spring when the *tremali* plums were ready and she did battle with a wizened little elder named Marina who lived in a forgotten compartment behind the lift shaft.

Marina had a perfectly good family further up the tower but she would not leave the little concrete walled space where she had spread shawls and rotten quilts on the floor. Her family brought her food and a bucket for a commode and had wired in a heater for the winter. The ancient's rivalry with Vera centred on a plum tree that had grown by itself on a patch of dry earth near the entrance to our tower. As the plums developed and the time came to harvest them Vera would peer down from the kitchen window checking they were still safely on the tree. The collecting must be timed so that the plums were still green and sour but not so unripe that the chutney would not set. This *tremali* chutney is an essential ingredient of our cuisine, indispensable and addictive. To eat without a dish of piquant *tremali* on the table is to be bereft indeed. Vera took great pride in her own particular recipe and she said that only the yard plums would do. They had a certain flavour drawn from the potash where men and boys made their cooked meat fires at the foot of the tower in the summer. The plums were hers by right of being the first to have collected them on the first season of the tree's fruiting maturity. So Vera said and so none in our family would have dreamt of challenging.

Last season old Marina had attacked Vera with her walking stick as she had been gathering the fruit, so this year I insisted on collecting them for her. It so happened that Maia was up and dressed and she offered to come down and help me.

We spread the cloth out and I shook the tree. The green plums fell. Marina came hobbling from the entrance hall. Maia took off her cardigan, laid it down and scooped some plums onto it. She was wearing her green dress. Now she tied the cardigan sleeves into a bundle and carried it to the dark doorway. I could not hear what she said, but Marina took the bundle, clasped it greedily to her scrawny chest and tottered back into the hall.

Poor old thing, said Maia when she returned to the tree.

And then she gave a little shiver and folded her arms around herself.

Here, I said, take my jacket.

As I draped the jacket around her shoulders my hands lingered for the slightest time, and she shivered again and lifted her hands to hold mine.

Eliso has been promoted, she said.

That's good.

Not for the ones in the observation ward. I can hardly stand to go home any more. She's convinced that my baby's going to be born with some awful defect. Dad does his best to make me feel alright, but he's no match for her tongue. I don't know what to do. Poliko just laughs it off. He doesn't want to think about anything that might go wrong, you know, after what happened to him . . .

She looked me in the eyes. The plum tree dapples freckling on her face and splashing down her green dress.

Have you ever spoken about it with him? Does he remember do you think?

If he does he wants to forget it, she said.

But he's alright now, isn't he? You're both happy. And your baby will be fine.

And you? Are you happy?

Couldn't be better, I said, as I looked away towards the entrance where Marina stood leaning on her stick like a gatekeeper at the gloom of another type of world.

Remember the taxi?

And the bath house!

I never really believed we'd manage it.

I thought I'd messed it up.

Then I saw you staring up at the stars as if nothing was unusual.

That kitchen was full of cockroaches.

I know . . .

Listen Maia, I'd do anything for you.

So you and Tamoona are marrying soon?

She's told you?

And you'll stay here.

We'll probably move to the Vake region, near her family.

But you'll stay here, I mean in Georgia?

Of course, where else . . .?

Would you want to leave if you had the chance? I mean *really* leave this place? Even if it meant . . .

I had never seen Maia so serious. Her eyes glittered. She bit her lip and frowned.

What is it? I managed to say as my throat tightened with the sudden vertiginous feeling that I was not really part of what was happening around me, not even part of this little job of fruit collecting. I was not connected to the current of real life. I was some kind of prototype pretending to be human. Maia shook her head, gave a tiny laugh and turned to look up into the tree.

There are more up there, she said.

I gave the tree a hard shake. A scatter of plums came tumbling down and we folded the cloth around them.

That season's *tremali* was the best Vera had ever made. The glossy chutney filled the mouth with spice and garlic and lemon. Every time I took a spoonful I thought of Maia in her green dress. The dappled shadow on her face. The shape of her pregnancy visible beneath the taught fabric over her abdomen.

*

You can't wear that! I said as Poliko took his leather jacket from the door hook.

I'll take it off for the ceremony. You'll look after it for me, won't you? Please?

Alright, I expect it'll be useful on the coast. Might be chilly after sunset. Be careful you don't catch cold if you swim. Remember how deep the Black Sea is, and the sudden drop after a few paces from the tide line. Don't let Maia go too far out. Maybe she shouldn't swim in her condition. Have you got your plane tickets? Here, let me brush down your suit before you put that jacket on.

I flicked invisible threads from his shoulders. He stood still for a moment and then he reached up and held my wrist.

That's enough, he said.

Sorry, I think I'm more nervous than you are.

He had not let go of my wrist and suddenly his fingers clamped tight and they became very cold.

153

You won't change your mind? he asked.

You don't really want me with you on your honeymoon.

But we do. We both want you to come with us. You can buy a ticket at the airport. Please come with us. I need you. We both need you. We can't go without you.

He was very pale and grim looking and his fingers were bone cold.

Listen brother, I said. Whatever bad thing happened to you in the past is over and gone. You're the luckiest man in the world. You're going to have a wonderful future with Maia and the baby. You go and enjoy your honeymoon with her.

I won't forget you, he said through clenched teeth. And if you change your mind . . . Come with us . . .

Now now, let's have a drink. I'll let you in to a little secret. I'm spending the night with Tamoona at her family apartment tonight. Her parents are away. We'll have a decent bed for once!

So you'll be alright with Tamoona?

Of course!

You'll have a family?

Why this interrogation? This is your wedding day!

I shook his hand from my wrist and slapped him on the back jovially. The smile widened on my lips. I gestured, palm up, to express the limitless visions of happiness to come. But my teeth ached from the roots to my sinuses and into my ears.

An open staircase wound around the polished concrete spiral of the Palace of Weddings. Pairs of brides and grooms processed up the staircase and disappeared into the formal agreement room. Coloured light fell through the windows showing couples bearing children, corn sheaves, pneumatic drills and shovels. Champagne corks popped in the feasting halls leading off the ground floor.

Toothache plagued me through the afternoon. I had the embarrassing impression that my breath was bad and I welcomed the guests from behind my hand or with my face averted. Relatives from my parent's town of Rustavi, neighbours from our tower, agents from the Musicians Union and Maia's family and relatives and neighbours. Tamoona met Vera and Givi for the first time. I saw her charming them where they sat at the long table. We Georgians like to be mobile at table. People get up and move around, chairs empty and fill with fresh arrangements of diners. We are messy eaters. We like our dishes to be layered, one resting on the rim of the other in a teetering china pathway down the table. Juices run down our fronts and chins. No-one takes the last morsel from a plate.

I realised that I was still clutching Poliko's rotten leather jacket. I placed the jacket on a chair. Undid the top button of my shirt and loosened my tie. After all, this was a celebration. I must make sure it all went smoothly. I must not give way to this sickness in the pit of my stomach. I had been wrong. My co-inhabitor had simply moved his quarters. And I had not attended to his new needs, so distracted had I been with tending the love that had blossomed around me and my family. He had crept down on tiptoe. Had found enough to entertain himself at first, with the contents of my guts at his disposal. But now, with the feast-laden tables, the overflowing wine jugs, the music striking up and dancers taking to the floor, he was not content to rest. He began dancing his manicured fingernails up and down my bowels. What with the toothache and the wine I had drunk to subdue the pain, I was not in a very good way.

Eliso came gliding towards me from the dance floor, coyly

called me her dear Iosif Dzhugashvili and tugged me to join her. It would be unmannerly to refuse. Everyone else is dancing. This is how we dance. A fast six-three beat. A straight back. Arms held high and wide with fingers and wrists twirling snakily. The knees and lower legs do most of the work. The feet make small steps hither and thither in various patterns which are often forgotten. The man is riding a galloping horse. The woman glides on castors in the soles of her feet. All is motion and yet all is static. The man may suddenly spread his arms like wings behind his back and fall forwards from the waist to pick up a glass of wine from the floor with his teeth. The women will circle now and sway their hips and twirl their arms and wrists and turn their heads to look slyly from side to side. Now the man with the wine glass in his teeth will rise up and throw back his head and drink the wine without spilling a drop. Everyone cries out *Hupaa*! The dance breaks up or continues with individual show-offs of twirls or chin raisings or more light-footed knitting.

I did my best. I do not think I am a bad dancer but my heart was not in it. Eliso kept casting meaningful glances at me. I became filled with anxiety that she would make some awful announcement about Poliko's previous mental collapse. So I made it my business to stay near her and distract her with murmured memories of the cupboard. I kept to the subject of her singing. But her eyes told me that she was thinking of the other thing we had done. My teeth felt loose in my mouth.

Time for us all to leave. A taxi at the kerb. Rain falling beyond the tree where we stand.

Get in the car. Why are you hesitating? I'll be following you as far as the airport. Rain dripping through the last few leaves.

Your bouquets sparkling in the street light. Mother made them especially. Red roses for the man's strength and white for the woman's wisdom. Mementos to carry on your honeymoon. You will throw them ceremonially to the sea, and you will laugh as they float away on the deep black waters.

Do get in the taxi. Come now, raise a smile. Why so solemn? Don't worry, I'm not going with you to spoil the fun. In you get now. It's raining hard. Maia, where are you? Ah my dear sister, there's no need to hold me quite so tight, your roses will be crushed. In those high heels you're a little bit taller than me. Haha, that's funny. Hee-hee. The rain tickles on the end of my nose. Do hurry up now or you'll miss your flight. See how the acacia turns to ebony in the wet. Let me hold your wedding dress from the gutter. Poliko? Your jacket. But he presses it back into my arms, begins to say something, changes his mind.

The procession of cars sets off. Tamoona and I in a taxi behind the newly-weds. I see two faces looking back through their rear window. How pale they look in the gathering gloom. I hold tight to Poliko's jacket as we swerve through traffic, our driver hooting his horn non-stop, and all the other drivers hooting their horns, the announcement of this happy day making pedestrians smile as we stampede past.

We all tumble out at the airport. A last glimpse of the newly-weds as they head for the VIP gate. Rose petals drifting behind them. Maia turning back and looking at me with an expression of sadness such as I have never seen on her face before. For a moment I think she will run to me and fold her arms around me. I will agree to go with them if she does. Drunk as I am I will agree to anything she asks. Poliko looks back now. They seem ill at ease. Nervous about married life,

I suppose. Don't worry, I call merrily. Everything's going to be alright.

Poliko frowns as if he cannot hear me, and takes a step in my direction. Maia says something hurriedly to him and they both take a few faltering steps toward me. Their roses drooping in their hands. Their little holdalls dragging on the floor. They will miss their flight. No time for any more farewells. No more thoughts of joining them. Tamoona's perfume is ripe with the promise of this night to come. Get going! I call merrily. Be off with you! They look at each other briefly and they turn away. A guard grins and nods them through the gate. I peer from the window with a view of the runway. There they are hurrying across the tarmac in the rain. Swinging their holdalls. Their roses bright as torches in the night. Petalled sparks falling as they go.

*

Tamoona left me early in the morning with a kiss and a whiff of starch from her lab coat. She was naked beneath. Wear it like that all day, I had commanded her. She threw back her head and laughed and I pulled her onto the bed and we made love again in the bed that she had slept in since a child. There was still an infantile aspect to her room in the pretty vases of plastic flowers, the oval framed print of a pair of kittens, the hairbrush and hand mirror backed with pink plastic, the slippers decorated with velvet ribbon bows that made me feel very tender towards my efficient clinician.

Why don't you stay here today, she said before she left. You could start getting used to the lifestyle, we have all the latest fittings, take a shower, relax. I want to imagine you being here while I'm away.

I prowled around barefoot, a towel around my hips. I drank a shot of brandy. Smoked one of her father's Cuban cigars. Here were the rewards of a lifetime's dedication to keeping the System from harm. The luxury of this apartment, the quiet street, the stately plane trees and the solid stone facades glimpsed through the lace curtains. Room led from room, scattered with finely woven rugs and furnished with gleaming mahogany antiques. A clock ticked with a soft monotonous tone. I poured myself one more brandy. Glanced at the family photographs on the walls. A painted portrait of a Count wearing a black embroidered costume and a Countess with her white lace headdress partly veiling her stern gaze. Sunlight reflected from the glass of a portrait hung high above the others.

I was not surprised to find a Stalin taking pride of place on the red flock wallpaper. I could not make out his expression for the reflections on the glass. He had been awake all night and like me was rather dazed and sated.

I stood at the lace curtains watching the rain pelting the gabled rooftops, the plane tree branches soughing and swaying as the drops bombarded the leaves. The dark brow of a rock-strewn ridge hung over this part of the city and continued towards the green haze of Vake Park. I pictured Tamoona and myself strolling with our baby in this park on our days off work. I felt immensely grown up. I had squandered a lot of time fretting about my internal organisation. He should not have been restricted to my lungs. It was all too exclusive, too richly furnished for his taste. No, he was better off ranging the long dark tunnels of my intestines, where he would find a more industrious atmosphere, less showy than his former rooms, more to his taste for plain surroundings.

As I stood tweaking apart the fine lace curtains, I heard a workman sawing something in a nearby yard. The heaving saw passed through my flesh. A magician flourished a white gloved hand. My head projected from the coffin-like contraption. A trick, which as I dwelt on the feasibility of it going wrong, caused a shudder of horror. The rain was relentless. A twinge of regret ran through me as I thought of Maia and Poliko frolicking on the stony beach of Batumi where it was certain to be sunny. I felt such love for them. I had become so used to their throw-away quips, their jesting tomfoolery that I even secretly looked forward to seeing how they would manage to drown their next victim in a lake of absurdity. I must watch out for them though. They might overstep the mark. There was still a way to go before they would be safely ensconced in the higher ranks of performers. When they returned in a few days time I would call a meeting at the Ministry and see if I could jump them up the quota queue. The telephone rang and I stubbed out the cigar and strolled over the room to answer it.

Come to my clinic straight away, Tamoona said. Don't stop to talk to anyone. Just come to me.

Before I could reply she put down the receiver. She had sounded thrilled, breathless with pent-up excitement. Last night she had been so different. She had needed time before she would allow me to touch her. Her inhibition had not lasted long. But now I suddenly thought of the reason. And it would make sense of her excited phone call just now. She must have just had the results of a test. She must be pregnant. She had been keeping it to herself until she was sure.

I rinsed out my brandy glass and emptied the ashtray. I was in no great hurry despite the urgency of her call. I wanted to savour this moment. I dressed carefully and so as not to get my suit wet I pulled Poliko's leather jacket around my shoulders. Before I left I went and stood before the Stalin. He was slightly crooked so I took the curtain rod and straightened him up.

Naturally I did not say a thing. Who in their right mind would hold a conversation with a portrait? No, I simply winked, man to man.

I burst into the clinic, gathered Tamoona in my arms and kissed her hair.

Let me go, she said. We have to make a plan.

She looked so serious, and she was right, this was a serious matter. I began preparing the words to propose to her. It should be simple but romantic. I mustn't bungle it.

Everything's alright isn't it? I asked as she continued pacing up and down frowning.

How can you ask that?

Yes of course, but how long have you known? Here, do sit down.

I dragged a chair for her to rest on, but she waved it away.

You'd better go to your Institute. Don't speak to anyone. Just carry on as normal for today.

Carry on as normal, keep it quiet for now, yes, alright. Oh, but Tamoona let's talk about it together! Can't we? Or are you afraid ... But look here, you really shouldn't be smoking.

I plucked the cigarette from her fingers and made a great show of stubbing it out.

What are you playing at? she shouted. Give me another cigarette. And what are you grinning for? I wouldn't think what Poliko and Maia have done was cause for laughter. Wait till it all comes out later today . . . Fancy, everyone still thinks they're on the beach at Batumi . . .

She gazed beyond me with a secretive look of bemused incredulity which caused me to spin round and hurry over to that shadowed corner at the end of the row of refrigerators where I now understood that Poliko and Maia were hiding with their fingers pressed over their lips to hold back their giggles, ready to pounce out at me, clutching their bottles of champagne, the glasses wrapped in a white napkin, a tasty snack tucked into a twist of newsprint. Hey! Surprise! We couldn't enjoy ourselves without you so we came back! And I also had my surprise, we, Tamoona and me.

We're having a baby too! I yelled as I lurched into the crowded air of that corner.

What are you talking about. Pull yourself together. There's no need for that, you don't have to act crazy, you should know that, you of all people.

Me of all people? I asked from my dusky corner where I had come across a cobweb which was sticking to my face. I plucked the insubstantial threads away. Her speech was calm, matter-of-fact, with a frisson of urgency, but calm. Yes, calm and so penetrating that I had to cover my ears with my cobwebby hands. And turn to search the cornered walls. But they were not there, my brother and his bride.

Imagine. They actually tried to defect. Your precious Bells tried to hijack the plane to Batumi. They'd hidden pistols in their bouquets. Incredible! My uncle is furious. He was there at the airport. He said it went badly wrong.

Went wrong, I echoed from my shadowy place.

Went badly wrong all round, she continued as if telling the story of some distant event far away in time, historical. My uncle said it was chaos in the night on the runway and every-one was reporting different versions of what had happened depending on which department they worked for and which chief they needed to protect – you know how it is. He's livid. He says it'll be blamed on his section. Several people were killed.

Killed, I uttered as I wiped at the sticky webs.

When the plane was grounded. An elite force was drafted in and there was a shoot-out, uncle says. The attack went a bit too far apparently. No-one seemed to have command.

I groped my way out of the corner. All right, I said jauntily. I give up, where are they hiding? You've all had your fun. Come on out now. A joke's a joke, but this is too much.

Tamoona advanced on me in her cool white lab coat, with her neatly plaited hair and her mouth shaped with the ripe-plum lipstick which she favoured. Calm down, she ordered. You don't need to worry. You'll be looked after. Uncle said they'll have to arrest you, but just for form, you know.

No! I shouted, furious now. I don't know. I don't know anything at all! I don't know what you're talking about. This has gone far enough. And you shouldn't be smoking in your state.

Once again I plucked the cigarette she had just lit from her fingers and dashed it angrily to the floor.

Innocent comrades have been shot dead, she said letting go the words like red hot coals.

Someone was hammering. A nail biting deeper with each blow. Images flashed through my mind. Last night in Tamoona's bed. Her pale body laced by the moonlight through the net curtains. The scent of her skin sinking into my skin. So I had been sawn in half after all. And this was death. This darkening, the ceiling lowering, the steel-topped benches tightening. This torpid not-air was what fills the mouth in the grave. And now my death-agony fury at her who dared to tell such sick lies to my face.

Not them. Not Poliko and Maia shot dead. Don't you dare say that! I yelled as I rushed into the office leading from the clinic and dialled our apartment. But there was no reply. Of course not, Givi and Vera would be at work. Tamoona stood in the doorway.

You're lying, I said coldly, tired of the way she would not give up the prank, a woman like her, like me, not cut out for making successful practical jokes.

You know I'm not. You don't have to pretend with me. I admire what you did. My uncle told me, although it's all hush hush of course. And, if you want to know, Poliko and Maia aren't amongst the dead. I'm not so mean that I'd want that for them, despite what they've done. I still can't believe they actually ... Their capture was a fiasco, according to uncle.

I'm going to Batumi to join my brother and sister-in-law. I'll get the next flight. If you want to come with me you're welcome. Why don't you come? We could do with a break. I know they wouldn't mind.

Don't make it more complicated than it already is. You're not the type to play double bluff.

I'm going out to buy cigarettes.

I'm opening the clinic in an hour.

I won't be long.

I'll make coffee. Oh, and did you really think I was ...? That's nice. Maybe I will be soon ...

That's right.

I walked robotically until I came to my Institute. The doorman perched on his three-legged stool as usual. I passed through the foyer and down the basement steps. I switched the light on. My office had not been disturbed. I sat at my desk and lit a cigarette. I told myself that this was a case of mistaken identity. There were many internal flights to the Black Sea coast. Many honeymoon couples wafting through the VIP gate. Some other pair of benighted lovers had attempted a mad-cap escape. Yes, I would go to Batumi and find Poliko and Maia and when we came home Tamoona would be sorry. My hands were shaking as I tidied my desk in preparation for my short holiday. I would leave a note for Vera and Givi. I might even take a jar of mother's *tremali* with me as a funny gift for the newly-weds. I finished my cigarette. Emptied the ashtray into the waste bin. My tapes were all in order.

When I reappeared in the foyer I knew at once that the two KGB operators had been there when I first came in. They stood side by side, wearing suits like mine. And they each had mirror-lens sunglasses clamped over their eyes even though it was raining. This caused an amused snicker to rise in my throat.

Come with us, said one.

Certainly, I replied with a smile.

We left the Institute. The doorman deliberately not watching us depart. An operator on either side of me, as usual in such a situation. We walked in silence. The rain came down but it did not touch me. Comrades hurried along beneath flowered umbrellas. The trolley buses were full. Extra passengers clung to the back steps and the opened side doors in exuberant abandon. The scaffolders were taking their early morning break sitting beneath tarpaulins, swinging their legs over the planks high above the streets. The house painters had fashioned newsprint hats in the shape of little boats. The red flags and the banners were getting a thorough wash in the downpour. The plane trees and acacias drank the rain with graceful dipping branches. Now that I was arrested I felt fine. All that panic about death had been just a nervous reaction after a sleepless night. I would soon sort out the mistake. I was, after all, not without my own connections and good name.

We came to a familiar street leading down to the river. The phage laboratory complex stood on one side behind the stone wall. Tamoona's clinic lay further along on the opposite side. I wondered briefly if she was looking from the window and might see me with these officials and think twice about her – and now I frowned to myself – somewhat patronising attitude toward me.

My two companions led me into the phage laboratory entrance. We passed through a gracious marble foyer and thence to a corridor of creaking parquet flooring and peeling cream walls. At the end of the dingy passage was a door giving out to a verdant garden where a gravelled path lay burnished in the wet. We crunched along the path, the three of us in step, the crunch, crunch, crunch beneath our feet a counterpoint to the beating drum of rain. And then a little building appeared from behind some shrubbery. Classical. Romantic. Shuttered windows on its chiselled rain-washed walls. Aha, the French Cottage.

We passed up a staircase and into an empty room where the shutters were open but the window glass was barred. The walls were damp and bare. The decorative ceiling moulding mostly fallen off. They left me there. I stood listening to the sparrows chirping in the cyprus tree beyond the bars. I noticed that I was standing in a little pool and that my shoes, which I had polished for the wedding, were not laced up. I stooped to do the laces. They were wet and my fingers were cold. Whilst I struggled to make the bows someone entered the room and I looked up into the silver-haired nostrils of Tamoona's uncle.

I did not present a very impressive figure. My teeth began chattering and nothing I could do would stop them. The Turkish cigarette he offered made me nauseous after the first drag.

As you know, he said, your brother and his wife have done a very foolish thing.

Before he could go any further I said, There's been a mistake. My brother and his wife are on their honeymoon.

He glanced at his wrist watch and said he did not have much time. He said that I must face facts. That since I had given him the useful bit of tittle-tattle – he used those words – I would be under his wing. Tittle-tattle, he muttered as if he had forgotten I was there. That's all they think it is. Mere scrapings and rotten cabbage of information. Takes a lifetime to study how to gather and they shove it in the pig-bin if it doesn't serve their purpose. Then they cook it up as some foul stew and serve it to the enemy. Huh! Enemy! As if we haven't got enough strife in the Party ranks. Back-stabbing bastards. At least in the old days you knew who your real foe was. Now there are all these smooth-chinned triple-double agents and they're all against the State. Who do they think they're fooling? Me, a loyal officer, never a wrong turn and what have I gained? There's more d'you see? Much more than anyone knows. Paranoia isn't the word my dear comrade. That tape of yours. Let's speak plainly, we won't get the chance again. Rot eh? Land of make-believe, was it? So they said, my wise masters, when I filed my report. There there, they said, don't concern yourself. Took it over. My case. My retirement dues. Bastards. Not much time. Listen young man, comrade. Keep a low profile. Don't make a fuss. Don't stir up the muck. Keep shtum that you ever made the tape and that even if you did make it there was nothing on it. Blank. See? Wiped. Bastards wiped my retirement. No evidence that I, you, we are the actual heroes with the original raw surveillance material. Nice quality recording by the way. That bloody elite force and their bloody invisible chiefs moving in and spraying the place with enough ammo to defeat the entire *mujahadin*. Good comrade, me. Never a foot wrong. Truth? Don't know the meaning of the word. Don't exist. Who cares if a handful of souls end up under the earth, Motherland, so long as the top echelons get to polish up more private jets to more posh *dachas* on the coast. My retirement. Up the chute. What's the time? Bit wet aren't you? How's Tamoona? Fine girl. Always been my pet. What was he thinking of, your brother? Was he mad? Been in the loony bin hadn't he? Not a killer though, neither of them. I know. I've seen real killers in my time. He might have managed it, him and that scrawny bride. Turbines within turbines. One cog turning the other. Never was much of a poet myself. But this I know. One set of cogs was all fine to let them go. Yes. Other cogs wouldn't have it though. One set of cogs planned to let them escape and blame it on the other set. Of cogs. The other set. Of Cogs. Turned the plane back in the sky to expose the first cog's turnings, not cogs' turnings that is but turning as in secret agent turning.

Secret be damned! Technical stuff. Shouldn't be telling you this. My bastard retirement down the tubes. It might not be true either. What one cog feeds to another is usually false. False is more reliable. The dear old Motherland eh! Keep calm. You'll be under my wing. Then again, maybe your tape wasn't wiped. It's out of my area now. I was informed of the wiping, but that could have been misinformation. Or it could be dis-misinformation just to get me riled. I am riled. My time in the sun pulled from under my boots. Go home and get dry. Have a drink or five. Tell your parents I'll try to see that they suffer the least possible demotions.

With that he shook my hand with those hardly-there fingers and ushered me out. He called for an umbrella and one of the operators came with one and gave it to me.

Off you go now, he said. Make sure you catch the news this evening, it's been decided to make this affair *transparent,* as they say in the West! *Transparent.* Haha!

I fumbled to open the umbrella. But then I changed my mind and I banged its brass tip on the marble floor and demanded to be told exactly what the hell was going on.

What the hell is going on, said Tamoona's uncle sliding his eyes towards the two watching operators and jabbing me in the ribs as he spoke, is an International terrorist attack on the Motherland co-ordinated and led by comrades Paolo Dzhugashvili and Maia Dolidze. A CIA plot is what's going on. An Aeroflot plane shot up by our own elite forces. Soviet Heroes killed. One hell of a cock-up. One hell of a stink. That's what's going on comrade. And my advice to you is go home and keep quiet.

*

A few months ago some local fan had scratched *THE BELLS* into the fake wood wall of the lift. I could not take my eyes from that graffiti as the lift juddered upwards. Dread seeped through the shaking floor as I rose slowly through the twenty-storey shaft. My visit to the French Cottage seemed part of a dream from which I could not wake. The things Tamoona had said, that excited smile on her lips, mingled in my mind with the confused thought of her being pregnant, even though I knew this was not the case. Guns? A hijack? The words sounded so improbable as I uttered them aloud. And people were dead. A shoot-out. None of this connected in my mind to Poliko and Maia. They had left through the VIP gate in their wedding clothes. They had hurried towards the runway. Their bouquets had shed petals as if something were disturbing the fragile blooms. Is that why they had hesitated? If I had gone with them on the spur of the moment – rushed to the ticket desk, kissed Tamoona goodbye before she could stop me leaving, joined Poliko and Maia to hurry towards the aeroplane ... If I had sat with them as the plane rose through the rainy night ... If I had glanced across the aisle and caught Maia's eye, and had said how wonderful it was going to be to see her with her baby soon, and could I help with a name? Could I choose a beautiful name as full of light and joy as its mother is ... If I had sat by the window next to Poliko and said, I've always admired you, always looked up to you, always wanted to be like you, so please stay close to me and teach me how to relax, we'll have fun together, we'll go out and explore the farthest lands that are open to us, on a motor-bike ... If I had gone with them – they surely wanted me to come – they said so many times – would I have changed everything? Did they want me to stop them hijacking the plane? Even as I think this I have to struggle to comprehend the fact. I did not go with them. They did not turn back at the VIP gate. They ran through the dark, the pale grasses waving on the far reaches of the runway, their rose torches lighting the way. They ran towards a fairytale where there are no bad wolves. But Poliko and Maia were more than bad. How could they have wanted to leave us like that? I spread my arms to steady myself on either side of the lift as a wave of nausea rocked me. This was no fairytale. My brother. My new sister. What did you plan to do? Did you plan to hold a gun to the pilot's head? Threaten the stewardess with death? Terrify the passengers into silence? And what went wrong? Was there an agent on the flight, watching your every move, tipping the wink to the pilot to turn the plane back before you'd even begun fumbling amongst your flowers? Or did they let you take out the guns, knowing what you were planning, watching to make sure it all went smoothly, even the hold-up, the actual hijack, the crossing the border? Until it went wrong. I could not prevent a sickly laugh at that thought. Wrong? What else could be more wrong than my Poliko, my Maia with guns in their hands. It was not the shock of a gun which sent me reeling from side to side in the shuddering tin box, guns are part of our lives. This is how it is. Fake Kalashnikovs on our shoulders as Young Pioneers. Pop-shot target practice with vodka bottles. Hunting rifles aimed at birds and rabbits, wolves, bears, the last panther in a distant forest. The rubbishy weapons handed out to conscripts. But to think of the two I loved more than anyone – this was clear to me now – more than anyone in the world – the two stars of my life – the two I had thought would always be near – the two funny madcaps who would not hurt a fly –

the two who could sing a Paradise – taking those toys into their hands and making them deadly serious – even as I reached for reasons why it could not be, I knew it to be true. Tamoona and her uncle were not fabrications of my maddened brain. And even worse. Beneath all this struggle with the horrible truth was another even worse.

In my darkened mind I kept a locked store of bright voices. Leaping out like the add-on pop videos after a banned film. I used my ears to visualise my Edens. Ever since I could remember I had been the ear-full look-out. Poliko and Maia whispered fabulous stories in the dark. They played with dice to see how those stories ended. Would this lift never reach the top floor? Must I stand here shuddering for the rest of my life while the world proceeds with its relentless business? Scenes discarded from a film sped past my eyes. Broken frames I could not piece together. My tower blocks. My balcony. My dust-filled vista of wheat. My brother singing in the streets. This woman with a face like a saint in an icon. A brightly lit cabin in a small aeroplane. They stand up in the narrow aisle. Let's go! Poliko says, waving a pistol. Now, says Maia brandishing a pistol. And it goes wrong. It had gone horribly wrong. Again that ugly laugh in my mouth. Wrong? I clutched my stomach as a sickening pain shot through me. Him, up to no good down there. But he was a fine distraction. A fine relief to lay any blame at his twinkling toes. I was the one who had given away that tape of them whispering their plan in the private world of night. I was the one who had chosen not to go with them. I was the one who had allowed the horror to happen. I beat my fists upon the dented wall. THE BELLS ... Come back, come back, I sobbed.

When I stepped out of the lift I stood quietly for some time in the cool dark landing. The pulley wheel turned and the lift dropped away. Setting my face into a neutral expression I turned the key in the apartment door.

Vera ran at me in the hallway and clutched the collar of Poliko's leather jacket.

Poliko! she cried. It's you! You've come home after all!

It's me, Iosif. Be calm now.

No, don't tease me, it's you Poliko. It's you, isn't it?

But even as she spoke her eyes darted away from my face and she pressed her knuckles into her mouth.

Who is it? Givi called coming to the hallway. When he saw that it was me he began shouting in breathless gasps. Where have you been? The KGB took us in the night . . . They made us look at photographs . . . Poliko and Maia in their wedding clothes . . . We had to say it was them . . . They say they had guns hidden in their bouquets. *Guns!* They say my son is a bandit. Both of them. *Bandits!* They held up the plane . . . They wanted to run away . . . With guns . . . You're his older brother. You're supposed to look after him. But you turned his head. He was alright in the packing plant . . . Why didn't you leave him alone? You and your ambition . . . Pushing him away from normal life . . .

Then he collapsed and sobbed into his hands. They were having a baby . . . Our grandchild . . . What have they done? What have they done . . .

Vera held him and they rocked together, weeping in our hallway.

The following day Givi was demoted to gate-keeper of the trolley bus compound. He took down his timetable, folded it carefully and then did not seem to know what to do with it.

I found it on the coat-rack shelf. I left it there for a while. Then I changed my mind and threw it away. Father spent hours standing in the hallway, tapping his teeth and gazing into the window of brighter paint where the timetable had been. Vera was demoted to cleaning the library floors. Forbidden to take out books. Long hours and not enough floor to clean. One evening she came home and quietly emptied her cacti collection into the rubbish bucket. The resigned look on my mother's face was unbearable. I swept up grit she had spilled, salvaged a cactus, poured the grit into a tin and pushed the spiky thing in. As I worked she asked me for the hundredth time why you would want to leave us forever. I could not find an answer. My re-potted cactus became grey, and day by day it shrank and was soon no more.

If by night I gave way to pillow-hugging it was an act of melodrama on the stage of an abandoned theatre. I had my parents' welfare to think of. If I found Vera or Givi wringing their hands or gazing into space I felt duty bound to bring them round to a rational outlook on what had happened – for we did not say the actual thing aloud.

I flung open a window to demonstrate my point. Look at what they rejected, I said. And didn't we also love them as much if not more than the State did? Aren't we as steadfast as the towers of our settlement? Pull yourselves together. There are still many good things to come. Vera, I insist on you allowing me to procure more phage for that leg. It's become very inflamed again. Your work will suffer. And Givi, I've found an old tin of paint on the balcony. Here, take the brush and paint the hallway wall, I insist.

When the telephone rang and it was a relative from Rustavi, sounding muted but secretly gleeful at the bad luck that had befallen their successful branch of the family, I was firm in my rejection of their forced sympathy. The earpiece gave out a hollow sound. I unscrewed the hand set but could find no device inside.

I spent a day running my finger along the back of every piece of furniture in the apartment. I took down the chandeliers and unscrewed the back of the television set. I opened up the State Radio speaker. I held a torch to the underside of our beds and to the workings of the bathroom geyser. Only spider webs and papery wings, dust and cigarette ash.

I telephoned Maia's parents only once. Dato answered, stuttering, dismayed. He said that Eliso was under sedation. I could hear her groaning in the background. I advised him to accept the situation for what it was.

Carry on as normal, I said.

We've been allocated work in the Astra plant, he stammered.

Good honest labour, I replied.

But all her friends are there, he sobbed.

Your daughter was not a loyal comrade to them, I reminded him.

I replaced the receiver. Autumn fog obscured the towers. Mist seeped through the gaps between the windows and their frames. Its clammy breath brushed my face and sighed in the corners of our home. I set about removing the good chandelier crystals to clean before I re-hung them. The wooden chandelier in my bedroom had fallen to pieces when I had taken it down. I decided it was beyond repair and wired in a single light fitting with a bare bulb which was perfectly adequate. Mother and father's bedroom had needed a thorough tidying, which I did as best I could.

They were not eating properly despite the dishes I pre-pared. And despite the regular dousing with phage, Vera's leg was bad again. She did not want the medicine I brought her. But I had found the Blue Horns Anthology secreted in her bedside cabinet. I sat at the kitchen table with a spoonful of antibiotics and warned Vera that I would return the Anthology to the library if she did not agree to take it. She opened her mouth. I tipped in the dose. I made sure she continued taking the medicine at the correct time of day. We were all taking medicines now. Givi swigged at a bottle of syrup based on aniseed and alcohol. I took a variety of lax-atives, none of which did much good.

*

I was in my office trying to concentrate on work when Tamoona's uncle walked in and said he was taking me to lunch.

We hardly spoke as we guzzled the food and wine. Our chins were greasy. Heaps of food still to eat. We leant back in our private booth and lit Cuban cigars. I listened to the key-board player fingering a melody over a woozy electronic orchestration. Was that one of their songs? Surely this is the moment when Poliko will slide his voice over the tune and Maia will join him, lagging slightly, so her voice seems an echo of his. I shivered.

How are you doing in light of the *situation*? Tamoona's uncle asked.

I want to see my brother, I replied without thinking.

Not possible.

And Maia?

No visitors permitted.

But at least, what can you tell me about them? How are they? *How are they?*

My dear young comrade, how do you think they are? They're locked up in the highest security jail . . . Solitary confinement . . .

He leant forward to pluck a dumpling. It was cold.

Waiter! Take these and refry them, he called, and in the same breath, You should just carry on as you are.

As I am?

Exactly. Keep up the good work. It might not turn out as bad for me as I thought. Any bit of tittle-tattle all goes in my new stew pot. After the trial we'll move you into a nice comfy post behind a desk. Get you settled somewhere suitable with Tamoona. But for now see what you can find out about the CIA spies in your region of blocks.

He laughed loudly. I laughed along with him. I slopped more wine into our glasses. The waiter came with the fried dumplings. We sucked on them. But comrade Kabakidze had to drop his on the table because he could not stop laughing, The CIA! Oh my! C . . . I . . . A . . . indeed!

What on earth were they thinking? he murmured when he had gained control of himself. Well, it's all over for them now. She was pregnant you know. Foolish little thing. Claimed to have nothing to do with it at first. Soon broke down though. They always do. Give 'em a few days alone. Plenty of tears. No sleep. Waiter! More wine.

Was? Was pregnant!

The shock jerked me upright. The table cloth rushed away. Plates and glasses clattered to the floor.

You bastards!

He dabbed his napkin at his suit front and beckoned a

waiter. I reeled away, staggered up the steps and out into the bright afternoon.

In one heartbeat I was at my Institute. In a second heartbeat I had mounted the marble staircase to the Rector's office. In a third I had barged in and loomed over him at his desk. And fourthly. Fourthly I resign. I am not fit. Thumping the desk with my fist. Not fit, d'you hear?

From a long way off I heard the Rector say, I regret losing you but I'm relieved you've done this Iosif. In the end it will be better for you that you didn't cling on in a false position.

In the next heartbeat I had arrived at Tamoona's clinic.

Do you know what they've done to her? I yelled.

Tamoona directed her patient out, washed her hands, folded away a length of lint, set a flask of phage back in the refrigerator.

Naturally, they had to take it out, she said.

It?

Well, whatever, boy, girl. You know it's forbidden to have a baby in prison. It was better for it to be aborted. Female prisoner's children are sent to orphanages. You look terrible. What's the matter? Did my uncle come to see you? He said he was going to offer you an interesting position. Did you speak about us?

She smiled and spoke my name.

I've got to be alone, I said.

Alright. I'll see you tomorrow. Try not to think about them any more. It's best that way.

No. Not tomorrow. I can't see you again.

She looked into my face. Then she turned away.

I returned to my office. The door was locked. I had never owned a key. It had never been locked before. I went back to the vestibule where the doorman sat on his three-legged stool. I asked for a key. He peered up at me and said there was no key to be had. I suddenly remembered those dusty artefacts in the niches on the staircase, and I made for the stairs because I would like to take one away with me.

Hey, called the doorman, where d'you think you're going? Only members of the Institute are allowed up there.

He rose from his stool. So I left empty handed.

*

You look terrible said Alik. Here, have a sip.

He flourished a brandy bottle but I shook my head. So Alik stuffed the bottle into one of my pockets. Pulled the zipper up to my chin. Turned the collar up. The pocket was ripped but the bottle stayed put. If I hoped that in wearing my brother's jacket I would be connected to his thoughts I was wrong. But I wore it anyway.

What d'you think really happened? I asked.

I don't think anything. Maybe Poliko and Maia just wanted to be young for once. You can't be young here. I myself have never been young. To be Soviet is to be old. It was only possible to be young for the first few years of Revolution. After that everyone aged overnight. Senile dementia. Organ failure. Tooth rot. Penis malfunction. Ancient babies.

He laughed without mirth. A funeral march came echoing from the public broadcast. The sky was a muted grey of infinite depth. A solemn voice boomed from the loudspeakers. A flock of sparrows came tumbling downwards as if they had been tossed from the top of a tower. And who amongst those sparrows, each dressed in similar feathers and with similar wing beats and similar voices stood out as the one who had knives attached to its feet and a poisoned needle hidden in its beak? Which of all the sparrows was a mass killer? An outrage to sparrow-hood who merely nibbled seeds or plucked lone flies from the centre of daisies? I watched them tumble through the air, my thoughts as scattered as their flight. I had been born on a day of mourning. The drum beat announced the deaths of eight innocent souls. And who had really slain them? They were dead of gunshot. Six passengers. The stewardess. The Captain. The Motherland had been told that two terrorists had carried weapons onto the plane. The Motherland had been told that an elite troop had been forced to attack the plane. The drum beat followed the falling sparrows as they sped towards the earth. They would penetrate it like bullets. I made a tape of them talking in private, I said not looking at Alik. I made lots of tapes of them. But that one was different. They were really planning it. The way they'd get out. It was at night. I couldn't help overhearing. Or was I dreaming? It was night. I was asleep. No, I was awake. The tape was turning. I gave it to . . .

Don't tell me any more.

I gave the tape to the KGB.

Don't blame yourself.

They might have got over the border if I hadn't . . .

Or not. Look around you. All those windows . . . Poliko was on friendly terms with everyone. He might have hinted at what they were planning to anyone. Or Maia might have let something slip. They might have bragged about the great things they were going to do in the West. I've noticed in my line of work how even the most careful of comrades can't keep a secret. Come and work for me Iosif. They'll arrest you if you don't get a job. Think about your parents.

Do you ever feel as though there's someone hiding inside you?

All the time. That's what's great about wrestling. Each match needs a different persona. You have to gauge your opponent and be the wrestler he can't predict. Different every time. Listen my friend, why don't you let me get rid of that jacket? I've got a nice black denim that would suit you fine.

They've taken her baby out.

They would.

If only Givi and Vera were allowed to visit him . . .

No chance.

It's as if they're still up there in the sky. Still on their way to Batumi.

Best to think of them like that. We won't be seeing them again.

Where did they get the guns?

You think it was me?

I slammed my fist into his grinning face. But before I touched him he had me pinned down on the ground.

Don't ever try that again, he said softly.

The thump thump of the funeral drum came up from deep in the earth. I could not move beneath Alik's weight. The drum was getting louder.

Why don't you finish me off, I choked.

Alik tugged me to sit up. Fished in my pocket. Poured brandy into my mouth.

Relax comrade steel man, he said.

The following day one of Alik's men found me on the bench set over the stack of tyres. He gave me the name of a relative of his who worked at the ground keepers' compound. He said I should go there and I would be found work. I thanked the man. He placed a hand over his heart and left me alone. I sat for a while. The early winter wheat lay rank and spoiled by rain. The plain was empty. All active life was at my back in the towers. Her block was close by. Her song still haunting the furrows where my brother had cut a swathe of speed through a wheat which covered the world.

I have kept this wheat in my heart as far back as I can remember. When the combine harvesters have done their worst the wheat springs up unharmed. Five years and five years and five and five forever. I had drunk a purgative brew of herbs that morning. I do not like to talk of such private things. But I felt compelled to take myself to a solitary piece of earth and wait there for the herbs to take effect. I had no appetite. I forced myself to eat. I had to maintain my condition for the difficult days ahead.

I lifted a handful of mouldering straw to my face. Darkness was coming on. The pylons fading on the tops of the foothills beyond the plain. If you had reached the border and been set down on non-Soviet soil. If you had been whisked away for questioning only to be set free as defecting heroes. Perhaps Vera and Givi would not have been hit so hard. At least they would have been able to imagine you in your new life.

I turned and tramped back over the soggy field. I wanted to reach home before mother and father got back from work. I had a stew cooking on the stove. They did not eat unless I put the spoon into their hand. We had heard nothing official about Poliko. We had no more visits from the KGB. Tamoona's uncle had seen to that. Oh yes, I had made it up with her. It was necessary to be on good terms.

At night I lay on my brother's bed and held his pillow to my chest. I allowed the dry sobs to rack me. I touched my face to check for tears. There were none.

*

My ground-worker comrades took me to their hearts, enjoying the frisson of my name without any trace of irony or suspicion. They all knew who else I was – the brother of the infamous terrorist Bells – but they did not speak openly of this with me. Our base was a hut in Vake Park from where I could see the grand rooftops of the street where Tamoona lived.

I turned the earth around the city trees. My hands became calloused and used to the cold. I wore the regulation khaki overalls, grey flannel shirt and heavy boots. And it was not long before I found that joining the ground workers had its compensations.

I was now one of the very comrades I had once so avidly collected. I even allowed myself to warble a song or two as I worked. No-one noticed if my voice was imperfect. No-one glanced in my direction. Only Tamoona found my new vocation hard to accept. I went along with her plans for my future re-integration. Her uncle had taken a liking to me and had promised that after a respectable amount of time had passed he would find me a position in the ranks of his business. But in my heart I did not want to leave digging for I had located certain trees which had a singing in their branches.

As I worked up and down the long stretch of Rustaveli Avenue I passed by the circular poster stands. The Bells had been pasted over now. Only sometimes, a tiny portion of a red sunbeam, a blond strand, a dark curl. I made it my business to tear away these accidentals.

My house-guest? My ear was not so deadened by worry that it did not pick up his chortlings and guffaws even though they be disguised as the rumblings of my stomach, or (excuse me) the passing of my wind. I considered trying my bell trick to tempt him out and even try to lose him. But I could not concentrate on anything so arduous. It was taking all my strength to maintain a modicum of order in the life of our apartment. A graph of shock waves marked the air we breathed. They stood steeply peaked and motionless. And we made our way blindly around them, blundered into them, fell victim to their razor edges. And even if I had the strength, it was safer not to risk luring out the little tyrant twisting in my guts, when such weapons as these frozen diagrams of damage lay all around.

A long, exceptionally cold winter passed into a false spring where the sudden warmth brought out the cherry blossom. Then the snow fell overnight and clung frozen on the trees for days until the sun came with enough warmth to begin the thaw. Mouldering blossom. Slush melting to grey pools in shady corners of the settlement. And it was early morning on this melting day when a defence lawyer telephoned to say that she had been allocated to the case and must visit us. I arranged for her to come that evening after work.

I dug the sodden soil. Nothing to hope for yet. The planes and acacias stiff and naked as my fingers. I had caught the habits of my ground work comrades. I gathered my jaw muscles and aimed the spittle to the side of my boots on the paving where people trudged past without seeing me. I did not see them either. I saw Poliko and Maia with the VIP gate behind them as they turned back, took a few steps toward me, then changed their minds and departed. The clods of earth stuck to my spade. I dragged it across the tree to clear them off. The mud clung to the bark so I scraped it off with my boot heel. Each tree is divided between the dark and light, the hidden and the seen.

I came home to find that Vera had laid a spread of cakes and sweets on a lace cloth over the best table. Her leg was still inflamed despite the treatments I had been giving her. It cut my heart to see her hobbling from the kitchen to the table with a look of hope brightening her face. I found her Anthology open on the kitchen shelf. Father had bought good brandy and sweet red wine. We were not to be found wanting in our hospitality despite the shameful circumstances.

The defence lawyer, a comrade Muhkashvili, sat at the table sucking sugar from her fingers. She wore wire spectacles with thick lenses which enlarged her eyes. Her hair was cut into a grey helmet pinned to one side with a black grip. When she had eaten her cake she opened an attaché case and drew out a bulging file.

I am to represent both of the accused, she said. I must warn you not to hold out any hope. Your son was the cause of death for many honourable comrades. He doesn't deserve leniency in any form.

But you're supposed to be defending him! You shouldn't say such things about my boy, said Givi pushing his plate to one side as if to clear a way forwards. Poliko must have been led astray. There must be other people behind what happened. I've been thinking about it. He couldn't have done it by himself and nor could his wife, she wasn't the violent type, nor was he. Impossible! She was having a baby. He served in the army. He was patriotic, a good working comrade. When he came back he was different . . .

Different? In what way exactly?

185

Givi mumbled that he couldn't put his finger on it. I broke in quickly, explaining that my brother had been overtired. Had exerted himself in the service of the Motherland. Had just needed a rest before returning to work.

The lawyer stared at me. I gave her a discreet smile. Between ourselves. A little understanding of my position and connections. She did not return the smile. She reached for another cake. Vera re-filled the plate from the bowl of assorted sweetmeats. We waited as the cake disappeared in two mouthfuls. I had a stomach ache. The sight of that cake being masticated was almost too much. I sipped some brandy. Vera gave the lawyer another napkin and she dabbed her lips with it and the linen was stained with a faint smear of saliva when she placed it back on the table. Now she took out a document of three or four pages held with a paper clip. She glanced through the pages.

This is the confession, she murmured as she read. It's not necessary for you to know the details. Ah, here it is. Paulo Dzhugashvili pleads guilty to the highest crime of treason against the Soviet Union. As does Maia Dzhugashvili nee Dolidze.

Let me read that! said Givi reaching for the papers.

Not permitted, she said, stuffing them back into the file.

What did he say? What did she say? At least give us the gist, I asked.

The lawyer meditated on her plate of cake crumbs. Then she looked up but her glasses hid her eyes. A couple of dreamers ... she murmured. But of course, that's not ... that's ... I mean to say ... Had they ever been abroad? I mean to the *West*?

I shook my head.

I have, you know. Yes, to London actually. Official visit of course. We all went to *Harrods*! I bought a piece of *porkpie*. Still have the bag! It was delicious, the *porkpie* I mean. It was good to get home though. It's terribly hard over there. Beggars on the streets. Rain all the time. Sorry, now then where were we? Ah, yes, the accused. The Bells . . .

Could you just tell us what they said about why they did it? I interrupted.

She looked at me as if she had not understood.

Why did they do it! I shouted and slammed my hand on the table.

Now then, no need for that, she said. Your brother is a terrorist and there are no good reasons for that. His wife too. Mindless violence against the State. That's what they did. It's an arduous duty defending them.

Alright. Just tell us what really happened, I said, trying to contain my frustration. You must know. You've talked to Poliko and Maia. What did they say?

She began sorting through her file of papers. Let me see, she mumbled.

But you must remember.

She looked up though her myopic spectacles. A crumb of cake adhered to her chin.

It was a while ago. And only briefly. They were each a bit upset.

A bit!

Now if you're going to keep interrupting, I shall have to leave. As a matter of fact neither of them said anything to me of value to the case that I can recall. I have no actual record of what they said to anyone else. I have their confessions and that's that.

But did they shoot anyone? Did you ask if they used their guns? Did you ask if they even aimed them at anyone? Did you ask them anything at all?

Not as such I didn't ask. I had only a few moments with each of the accused. We were not alone. D'you see? The answers to your questions are not recorded. The questions don't seem to have been asked. They're not in the files I've been given. I can only work with what I have. I can't fabricate words where there are none can I?

Then what do they say in their confessions?

That is privileged material.

I shook my head and turned to look out of the window, or else I might slap this comrade, with her cake-crumbed chin and her dabbing the napkin at her lips and reaching for a biscuit.

Vera had been sitting tense and quiet attending to the table things, but now she stood and cried out, Let me visit my little boy! Please help me to see him. Just once!

Not permitted, snapped the lawyer. I advise you to keep calm. You'll be allowed to attend the hearing but any disturbance, the slightest sound and you'll be ejected and not allowed to re-enter. You can send clean clothes to the accused via my office. This is my card. By the way, that cake was delicious. Homemade? Thank you, another glass of wine, I won't say no. What a lovely apartment. My daughter adored The Bells. I don't suppose you have a signed fan-club photo? No? Well I shall be there at the hearing but I won't be permitted to speak with you. Any questions? Then I'll take my leave.

Vera and Givi followed her to the door with breathless gasps. Have you seen him recently? How is he? Is he eating?

Is he well? And Maia? She'll have had the baby by now. Girl or boy, d'you know? Perhaps – if it comes to it – we could take the child? Please pass on a message. We're thinking of them all the time. We love them both. We . . .

The front door closed. I heard the lift mechanism whirring in the shaft. They came back to the table and sat down and wept.

There, there. Dry your eyes, I muttered as I cleared away the plates, at least it will all be over soon.

But they wept all the more despairingly.

*

It was high summer when the trial date was finally announced. The decision had been taken at the highest level not to conceal the terrorist attack, as the hijack was officially labelled. We live, as Tamoona's uncle likes to repeat, in the modern world of transparency and fair justice. The trial was going to be filmed daily. Selected parts would be aired on the evening news across the Soviet Union. Foreign reporters would have access to the footage. This was all highly unusual. This unfamiliar frisson of openness gave the case a kind of stage-struck glamour.

The courthouse was packed with military personnel, police, KGB operators and Party officials. We had been allocated seats at the very rear and could see nothing but the backs of the heads in front of us. The courtroom was insufferably hot and airless, despite the huge ceiling fan slowly revolving on a gyrating spindle.

Dato and Eliso sat across the aisle from us but we did not communicate. Eliso's tranquillised eyes were puffy. Dato looked diminished in his overlarge suit. Vera and Givi were also in their best clothes. I had pressed and repaired my grey suit. These same clothes we had worn to the wedding, adorned with buttonholes and perfume.

A ripple went through the courtroom when Poliko and Maia were brought up to the dock. From our places at the back we could not see them. Not the slightest glimpse. We saw them on the television in the evenings. The news was always preceded by a stern-faced announcer reminding viewers of the continued subversive threat to the Motherland. Patriotic music blaring and fading as the courtroom footage began. Mother and father cried out and touched the screen where Poliko and Maia stared straight ahead with no outward sign of emotion. They looked so small and thin. They were perspiring and ashen faced. I longed for those blank faces to belong to a different couple. They stood side by side in the dock. They were not handcuffed. I saw the slightest motion of their arms as they discreetly brushed the backs of their hands together. It suddenly hit me that it would be the first time since their arrest they had seen each other. These bright stars of my life brought to stand before the grim-faced judges. And even as this anguish filled my heart, my throat tightened with impotent anger. They should be sobbing with remorse. They should be bowed down by sorrow at the pain they had caused. How can they stand there looking so remote?

Four days passed like the glance of a shadow racing beneath a windswept cloud. At home we were virtually speechless, going about the routines of life with mechanical actions. We had been allocated this time from work. I do not, to this day, know if it would have been easier if we had been banned from attending, if the trial had been held behind closed doors. If we had not glimpsed Poliko and Maia, miniaturised on our television screen. Torn away from our view on an editor's whim. Replaced by three implacable judges. Overlarge military personnel. Nervous passengers who had been on the flight. The outcome would have been the same. We were not there to participate in any way. And if we were there to learn the lesson of our association with these two comrades who so hated the Motherland they had plotted to flee from her loving care, the court was too late. Nothing could teach us any more on the subject of associating with love and loss.

In court we sat quietly, afraid of drawing attention and being ejected. The legal jargon was difficult to follow. The two handguns used by Poliko and Maia were produced. The shrivelled stem of a rose was produced.

This was no spontaneous youthful folly but a premeditated plot with CIA know-how behind it, said the prosecutor, flourishing the dead rose stem with a look of covert admiration – as if only the CIA could have come up with such a brilliant secret weapon.

The court heard a departmental KGB chief say he had been forewarned about a plot to steal an Aeroflot plane and fly it over the border, but his superiors had not taken the supposed threat seriously when he reported it. And then his superior said that he had known nothing about any plot or about the hijack until he had been rung in the middle of the night by the airport control tower manager. Then this same control tower manager said that five minutes after take-off he had received a may-day signal from the Aeroflot flight in question. Another control tower operator said there had been no such signal but that the plane had turned back and been given permission to land by an unknown authority. When the judge asked to hear the black box recording from the flight deck he was told that it had been accidently damaged beyond repair.

Each day brought less oxygen in the courtroom. The previous day's sighs and huffs, suppressed guffaws, held-back sobs, gasps of disbelief, grunts of indignation and exhalations of boredom were stirred into each passing second of the present by the huge wobbling fan blades above our heads. Even though each word was vital to my understanding of what Poliko and Maia had dreamt of doing – and what they had really done – words slipped away, phrases were lost on me, entire sentences were spoken and immediately drowned. You do not think I did not try to contact them? So near as they were, even if hidden by the crowd in front? I sent out hundreds of telepathic brainwaves to tell them I was there. But I did not know how to believe in anything any more.

The tower blocks are grounded in rumour. Gossip cements the facades. Overheard chatter glazes the windows. The cables and pipes beneath the plaster fizz with a billion versions of events. There had been much talk in the settlement of the shoot-out at the airport on that night of Poliko and Maia's escape attempt. But another rumour had also gone the rounds until fading away under the weight of official information. A cleaner had been swabbing the steps leading out to the runway and had witnessed what took place. She was a very old lady with a whiskered chin. Her grand-daughter lived in our settlement. The old cleaner swore, as only old cleaners can, that she had overheard a policeman laughing at the fake guns the hijackers had used. When that rumour reached my ears I had grabbed it and forced it into the shape of a fact. I had caught a glimpse of the same cleaner with her long stick and rag flipping the marble floor near the VIP exit as I had waved a fond goodbye to my brother and his new wife, as I had called out a jaunty word or two about the new life they were embarking on. I have already told what followed. But fake guns? Let it be true. Let it be a fact to cement to the memory of my brother and his wife.

I will never forget those other official facts though. The immediate announcement on television news of a terrorist attack. The public funerals of the eight victims. Shevardnadze's grim faced attendance – a man with a blood-link to Georgia whilst deep in the politics of Moscow. Scenes flash before my inner eye as if clips from a gangster movie. Poliko loved such films. The Godfather was his favourite. He and Maia often went to watch films in Victor's apartment. He had given them a key. They went down in the afternoons. If I was at home they sometimes persuaded me to go with them. I went purely in the spirit of observer. I had decided not to file a report. After all it was not a bad idea to keep an eye on the latest gadgets. It turned out that Victor's mother had acquired quite an illegal collection of Marlon Brando films. Very soon Maia had also fallen in love with the film star, especially in his early roles. The handsome young rebel astride a motorbike. The tragic failure of the talented boxer. The drama of the actors' voices lost beneath a single hypnotic monotone as the narrator pinched his nose to disguise his identity.

I do not have that tape of them whispering in the night. If it has not been erased and if I had it now I would listen to it and relay every word here even though it would use up the last of my stock. They should have the right to speak. But I gave their voices to Tamoona's KGB uncle. He seems to have done well out of it after all his claims of being outmanoeuvred. He did not appear at the trial. Was never called to account. Has a new post in a relaxed district on the Black Sea coast where he has moved in to a *dacha* and is making his own wine. Everything exists for the good of the system. We live in a fairy-tale with a nice wolf. There are no official stories of rogue wolves thriving in the wilderness. No man-eaters who escape from the public zoo. That spool of audio tape ran for two hours. The same time as a VHS spool with a banned film plus several illegal pop video clips. In that film all is compressed into bright sequences of action. A wedding. A regretful farewell at an airport. Bouquets where guns lie secreted amongst thorns. A brother is supposed to step into the picture now. He is sup-posed to have fathomed the plot and in an act of double bluff he goes with the newly-weds onto the aeroplane. Now the screen splits as it did in some of the pop videos. One side shows a surfing ocean breaking on a sandy beach. The other has a sky of fluffy clouds where a tiny craft flies ever onwards towards a blue horizon. Did you do such a terrible thing for a vapid dream?

The court heard a version of the shoot-out given by a tight-lipped General speaking for the regular militia. Accord-ing to him an elite Alpha force, beyond his command, had been flown in from Moscow. Their gunfire consisted only of a few warning shots to subdue the terrorists onboard. We then heard a forensic scientist say that all eight dead had been shot by bullets from the elite force weaponry, which had penetrated the fuselage in a pattern consistent with the order to fire at will. A police chief said that his hands had been tied the moment the Alpha force arrived. No-one was called to speak on behalf of the Alpha force. A passenger said that whoever the militia were they had continued shooting for twenty minutes and there was no return fire from inside the plane. We were screaming for them outside to stop killing us, the passenger added in a flash of bravado before he was ordered to stand down. As this evidence came to my ears, muffled by the crowded backs and heads of those in front of me where I sat between mother and father, I could not feel any sorrow for those numbers of dead. All I could do was inscribe the facts of the manner of their deaths on the tombstone of my heart, and not a man or woman alive would ever erase them.

The fourth day. A subdued crowd. The fan turned ever more wearily until it ceased spinning completely and hung wobbling slightly in the rising heat. Our defence lawyer had been called to speak. Through the crowded rows of observers, specialists and witnesses I could just see a part of her head, that grey cap of hair, the glint of her spectacles, the corner of a manilla file. She has practised this in front of a mirror, I thought, as she spoke with theatrical cadence, each word standing alone, trembling slightly with the burden of meaning.

These two young comrades are not crazed drug addicts or mental cases, they were the famously charming Bells, and we should only weep and wonder at how they have thrown their success away.

Silence as the court waited for her to continue. She would remind the court that Poliko and Maia had not rained bullets at innocent passengers. Had not shot dead eight unarmed comrades. But she stepped back to her bench. Now, I thought, now Poliko and Maia will have their moment to speak. But the moment did not come and the day dragged to an end amidst a technical exchange between two two-way radio specialists.

The start of the fifth day. I had not expected it so soon. The verdict was to be announced. I sat between Vera and Givi, clasping their sweating hands as Poliko was found guilty of high treason and sentenced to death. Then Maia was found guilty of high treason and was sentenced to life imprisonment. My parents sat still as stone. I held their clammy hands. The fan wobbled above us. Murmured voices came from far away. Papery whispers of documents being shuffled back together. Chairs scraping as people began filing out.

Don't worry, I croaked. It doesn't really mean that. You stay there. I'll go and find out what it really means.

I found the defence lawyer with Eliso and Dato in the crowded lobby.

I was just explaining to comrades Dolidze, she said. There'll be an appeal. That's the law. The judge had to give the harshest sentences for now so that the State can be seen to show mercy in the appeal court. D'you see the logic?

Suddenly Eliso gave a cry.

It's all your fault, she screamed into my face.

Heads turned to look. The defence lawyer spoke to Eliso in a cold level tone.

I advise you not to make a fuss if you want to help your daughter. Go home all of you and wait for the appeal notice. I repeat, don't make waves. Continue as normal and wait to be contacted.

Givi came shouldering through the crowd with Vera behind him. He stood very upright, reaching for Vera's hand as he spoke.

We've been talking, me and my wife here, and we both

agree. We're getting on a bit but we're both healthy and we have a good apartment and good solid work. We want to take the baby in. We'll do it officially. Adopt. We can't have the child growing up in an orphanage.

Vera glanced at Eliso and said, We don't mean to be unkind. But we think we'd make the more stable family. We've had three children you know, the first passed away but . . .

The defence lawyer held up her hand.

Stop this! she said. There is no child. It was got rid of immediately. Now, go to your homes and wait and don't make a fuss.

Vera and Eliso fell into each other's arms and began rocking and keening. Our lawyer walked away. Other people turned to look and then quickly turned away. Givi and Dato and I stood grimly speechless. Until at last Vera and Eliso quietened and we led them from the courthouse. I hailed taxis.

Locked in silence we went back to Nutzubidze Plateau. Everything in the city had been made by a child, and all the pattings and pinchings, the shorings and trenchings could not keep the walls of these sandcastles upright any more. Maia would not have given up her baby. She would have fought against them taking it. She was fierce and strong. They would have held her down to sedate her. She would wake to find that she had failed to save the infant inside her.

Our apartment had not changed since we left it that morning. The familiar furnishings stood in their usual positions. Vera went to the kitchen, ran water into the kettle. Givi retreated to the hallway. I came into this bedroom. Sat on the edge of your bed. Brother mine, as you always said.

That evening we gathered around the television screen like addicts needing one more fix of pain. Here were Poliko and

Maia as the judge pronounced those impossible sentences. They glanced briefly at each other. What passed between them I could not fathom. And then came something we had not been able to hear from the back of the courtroom. The judge turned to Poliko and Maia and asked quietly if they had any final words to say.

Poliko hitched his trousers up on his thin hips. He spoke in a dry whisper, his grey eyes flickering from side to side.

How can we apologise to the dead and their families? What happened can't be excused. We can't say anything to bring them back to life. Words are useless.

Maia was looking out into the courtroom, as if only now seeing the rows of onlookers, and she was searching, searching amongst them for a familiar face.

Here! I gasped to the screen.

She bit her lip – a habit so familiar to me – her narrow face, now ravaged as a martyred nun – bowed her head briefly and then looked up. For a dizzying second I thought she was going to sing but she spoke in a tiny voice as if in a trance.

We made up the plan by ourselves. No-one else is to blame. Then we were really doing it and we couldn't stop. But no-one would have got hurt if it had been up to us. That wasn't in our rules. We weren't going to really shoot anyone. We were going to live peacefully somewhere different. That's all.

Her hands went to the flatness of her abdomen. The guards stepped up and took hold of Poliko and Maia's arms. The four young guards took their arms gently. And led them out of sight.

We sat staring at the screen as the news reader went on to another subject. I stood to switch it off. Vera sobbed and rocked. I took Givi aside.

I'll find out what I can. I've got connections. I won't let it go at this, I said.

Keep out of it. Your sort only causes more trouble, he said.

Then I went to our bedroom and stood over your bed, Poliko.

*

Tamoona said I should put them out of my head until the appeal. But my head did not belong to me to put anything in or out of.

It sat on my shoulders. A wooden face painted on the front. A neat moustache. Well groomed hair. Rosy cheeks. If I, and I did, kiss Tamoona, my lips were stiff and could go no further than grazing the surface of hers, which were greedy for more. She liked my calloused hands. She liked me to go to certain places on her body, places where the rough nodules on my fingers thrilled her. I went to her in my worker's clothes, with earth under my fingernails and dirt in my socks where the boot soles had come loose.

I spent one of my off days hammering said soles down with cobbler's tacks. But the tacks soon fell out. I glued them instead.

Our neighbours treated us in the same friendly way as usual. No-one mentioned Poliko. Old Marina tottered out from behind the lift shaft when I was coming home one evening. She had a few withered plums in her hand.

Give these to Vera, she said, with no trace of dementia in her behaviour.

The phage treatment had failed to cure mother's leg this time. And neither had the antibiotics any good result. Givi and I took Vera to the hospital. Her leg was so painful that she agreed with no trouble. It had swollen up overnight to a tight purple balloon. The doctor said she should have come sooner. After the consultation he spoke to Givi and me privately.

I'm sorry, he said, but it's very likely she'll lose that leg. It's gone septic and there's a danger of gangrene setting in.

The nurse would not allow us to enter the ward where Vera lay at the far end. Givi called out her name, called that we would come to see her tomorrow during visiting hours. The nurse ordered us away and shut the ward doors.

The hospital corridor reeked of worry and false calm. Givi had hardly spoken to me since the end of the trial three weeks ago. But now he allowed me to put my arm around his shoulder and guide him down the corridor, and I murmured hopeful words about Vera's recovery.

Night without Vera in the apartment. Her Anthology lay ready on my bedside cupboard so I would not forget to take it to her in hospital tomorrow. Father stood in the moonlight. I rose from my bed and said I would make some tea.

Why did Poliko do it? he cried out. He had everything he could have wanted. Why did he want to go away to some strange country where he would have nothing? He couldn't speak any foreign language. Nor could Maia. How would they have managed?

I don't know dad, I replied wearily. I suppose they would have studied. I don't know why they did it. Why don't you rest here with me tonight? We'll go and see Vera first thing tomorrow. We have to think about her for after the operation. She's going to have to adjust.

He slumped onto the edge of Poliko's bed. I would hold

him and let him cry if he would allow me. But he suddenly straightened up and slammed his hand on the bed.

Adjust! he yelled, Where did you hear that word? This is the Soviet Union. That bastard KGB Andropov is Head of State. You don't make mistakes. You do your job. You climb as high as you're able. In return you get a decent standard of life, a decent home, decent education, decent health care, holidays. All free or practically free. That's the agreement. There is no give or take. There is no adjusting. What has it taught you, mooning about with that tape recorder, hoarding all those versions of the same song? There is only one version and this is it and you'd better come to your senses if you really want to help your mother!

I know! I shouted back. Don't you think I know! How do you think I feel! It hasn't been easy for me! Why did you let them saddle me with this name ...

But Givi tipped to one side and muttered that he was tired, and in a moment his eyes were closed and he slept.

I pulled him more comfortably onto the bed, tugged off his shoes and spread a cover over him. I rested my hand lightly on his forehead and the thought occurred that this was how a father might comfort his child into sleep.

Meagrely the moon dusted the wardrobe I had shared with Poliko, and the same dim moon showing the marks where our young hands had grazed the plaster walls, and the blurred stains reaching higher up the wall as we had grown to be men.

Next day at the hospital we were told that Vera had died in the night.

*

I have poured a drop of cooking oil over the ball bearing in my bedside cupboard door. The door is a tight fit and the ball bearing will not roll to allow it to open unless I keep it lubricated.

I have stored the spools of my life and those I love within this small cupboard. I wonder if Poliko and Maia would recognise me now. I have lost weight and I rather think my face has taken on a different set to its habitual expression of watchfulness. I do not recognise this man called Iosif when I look in the mirror. Each day brings a new stranger to stand on the other side of the looking glass.

Will the facts be safe stored on this fragile ribbon? But I must not allow myself to doubt. Once there were no tower blocks. No Nutzubidze Plateau. No plain of wheat. Once there was no Motherland. Once, a little boy called Iosif woke to hear footsteps in his chest. And in that instant the tower blocks, the plateau, the wheat flashed into life, sparkling on the Motherland's breast. He longed to sing in honour of this beauty. But his vocal chords were rotten and to hide his disappointment he used his ears instead.

A terrible thought has just occurred. I have said that this is supposed to be a record of facts, and have linked that with the faint hope of steam-rollering my relentless guest to smithereens with the weight of these facts. But were not those wayward conversations picked up by the sharp little ears of an aspiring Komsomol also facts? And did I not stack them in neat pillars just to please him? Ah, he raises his hand to cover his mouth. Not to hold back the germs he coughs but to hide a yawn. He is short of breath but I am not supposed to know. He has suffered from the stale airs of my lower parts. But I have not allowed him to climb the rungs of my ribs and re-enter his once airy apartment. There are terrifying rages. Endless tantrums. My digestive tract is twisted into knots. I frequently have to vomit. A note on inner hygiene. Swallow a dilute solution of iodine. It will coat your insides with a sunny glow, thus shedding sterilising beams on bed-bugs and other nuisances. Now will follow a few seconds of silence while I hold the microphone to the room. I am certain the microphone will have picked up his rumbled threats as he lands punches in the pit of my stomach. I have considered swallowing a drink to put an end to me and him. As a ground worker I have access to fluids in cannisters marked with the skull and cross-bones. But poison would be too much to the taste of the parasite I have been host to all my life. He does not like that title. He spits bile and scorches the lining of my stomach.

It is lucky, or no, for I do not believe in luck, rather it is fortunate that a small amount of blank tape remains on the last spool. I have numbered the reels in order of my narration but I will not play them back. The facts, such as I know them, must lie dormant. I dare not allow them to be overheard now. Not even if in playing them – like a secret weapon emitting sound unbearable to the human ear – they shatter my inmate's eardrums and cause him to bleed from the brain. Nothing I do must disturb those in charge of setting the appeal date. Legal matters take time. The news will come in an official letter. I will wait. Each passing second brings us closer to the day when Poliko and Maia must receive clemency.

Since mother is no more, father has taken to staying at the trolley bus depot where he has fixed up a corner of the repairs' shed. I often try to persuade him to come home. His work comrades have donated bits and pieces for his comfort. His boss has turned a blind eye to the corner. So I do not suppose father will come home after all.

Andropov died in the darkest month of winter. The banners took longer to be replaced than in previous years. Eventually they hauled the image of Konstantin Chernenko up against the dripping walls of State but almost as soon as they had got him up they draped him in black shawls and lowered him down again.

I was at my work on Rustaveli Avenue when they were winching the next banner on to its hooks. The huge canvas filled with wind and pulled away from the uppermost fixings, and the workers began shouting instructions to each other. We on the street stood staring up as Michael Gorbachev sailed out above us. The workers hauled him back, then they furled him up and amidst a great deal of shouting and arm waving they fixed only the topmost rings to the upper hooks. Having secured the banner they allowed it to unroll, and as the face of Gorbachev appeared a little cheer went up from the street.

This morning I received a telephone call from the administration of equipment department at my old Institute. The comrade on the line spoke coldly, even though I have known her for years. She had come across an unsigned docket allowing release of one portable tape recorder. My identity card number was attached to the docket. I must return the tape recorder immediately. I am only surprised that I have escaped her notice for so long.

The three motors are freshly cleaned and I have rubbed a shine to the clear plastic lid and worked some parquet polish into the leather carrying strap. I have not yet said everything I hoped to. The reels spin. The red needle stirs. The counter ticks to ever greater digits. My voice will soon be silenced.

Your pillow still gives off the faintest breath of your hair when I hold my face near to it. No answer when I call across time to you. No matter. You can rely on me. I promise to maintain you in the tip-top condition you will always be to me. And I promise you will be unharmed when we are reunited.

In my mind, in my heart, in my blood, I know they were not carrying fakes. Nothing they did was ever fake. Their games and jokes were authentic as the songs they composed. I cannot find a fact to prove this. A vapid dream. So slight. It fades so quickly. A sweet dream of a beloved brother and his lovely wife. Waking to find it was all an illusion. I no longer listen to rumours. No longer cock my ear to door cracks for suspicious versions of intimate life. I am not clean. I have this *thing* inside my guts. If I were laid out on the butcher's slab, as I saw the cow's lungs spill out when I was young, the *thing* would wriggle free and cause havoc in the market.

Quick now, the tape is running to the end. A slant of sun across our bedroom. Dust sinking through the wheaten band of light.

Life has settled into a routine. As soon as I give up the ground work and take the position offered by Tamoona's uncle we shall marry. But I am not sure I can give my ground work up.

The trees have music in their branches. The earth sings as I turn it.

Ah, the counter turns to the last digit.

PART II

oh my beloved country

1

The crowd had been gathering all day and now the evening starlings wheeled over the marble pediments of the Communist Party Headquarters.

Go away! shouted a voice, and people laughed because it seemed that this mad man was admonishing the birds when everyone else had gathered to ask the Russians to kindly leave.

The Berlin Wall had been torn down and people were stepping over its rubble unhindered. The Soviet Union was no longer bound with one ideology.

Time for us to stand alone, the starling man said to his neighbour.

That's right, time for Georgian Independence, the neighbour replied.

He spoke the last word like that, with a capital I.

Iosif stood beneath a plane tree between the church and the jovial crowd. He lit a cigarette, leant his back against the broad tree trunk, closed his eyes as a group of young men near him began to sing in close harmony. *Oh my beloved country, why do you weep? Your children will protect you . . .* Other voices joined, like the starlings wheeling overhead, each in tune with the next and each on its own path and the whole making this marvellous airborne carpet. He did not sing.

Someone brushed against him and he inhaled the scent of beeswax and incense.

The Orthodox Patriarch raised both arms to the sky. His robe fell away and a crucifix glinted on his chest.

You must leave! he called over the anthem.

The crowd turned to the churchly voice and many performed the sign of the cross. Parents lifted their children to their shoulders to see this leader of their faith, with his church doors wide open and no-one checking who went in or out any more.

Go home, you're all in terrible danger! There are Russian tanks on the river embankment! cried the Patriarch.

Even as he spoke the ground trembled. Some made towards the church. But most stood their ground, and continued singing and watching the starlings wheel above the red flags. Iosif was one of the first to see the tanks as they crawled up the steep road from the river. He yelled that they were coming and the word spread and men stood facing the river road as women gathered their children to them. By unspoken accord the crowd kept singing their anthem into the narrowing air between themselves and the armoured vehicles.

Iosif looked toward the church. He thought he saw Vera in the candlelight. He thought he heard Poliko's tenor rising above the chorale. In the seven years since his brother and wife had been imprisoned awaiting their appeals, Soviet daily life had carried on as usual, albeit much less restrictively under Gorbachev's era of Glasnost. And then suddenly this. Russian tanks bearing down on Georgians. Their anthem lost amid the racket of engines and caterpillar tracks grinding over cobbles. A canister clattered at Iosif's feet. Smoke came wisping and creeping around his leg. He kicked the cannister onto the grass verge away from the milling crowd. But more came tumbling through the air.

Now everyone had their hands over their faces, choking and blinded by clouds of pesticide. People ran in all directions trying to escape it. Children were separated from parents and stood screaming in the pandemonium. He picked up a child and a woman cried out its name and grabbed it from him. He felt the pesticide scorching his lungs.

He discovered that he was at the river, clinging to the stone embankment, retching into the water. Chemically induced tears streamed down his face. All along the embankment people clung and retched and sobbed these poisoned tears. Daybreak found twenty lifeless bodies on the ground by the steps of the former Communist Party Headquarters. Daybreak found faces grey with dismay. Throats burned black. Fists clenched in fury.

The young priest in charge of the bell stumbled up the few steps of the belfry, fumbled blindly for the short rope and rang the clapper back and forth. *Nau nana nana nau nana nau nana nau nau.* All day long the priest rang the single bell. *Nau nana nana nau nana nau nana nau nau.* Other single bells joined from small churches dotted around the city. *Nau nana nana nau nana nau nana nau nau.* Taken on the wind to all quarters of Tbilisi.

In his confusion Iosif talked aloud to Poliko. Sick laughter racked him as he joked about how the Motherland had mislaid her children. Because her children were just like Poliko now. All heading West. As if the East has ceased to exist and there is only West. All the way round the world. West West West West until you arrive back where you started.

Why didn't you hold on a bit longer brother mine? Look at us now! We're all free to go where we want. West of course. To the surfing beach! We'll get there before you! Can you hear me? Iosif shouted and then bent over in a paroxysm of coughing.

He could not remember how he found his way back to the towers. A horror-struck silence hung over the settlement. The central heating grew hotter and hotter until the pipes and radiators were untouchable and he opened all the windows wide and leant far out, because he needed the familiar touch of the wind as much as he needed oxygen. A strange popping sound came from the pipes and then the metal began ticking and within half an hour the pipes were cold and would never grow hot again.

A blue flame lit the bathroom as he sluiced water over himself. He held the sides of the sink and saw his blue-tinted face slowly fade into the blackening mirror as the gas flame diminished and then went out. He turned the pliers in the dark to switch off the geyser.

2

In the seven years that had passed since the trial, Iosif had tried to carry on as normal and wait for news of the appeal. He had ceased oiling the ball bearing in his bedside cupboard door. The door was stuck fast. He was a groundsman and had no need of spools of tape. It had not worked out with Tamoona. He had been wrong to think that his guest would be diminished by his lowly quarters. The entwined conduits leading to indigestion, stomach cramps, bilious attacks, wind, irregular bowel movements of both extremes had suited him, and Iosif was plagued by the tickling of those mischievous fingers on the insides of his belly. If he sometimes broke into fits of giggles it was not at the world around him but at the behest of a guest who had become too familiar, who had broken the codes of hospitality and had raided and dismantled his host's secret store of facts.

While Iosif watched the Soviet Union evaporate with such ebullient speed, his private life was choked with regret and loneliness. As he had seen the last scaffold planks around the old world rot and crumble away, it had felt as though his bones were turning to chalk and a lifetime of inhaling the residue of his tower blocks had finally clogged his arteries. But he was not given to self pity. He had waited doggedly for the appeal notice. This waiting had become the one positive thing that he could achieve.

He filled Vera's old shopping bag with persimmons and a round of bread and a bottle of wine. It was supposed to be curfew but people passed quietly along the tracks. His feet took him over pipes and ditches in pitch dark. Candle flames glowed at invisible windows in invisible towers. The night was riddled with never-ending yelps, high-pitched and desperate, as abandoned dogs padded from yard to yard.

He toiled on until he left the airborne candle flames behind and there was only the wind slamming a sheet of asbestos, the grey glimmer of the concrete slabs that would lead him to the gate. It was cold. The slabs had lifted and cracked and the tram lines were gone, leaving dark trenches filled with molten snow. The wind hissing in the grasses beyond the trolley bus yard. He rattled the gate and called for his father.

They sat in the repairs shed. A candle on the upturned bucket. A crate for a table where he spread the food and wine.

Why don't you come back home dad? It's going to get much colder. I've cooked beans as you like them done. Come back with me now, won't you?

Givi leant and poured wine into a tin mug. I'm alright here, he muttered, patting the bunk he'd made from trolley bus seats, the grubby quilt and pillow he'd carried from his bed.

On the floor stood a little heater with an electrical coil running through a firebrick, the wire spliced to the mains cable strung above and disappearing through a hole in the wall. The cable jolted as power suddenly came through. The wire quivered with the uneven surge and the coil and firebrick glowed red and stank of scorched dust. The old man rubbed his hands to the heat.

There's nothing to keep you here now the trolleys have stopped running. I don't like to see you in this state.

I'm fine as I am.

Come back home, at least for the nights.

You'd better be going. Shouldn't have come out in the curfew. Get yourself back while there's power.

I'll bring a light fitting and wire it in next time I come.

I'm alright as I am.

He stood and touched his father's shoulder and said he'd come back tomorrow. Givi shrugged him off. Sat there staring at the red electric coil.

At least take these matches.

The old man sat and gripped the edge of his bunk and Iosif placed the matchbox on the upturned bucket.

He let himself out of the gate and walked away and heard the rattle of keys as his father locked up after him.

He chose the longer route on the zigzag tarmac road. Now the towers were ablaze with light. Not a dark window, not a radio or television switched off, not a tap left dry, not a gas stove left cold nor a heater left dark. The coming of electricity and water and gas was like hunger satisfied. He climbed the twenty storeys of stairs because the lift might stop mid–floor when the next cut came.

He had left everything switched on in readiness for any brief period of power. The apartment lights were bright, the taps were gushing, the electric heaters warming the rooms as if someone was home and waiting for his return. He washed the pile of dirty dishes and pans. He had his cigarette standing at the kitchen window. The lights went out across the settlement. He opened the window. Darkness wrapped around him and thickened in the rooms at his back. Dogs howled as gunfire rattled from the city and shots were returned. The dull thwump of an explosion was followed by silence and then the distant glow of a fire like a beacon marking a living place in the void. Pale faces made strange by candlelight came hovering at windows high above the ground. He fumbled on the shelf for a box of matches and put it in his jacket pocket with his Astras.

He walked beneath the pine trees on either side of the road away from the settlement. The glow from oil lamps and candles illuminated ragged breaks in the black canopy. He kept watch for the deeper darkness at his feet where an open manhole or a crater waited. On either side were rows of squat buildings. Behind splintered window glass and shreds of net curtains single objects stood in the darkened shops like museum exhibits of life lived long ago. An abacus. A school exercise book. A polka-dot cup and saucer. A blood pressure gauge. A map of the Soviet Union. Still set out as if for sale in a city with no real currency.

He was thinking of his father alone in the trolley bus depot. He should have insisted, stayed with him, forced the old man to break down, cry like he used to and mutter harsh words of blame. A burst of gunfire made him flinch, even though it was common now, the gunfire in the city.

He hurried on towards Vake Park where he hoped his work mates might be sitting around a fire outside the hut. Others hurried along in the night, their heads bowed to watch out for the holes in the ground. He wondered how it was that these craters had appeared so suddenly. The stolen man-hole covers were one thing, but the way the roads and pavements had fallen into these pits was not man-made. The earth had given way almost overnight. The sulphurous mud had claimed headscarves and cafe chairs, kitchen utensils and monochrome photographs of Yuri Gagarin, identity cards and spectacles, ring binders and desktop calendars with drop-down dates lying amongst bitumen-bandaged conduits. He paused to strike a match and light a cigarette, peering down into one of these holes where something white glimmered in the depths, when he was suddenly aware of someone at his back and in that second someone jabbing something hard up under his chin and saying close to his ear, Don't make a sound.

Another man emerged from the dark. The gun man shoved him onwards and told him that he was going to die. The other man laughed and said, But not just yet. Both laughing in the backs of their throats, swallowing the sound into the dark. Now the fighters walked on either side of him and the pistol was taken from his throat. He walked between them, holding himself quiet. He was not afraid of dying, not now that it was upon him. He felt relieved to know it was all over. Only sad that he would not meet Poliko and Maia again.

He knew where they were taking him as soon as they turned along the side of Vake Park onto a steep road through trees, the road petering out to become a track, the branches touching with nervous shivers as they passed through. The city lost in darkness below the ridge where they walked. The clouds swept away now and the sky brilliant with stars. They came out to a clearing where men crouched around the flames of a camp fire, some with black caps on their heads, some cleaning weapons, the angular limbs of sub-machine guns moving in the firelight, the clink of metal and crackle of burning wood and a car engine grinding and failing somewhere amongst the trees. Smoke over a separate glow of cinders where a dark shape stooped to tend the cooking meat.

His captors felt in his pockets and took out his Astras, the matches, his last few roubles, his door keys. They pushed him on towards their captain who stood apart with the firelight at his back. Who did Iosif belong to? Whose brand of freedom did he believe in? They would ask and wait for the right answer. They would ask where he lived. They would have friends in the same towers. Some would be on the enemy side. Some would have been killed. Some changed sides several times and were still not sure. Their captain looked into his face. The smell of gum on his breath as he uttered a low laugh of recognition and turned to the firelight and called out to his men, Look who we have here, it's the man of steel himself!

Iosif saw the captain's face clearly now. He cursed aloud and went for Alik with his fists. He felt the grip of hands on his arms and shoulders but he fought against them and cursed in their faces because now he could not move and his arms were twisted up behind his back. He was pushed to the ground. The pressure of a gun at his temple. He smelled the old season's leaves under his face and waited for it to be over. But the pressure went away and he was yanked up and made to kneel and held there. Alik spoke quietly.

You want to blame me? Alright then. But Poliko could have found the handguns anywhere. You know how the system operated. He could have been a leader like me if he'd wanted. He was gifted. Not only his voice, he had something else. That's why Maia was attracted to him. Oh, you think she was innocent? But no-one was innocent back then, were they? No-one actually believed the Motherland myth. We all play-acted, but some of us gave a better performance than others. The great thing about what Poliko and Maia did was that it wasn't an act. It was authentic. But that's enough about the past. Those times are dead and gone forever. Let him go. Give him back his things.

And so he was set free on the track in the trees. He stumbled but did not allow himself to fall. A car rolled alongside him. Alik was at the wheel.

Get in, he called. It's not safe to be out alone.

3

Although it was the wrong time of year he was washing the trees with lime. He had gone the entire length of Rustaveli Avenue, counting five trees and marking the sixth. Now he was using the last batch of the lime, and when it was finished there would be no more. He had decided to wash the trees on the back streets around Vake Park where it was blacker than pitch at night. He counted five and walked on to the sixth, reckoning that this distance would be enough for the lime to light the way as it glowed fluorescent in the dark.

A man came past carrying bread and paused to offer him a cigarette. They stood smoking together, saying nothing but looking up towards the ridge where the fighters were camped. The man bade him good luck and passed on. Iosif dipped his brush into the bucket and painted the lime wash to waist height around the bole.

As the lime dried he saw continents and islands forming from the camouflage texture of the plane tree bark. He stood and looked into the white sea and saw the maps of land masses with their coast lines and their inland geographies and each land floated alone and complex in the dry white sea and he thought that each tree contained such places, each tree contained the entire world and you only had to brush your hand over the bark to know it.

No-one came to pollard the planes any more. Their branches had grown muscular, reaching to the buildings on either side, fingering carved balustrades, pediments with Grecian urns, medallions of Bacchus wreathed in vines. Here and there someone had hacked off a branch that had grown over their balcony and the smoke from these burning green limbs poured from sooted tin chimneys jutting from holes in the tar-smeared walls.

He moved on, counting five and stopping at the sixth. Gunfire rattled from the ridge and he looked up and saw the glint of water rushing down a gulley and lost in the jumble of rocks and clinging pines. He had no right to behold this bright falling stream and the clenched skyward crags and the clouds pregnant with snow. He was ready for the stray bullet. The whine of a ricochet. The blast that would blow him to smithereens.

He could not remember when the gates to Vake Park had been taken nor when the mowers had disappeared from the store. He sat on the bench and rubbed the dry lime from his fingers. He closed his eyes and listened to the rustle of cinders swirling in the cold fire. He had the ground workers' compound to himself now and he rarely went back to the tower block apartment. He had the draughty hut for shelter and the plot of earth for vegetables. He was able to sleep deeply on the low pallet. And he woke expecting nothing but a bite to eat and drink, the warmth of the fire he would light outside, his toilet amongst the trees, the need to chop wood, tend the vegetable plot, smoke a cigarette.

The fighters came down from the ridge at dawn, dropping down monolithic steps on either side of the dry tiers of a fountain, crossing through the park, bearded and dark-eyed, their makeshift uniforms damp with dew and their once fashionable shoes leaving soft footprints on the paths. They were going home for clean clothing and food, a wash, a sleep. He recognised faces from the settlement of Nutzubidze Plateau, and they knew him and nodded to him in bleak greeting.

The first thing he did after rising and washing his face was to fill two buckets with water. If the tap ran wet that was good, but if not there would be rain stored in the butt. Then he carried the buckets across to the mower store where two refugee families were now living. He called out that he had brought some water and put down the buckets and waited for one of the children to take them in and return them empty. But this time a woman came hobbling out, and because she needed to lean on her stick she let him carry the buckets for her.

He had seen her before, making her way across the park wrapped in shawls with her leg swathed in dirty bandages. And the sight of the limping woman had seared him with memories of his mother in better days. But his memories had the flimsy texture of a dream, floating out of reach, and even as he tried to recapture the truth of the memory it was swept away by the present moment.

He followed the refugee woman into the store. The city was full of refugees now and those that found a private shelter like this were fortunate. They had made a home of the corrugated barn. Straw mattresses were laid on pallets, there was a rickety table, three-legged stools, a tin stove to cook on, their few clothes hanging on nails, a paper icon of Saint George hooked onto a splinter of wood from an upright support.

He said a greeting to the two men sitting at the table and they thanked him for the water. He could not refuse when the woman asked him to sit and eat with them. She set the bucket to warm on the stove and brought a dish of beans and some dry bread. The men left the table and she sat with a sigh and rubbed her leg. He spooned out some beans and tore a crust of bread and ate as she watched him.

When he was finished he thanked her and went to leave but she said, No, stay. And she leaned towards him and thumped her chest and said, I was a teacher. Things were good, we had a fine home. Look at him, my husband, a worthless drunk now but he was famous not so long ago.

She turned to the man who was her husband and he grinned foolishly and nodded.

His friend slapped him on the back saying, Aye, you were famous not so long ago. Why not show our visitor? Come on man, stand up and do your best.

The man looked puzzled for a moment but then he stood, took a small breath and began to sing. His wife covered her face and kneaded her brow. The voice rose high and tender as the man sang of a small industrial town and how he must leave and not return to the beloved vines he had planted in his garden there.

When the song was over the man's friend passed a bag of tobacco around and they rolled it in strips of yellowed newspaper and sat smoking and flicking the strands of burning tobacco from the unfurling paper. Iosif told them that he had been an ethnomusicologist. He said that in the old days he would have recorded that song for posterity.

Aye, said the singer's friend, this is what we carried when we fled over the mountains, our tobacco and our songs.

He took his leave and said he would bring them water when he could and they thanked him.

The woman with the bandaged leg came outside with him and looked into his face and said, You come back and sit with us whenever you want.

They had not exchanged names because names belonged to what they had lost.

Curfew, but he watched the headlights of a lone car beam across the wall of a tall building. He watched the black shadows of cables and a lamp post sliding across the wall as the car slipped away. He must be careful not to surprise a patrolling militia group in the dark. The air was soured from burnt timbers and scorched masonry. In the half fallen dwellings he saw candle flames and people passing behind net curtains at the shattered windows. He saw the candle-lit sheen of a gilt-framed mirror reflecting a crystal chandelier and part of an ornate cornice and the top of a mahogany cabinet. The darkness was close as a cloth held over his eyes and he went on by instinct, by the generational knowledge of his city, his feet finding the way through the ruins toward his Institute.

He had not been here for years. He found ways to avoid this street. He stumbled for a second as his feet came to a heap of masonry. Here was the Institute, a jagged shape against the sky where the pediments had been. Now he could just make out the ends of timbers sagging under the weight of the unsupported roof. And there, high up in the dark, was an exposed wall that had once been part of a lecture hall, the ghost shape of a framed portrait hanging on the wall in the night air.

He went on, over the rubble and into the shell of the foyer

and found the steps to the basement. He forced the door to his office open. Broken brick and grit slid beneath his feet and it was absolutely dark and underfoot was wet. He struck a match. There was his desk, his typewriter and his papers, and there were his shelves of tapes in their labelled boxes. Dusty but the same! The match burned out. He lit another. The glassy balloon of the 500-watt lamp reflected the yellow flare. He opened the desk cupboard where he kept his batteries and blank tapes and the back-up tape recorder. It did not matter that it was dark when the match went out now. He filled his pockets with batteries and reels and rubbed the dust from the tape recorder casing with his jacket sleeve. And then he sat on the chair and rested his head on his arms on the filthy desk top. He longed for the past.

He woke with a shudder and stumbled out with the things he needed. The female cats were dragging their kittens to their dens in the ruins. The stray dogs already lay asleep, stretched on their flanks in the angle of the gutters. And in the dim dawn light he saw the naked plane trees and their trembling twigs over his battered city. He strode on, raising his haunted face to feel the wind. Snow began falling. The white flakes settling on his black hair.

The two refugee families were gathered as before. The children were quiet and solemn eyed as he set out the tape recorder and the man stood to sing. When the man was finished he re-wound the tape and played the recording for them. They listened without comment, but the singer tugged at the skin of his throat and closed his eyes. Iosif asked, could he keep this recording, archive the song? The singer nodded and his friend got out the tobacco and they rolled cigarettes. He noticed how the singer's wife limped as she went to the stove. The children returned to their games and the men set out a chess board. He said his goodbyes and the singer's friend asked if he had more batteries and would he be prepared to barter them? But Iosif lied and said no. The wife followed him out.

Look here, she said, I know of other singers. I could take you to them if you want. She touched his sleeve and looked hard into his face. We've become nothing more than chaff blown hither and thither. Your recordings might give us back our immortality, she said.

I only have enough batteries for a few hours, he said.

A few hours of immortality is plenty, she smiled.

He lay awake that night watching the snowflakes drift through the gaps in the hut roof. But he was warm beneath his quilts and the flakes lay only briefly on the floor before melting. He thought of the refugees' flight across the mountains and how some had perished on the frozen scree. They had walked over the glaciers and then walked around this city where they knew no-one and had lain to sleep in the chaos with their cuts and blisters turning sore before they found refuge. He would try to save some of their songs. But his heart was beating fast because he knew what he must also do for the singer's wife. Her festering wound needed phage treatment. And at last he fell asleep and there was his mother and in her hands she had gathered the thready roots of a cactus.

He saw the flicker of a candle flame through the translucent glass in the clinic window. His clenched his hands because she was there and he had imagined she would not be and that after all he would not have to see her again. He tapped three times on the outer hatch. The old signal. He stood shivering and watching the door. He thought that if she did come he would have to kill her. He imagined the struggle beneath his fingers as he did it. He was capable of it, he knew that. But now the door opened a chink and he said, It's me. And after a short silence she replied, Then you'd better come inside.

He would not allow himself to look at her. She was thinner than before. He stood in the doorway. She was wearing her lab coat.

I need some phage, he said.

I see.

Yes, it's for a woman with a bad leg.

A woman with a bad leg.

That's right.

Pricked by a cactus I suppose.

No. She's a refugee.

And she's got you running around after her.

No, that's not it. I . . . listen, can I just have some phage?

Come in properly.

He followed her across the waiting room and into the clinic. They stood each with their back to a work top, each gripping the surface behind them. They did not speak but stood looking and remembering. When Tamoona raised her hands to the back of her neck and tugged the plait around and began undoing the strands, he uttered a dry sob. No, he said. But he was already kissing her. Already lost after so long without a woman. And she was as lost as him. These kisses, this defeat, this lust. Everything was lost – this is for all we have lost – all we have not forgotten – all we once were.

When it was over he wondered again if he was going to kill her. Tamoona straightened her lab coat.

I've missed you, she said and waited for his reply.

He gazed around the clinic. It was clean and the shelves were stacked with organised petri dishes, rolls of lint, glass beakers.

Could I have some phage? he asked.

She raised one eyebrow. How familiar that was to him. She was so much more clever than him. Always one step ahead. But not this time. He ploughed on with his idea.

I thought we could help the refugees. There are so many with ulcerated legs. They don't know about your phage clinic. But I could tell them. We could . . .

You seem to have forgotten something, she interrupted with an expression of incredulity.

I have not forgotten a thing.

Just tell me one thing. Is this *darkness* what people call freedom? How can you come to me and ask for phage when nothing works any more? Everything's destroyed. Our phage library is ruined. It's criminal what's happened to the labs. We can't keep them running without electricity. I can't bear to think about it. Years of dedication. Years of research. Everything that Eliava gave his life for has been poured down the drain. And what do we have in its place? Fear. Chaos. Anarchy. Civil war. People running riot because they have no rules to guide them. You come to me and ask for phage like a child asking for ice cream. But I can't store the phage any more. Don't you hear the silence! No refrigerators equals no phage! I come to my clinic every day because I don't know what else to do. But there's nothing here anymore. Are you going to restore the power? Can you fix up the lines people have torn down? Why did people want to destroy a system that provided everything they needed? It's such a waste. Such a stupid waste.

She turned from him and her shoulders shook. He went to her and held her in his arms.

I'm so tired, she said. Let's not argue, Iosif.

I'm not the same as I was.

You are to me.

I'm going now.

I'll be waiting for you.

The camp was deserted. The snow was melting on the ashes of the fire. There were tyre marks and fresh footprints and urine stains in the snow so he knew that they had only recently moved on. He was alone and unarmed and he ought to go back to the safety of Vake Park. But he followed the track from the camp up along the spine of the ridge. He thought it would be safer if he did not try to hide so he sang as he went, tramping through the snow. He slapped his hands together and threw back his head. His voice was atrocious. They might kill him just for that.

Late in the day and the dogs calling down in the city, their thin yelps piercing through the muffled grey air. A distant voice pitched to a melody in a minor key. He wished he had more than the few reels of tape he had salvaged. Already half gone, but the recordings were the best he had ever made. The refugees' songs came from Abkhazia where citrus groves and tobacco plantations grew down to the Black Sea and the melodies were filled with light and warmth, and when the refugees sang it was a refusal of all the sorrow that had come to them. And always in the background the sudden crack of gunfire and the singer continuing without the slightest hesitation. He did not dare replay the tapes too many times.

He could smell acrid gas leaking from the magnetic ribbon.

He did not like to think of the years that had passed by. If he sometimes bent over and held his hand to his stomach, he was not unlike many others suffering from the stress of these dazed times. Iosif had learned to live with these pains, these twists and wrenches in his guts, this stone-like coldness in his abdomen, the weight of that rough boulder cutting into his bowels. He was always shy about this sort of thing. He would not have gone to a doctor even if there had been any around. A certain visitor, who Iosif never named to himself these days, was camped in the midst of Iosif's humiliation. He had settled in a dirty place. A vagabond in a grim site of slime and foul airs. Iosif heard him cackling and felt him picking at his sores. Blood sometimes came when he crouched to the toilet. And Iosif would see the red smear and would comfort himself with the hope that a bit more of his guest had leaked away. He was not insane. This is just how it was for him, and he never spoke of it.

He had become so accustomed to the loss of Poliko and Maia that he hardly felt it any more. The waiting had acted like an anaesthetic. Their faces had faded as imperceptibly as the colours fade in a print. But after what had happened with Tamoona their faces were reappearing, flash-lit, glimpsed and gone only to appear again, briefly brilliant, in another room of his mind. He sang as if he really were a mad man. And he came to the fighters like that, singing out of tune, waving his arms about, his face deathly pale, his hair wet with snow.

They were drinking *chacha* spirit. Silently passing the bottle round and pulling hard on the neck. Their ill assorted uniforms were sodden and they were all bearded and red eyed. Victory, said Alik, passing the bottle to him. He drank the spirit. Victory, he replied. No-one asked what he was doing wandering around where he could get shot. They lit up smokes and stood together looking out over Tbilisi.

It'll be over soon, Alik said. Then we'll get the city back on its feet.

One of the men began the anthem and the others joined. *Oh, my beloved country why are you so sad?* he sang with them.

They walked along the track down to the city and on the way Iosif explained his plan and asked Alik to find him a generator.

And a supply of benzene, he added as an afterthought.

Alik laughed without mirth. I led my men to victory today, the ridge is ours, our brothers are in control of the communications tower, but now the man of steel wants more.

He aimed for the sky and shot a round. The dogs howled from the dark streets below and the fighters stood watching quietly.

Alik came with two of his men lugging the generator and three jerry-cans of benzene adulterated with paraffin. He promised there'd be more fuel when Tamoona needed it and he made a great show of hooking up the power line and getting the thing running smoothly. The noise from the generator filled the clinic. The refrigerators trembled as they started up. Alik produced a bottle of vodka and Tamoona found beakers for glasses and they all drank the spirit in one gulp, wordlessly acknowledging the chemistry in the beakers and the crazed throbbing of the generator and the soundless shivering of the refrigerators. One of Alik's men knocked a hole in the window glass and put the exhaust pipe to it. Are you satisfied mister steel man? Alik shouted above the din. Tamoona threw back her head and laughed. Iosif wished Alik would not call him that. But he laughed along with them. Now Alik switched the generator off and explained its workings, the place to pour the fuel, the parts not to touch when it was on. You could run it at night, he said, eyeing the quilt and blankets on the floor over by the wall where Tamoona had draped some of her clothes on a chair. Iosif saw how Alik eyed her too. She wore her white lab coat and she looked efficient and untouched amidst the ruin that had befallen every corner of their city. He did not feel angry with her now.

Perhaps Alik was right and he was indeed made of steel. He barely felt a thing now that he had accomplished this. He felt inflexible deep in his bones. In the old days the workers had rolled out mile upon endless mile of steel and it had been cheap as paper. There had been such a glut of steel that it was used for garden fences, for paving muddy tracks, for workmen's huts, and he was part of that over-production. He was excess material. He was an end-cut from the smooth glistening blade. Even now, with Tamoona looking exultant and Alik obviously impressed with her, he did not feel any pride or joy in bringing about the rejuvenation of her phage clinic. He was glad for the refugees who would benefit. That was the most he could manage.

4

When the refugees came to Tamoona's clinic with their sores rubbing beneath their soiled clothes, it was not just her phage tinctures that saw them leave with a more determined set to the mouth. She would not permit failure and she passed on this refusal to submit to the chaos of a country that was like a stroke victim painfully inching backwards in the dark. A stunned nation seeking something intangible but familiar, something like a name, something less than an identity, some minor memory of childhood, some recalled scene steeped in the simple emotions of a homely voice calling from a balcony. Something ordinary to confirm they were still who they always were.

The generator crouched below the window. It was encrusted with engine oil and rust and it stank despite the exhaust pipe exiting from the hole in the glass. The racket of its motor caused beakers and petri dishes to tremble towards the edge of the shelves, lint slid across the steel-top surfaces and fell unrolling to the grey tiled floor. Iosif felt the vibration in his teeth even when he had switched the generator off after the last of Tamoona's patients had gone. He felt it in her lips when they kissed. Yes, he came to her before curfew. They lay together on the quilt, more quilts piled on top of them, a candle burning.

Now Poliko and Maia sang to him in dreams. He was terrified of the years that had separated them and the way they had gradually faded. He vowed to take every breath on their behalf from now on. He promised to breathe with the same rhythm as their breaths, and then they would not be separate any more. He knew it was too late. He had already lost them. But this did not prevent him breathing in time with them. It was exhausting and he often failed. He needed every breath to be shared with them, even in sleep, waking tired, fearful lest he had dreamt too deeply and forgotten.

He was glad of the ungiving clinic floor beneath him. He woke at dawn and left Tamoona like a husband leaving his wife for paid work. He worked until his back ached and his arms and legs felt leaden. Digging and turning the stubborn earth around the trees along Rustaveli Avenue and the streets of the old city. He had a long-handled shovel, better for pitching up sand or gravel than this type of digging but his hands were calloused and familiar with the grip and the strike, and his back was used to the stoop and his shoulders and arms to the leverage. Probably the trees would survive just as well without his care, but this was his work, he was a groundsman and he wanted nothing else.

He continued working even though there was no pay. It was not hard for him to simply continue the never-ending round of applying fresh limewash and loosening the earth. He also gathered windstrewn household rubbish, cigarette stubs, the scuffed glove of a dead puppy or kitten. He set light to the rubbish in the gutter and stood over the smoke to warm his hands if it was cold. Since the outbreak of fighting he sometimes found spent cartridges. Sometimes the tree would be splintered from a bullet and there might be a dark stain on the bark and a pool of dried blood at the base and he would strike the clods open and mix the blood in. He worked for the need to work and for the respite he received from the softened earth and the supporting trees.

5

He was on his way to the trolley bus depot to visit his father. He had some food, a jar of cooked beans, a bunch of spring onions that he'd grown himself, a chunk of *chadi* that he'd made from the last cornflour he had found in the back of the kitchen cupboard where Vera had stored it all those years ago. A spring day. People were tending the vegetable plots they had made alongside the footpaths and overground sulphur water pipes. The pipes were empty. Their silver aluminium lagging had been torn away by the wind. The fat steel conduits had become burnished where people clambered over, going up and down on the footpaths. Starving dogs lay sleeping in the dry paddling pool. He was singing softly to himself. The song from the poem had come without warning and he sang almost without knowing it, his tuneless voice droning along like the bumblebees that flew past his ears. The wind was whisking the blossom from the cherry trees, falling in pink drifts, lacing the track ahead of him, as if falling for him alone, as if to soften the way. Petals fell onto his black hair. *Nau nau nani nau nani nana . . . Somewhere in the distance a flower has fallen fast asleep beneath a bush . . . Nau nau nani nau nani na . . .*

He was going to say goodbye, and if Givi wanted to say goodbye and hug him and wish him well, that would be a bonus and if not then he would leave the food and the spare key to the apartment and promise to keep in touch and send money as soon as possible. I'll send the money via the post office, he prepared to tell his father as he walked. I'll send letters by fax. You must pick up the faxes at the central post office. You can write fax messages back to me using the number on my fax to you. The money will be enough to pay for international phone calls as well, you can make them at the post office. I'll send my number with the first fax. There'll always be a home for you with me and Tamoona, and as soon as we're settled I'll send money for your ticket.

He let the tracks take him to the upper terraces of the settlement. It was pleasant to see the vegetables growing in the nicely tilled earth, to bid good-day to the grandfathers and grandmothers working the plots with their grandchildren. And here were the last ranks of towers. And here the aerial walkway hanging unhinged above the view of the plain beyond. He stood clutching his bag of food. In the low rays of the morning sun he saw undulations beneath the grass and they were the old ploughed furrows. These ribbony humps were all that was left of six decades of intensive wheat production. Now the plain was wild with grasses, poppies, thistles. The wind had a new voice, a new interplay of shushings and whisperings, variations and improvisations that he had never heard in the steady hiss of the old voice of wind in the wheat. *Have a nice day*, he said to the sunstrewn plain. Tamoona had taught him the words, getting him to repeat them to her satisfaction, rewarding him with a jokey kiss, *have a nice day* laughing between their lips as they kissed.

Was it so wrong to think of happiness? Even though he did not deserve to be happy? Wasn't he allowed to forgive himself? Couldn't he be permitted to start afresh in another country, far from here, a place where he would have only a generic history, be a curiosity, an exotic figure, a specialist in folk songs from a land that nobody had ever heard of? It wasn't as if he was going to run away without telling anyone who cared about him. He wasn't going to get people killed by leaving. He wasn't going to lie to anyone. They would wait until they were settled and then they would have a baby. The child would grow up so free that the idea of freedom would never have to occur to it. But we'll come back to visit, they had agreed, we'll bring up our child to be bilingual, we'll teach it our history.

Tamoona was less convinced about the child than he was. It hasn't happened in all this time, she said. You know I've had lovers since we parted, and before I met you there were some, and all this time I haven't become pregnant, and that's not because of contraception, if you want to know the truth I like it better without, it's more erotic for me, the thought of a sperm finding me defenceless. But we must be practical now, there's a lot to organise before we can really leave.

Once again she related the lucky story of how it was that she had met an American Professor, a pharmacist who was here to research bacteriophage. And how he had been directed to the phage laboratory complex and how she had been there at that very moment, looking through the shelves of the silent refrigerators in the hopes of finding flasks of viable phage.

There was no light and the laboratory was strewn with damp papers and files that smelled of mouse droppings, but this American had sat on a dusty lab-stool talking eagerly with Tamoona about patenting bacteriophage. He was impressed with her first-hand experience of raising the cultures and developing a steady state material that could be applied to medicine. She had taken him to collect raw river water. Her battered bucket had caused him to laugh with embarrassment at first. But when she led him to her refugee clinic and he saw the clean wounds, the healing feet, the tubercular sores drying up, Professor Ted Huwbright, who spoke passable Russian, became ardent in his praise. Before he left he promised to keep in touch.

True to his word he sent a fax to Tamoona via the post office. It was an invitation to take up a research post at Emory University in Atlanta.

I saw how impossible life is for you with the demise of the Soviet Union, he wrote. I'm wiring some money which I want you to use as you see fit. As soon as we've done with the sponsorship formalities I'll wire a second amount for the air-fares. Tell me how much you'll need and the names and passport numbers of your family members who'll travel with you.

But Tamoona's family had fled to Moscow when the French Cottage had been ransacked, secret documents revealed and revenge attacks taken place and she had hugged Iosif and laughed, You'll be the only one travelling with me.

Iosif applied for a brand new passport and when the officer handed it to him they each exchanged a glancing smile because the passport cover was embossed with their own unique language whose looped and hooked lettering said *Independent State of Georgia*. After a painless visit to the American Embassy his passport was stamped with a United States visa. They would live as guests in Professor Ted's house at first. They would study the language. It would not take long before they were properly settled.

For Tamoona the departure was about escaping the ruins of her work and re-building it in a place where things ran smoothly. Her old antipathies to the West were of no use any more, so she ditched them. Iosif had not needed much persuasion. Seeing Tamoona again had brought Poliko and Maia to the front of his mind – but the torture was that he could not reach into that dark space and touch them or speak to them. They hovered ghostily looking like they had been back then. But they would be changed.

Iosif was changed. The moustache had long gone. His jet black hair was no longer shorn and was greying at the temples. His outdoor life had weathered his skin where it was exposed. His eyes were extremely black and hard to read. His lungs did their job well enough. His throat was hardly ever sore. His ears, which had always stuck out slightly, never ached. He was leaner than ever. The cramp and twists in his stomach had eased. He had not felt so well for a long time. He did not bleed any more. His bowels were regular. He was not that deluded to think that his guest had gone away of his own free will. Nor to imagine that he had imagined the guest and that the guest had never existed, or that he had been like a phony clairvoyant talking to spirits made of the client's hopes. As Iosif's health had improved so had his namesake's declined and the guest lay curled in a foetal position, only occasionally mumbling garbled orders and weakly thumping the pillow of his host's stomach lining.

Iosif held on to what he knew was a naive hope, that the new life ahead would somehow eradicate his lifetime pest. Maybe they'll spray us at immigration, he mused, and the American fumigant will evaporate him. After all, he hasn't got a visa . . . He kept those thoughts locked away in a part of his mind unavailable to his namesake or anyone else.

He had been gripped by the desire to be done with it all. He longed to deal with life as simply and nicely as Professor Ted was so generously doing for them. He stood at the edge of the plain with the towers at his back. The soft swishing of grasses filled the sunlit air and he knew he must not turn to see the block where Maia had lived, or the balcony where she had sung. Try as he might to breathe in time with them, he could not reach out and hold her, he could not reach out and hold his brother. It was too late. It was too long ago that he had lost them. They were gone and he was going. That was that.

He followed the perimeter track to where it led back down towards the rattling tin roofs of light industrial sheds and concrete blocks that had once housed pumps and transformers, empty stores that had once sheltered the combine harvesters and tractors, ransacked repair sheds, a chicken shed denuded of everything but a crust of white feathers and white droppings. He came to the trolley bus depot and called out even though the gates had been stolen and he could have walked right in.

Dad, he called, it's me, Iosif.

He found his father hanging from a cross beam in the repairs' shed. He stood the upturned chair upright and climbed onto it but it wobbled and fell apart and he fell with it and lay dazed for a moment on the concrete floor. He pulled himself up and went out and found an empty oil drum and rolled it in and stood on it to reach up to the noose. The old man was light as a few sticks in Iosif's arms as he jumped off the oil drum. He carried his father out into the sunlight, laid him on the earth and knelt down. The sun shone on them, warming Iosif's back, the top of his head, his neck. He looked into his father's agonised face. In life it had been the face of an ordinary comrade, a comrade who had wanted to keep the trolley buses running on time so his fellows could get to work on time. But time had outwitted the old man. The times he had lived for had fled and left him alone in a ransacked depot where no-one came to check if the gate was locked, and then the gate itself had been stolen. Iosif touched his father gently on the forehead but he quickly withdrew his hand from a skull which contained nothing now but death.

He sat in the driver's seat of the old Lada but he could not get it to start up nor did he know how to drive it even if it had. He ran across the yard and out of the gateway and then turned back and ran to his father and took off his leather jacket to spread over his face. There were rats. Wild dogs. Starving cats. Rooks. Crows. Ravens. White-winged vultures from India. He could not leave Givi exposed to them so he began to dig a grave in his father's vegetable plot. He dragged the corpse to the shallow trough and tried to organise the limbs and the lie of the head. Then he spaded the earth over the body and over the leather jacket hiding the face.

As his brother's jacket disappeared beneath the earth, Iosif told him that his father was dead. He asked Poliko if he knew that Vera was also dead. She died a long time ago, he told Poliko. Not long after you and Maia were taken. Have you been picturing our family alive and happy? Just like we used to be? Have you been seeing Maia pregnant with your child? Even though they aborted it? Have you been picturing me mooning about on the balcony with my tape recorder? Where are you? Answer me! I'm leaving Georgia. I'm leaving you and Maia behind. I'm going to America, where you always wanted to go. Say something!

He stumbled back along the footpaths. His boots were caked with soil and his hands were muddy and his trousers stained. He must have shed tears even though he could not feel them because there were pale tracks running down the smudges on his face. He came to a sudden standstill somewhere in the settlement. His fists clenched at his sides. His eyes unseeing. The hot dry wind tore bits of concrete from the serrated edges of the blocks. A sheep bleated mournfully from a balcony. The tannoys scraped the posts where they hung on brittle wires. The rubbish mounds reeked and ruckled where the maggots seethed. Why shouldn't Poliko weep for the damage he had done? Why shouldn't Maia weep for the harm she had caused? But they had both stood there dry eyed. The huge creaking fan had revolved on a bent spindle hanging from the ceiling. It had been so hot in the courtroom that even to swallow was an effort.

6

Edward Shevardnadze and members of his fledgling Democratic government were bunkered in the Communist Party Headquarters. The tall triangulated girders of the communications tower puffed scrolls of black gas over the city from its smouldering bundles of cables. Fighters went home to their tower blocks or to their old apartments of gracious dilapidation. They greeted each other as neighbours, none talking of who they supported. People spoke instead of a UFO hovering above Tbilisi. The alien craft was seen only at night when the city was pitch black and the spacemen's lights shone bleak blueish pathways for adventurers to tread upon.

Most people walked nowadays. What cars remained were demented reinventions of found materials. Passengers reclined in aviation seats, doors were hinged with jute straps, the cars had glassless windows, mismatched panels beaten to fit with a blunt axe, flat-tyred acts of will, running on paraffin, engines missing vital parts and still turning. No-one understood how their vehicles had deteriorated so quickly. The trolley buses stood stranded where the power had failed in the overhead lines. Their doors were forced open, anything useful removed. The roads were blocked by sprawling markets of open tables and metal kiosks. Here the new entrepreneurs dealt in tatty scraps of paper issued as emergency coupons as they sold their out-of-date tins, misshapen candles, false spirits, carboys of good homemade wine. Pyramids of pink tomatoes. Rounds of wet white cheese. Car-loads of muddy potatoes. Cones of flour decorated with calendula heads. Bunched dill, tarragon, coriander and parsley tied with woody stems. No-one need go hungry.

Iosif went back to the apartment. He tied the window latches together across the central window bars because they had blown open and rain had come in and the net curtains were grey and ragged by the floor. He swept the floors. Trod on the cockroaches. He made sure any electrical plugs were out of the sockets. He picked up the telephone receiver with a sudden desire to speak to someone, a relative in Rustavi, anyone. But the line was filled with static and a great muddle of voices calling out names and mistaking stranger's conversations for their own. He replaced the receiver and pulled the cable from the wall. He looked into his parents' bedroom.

The bed had no quilt and so he found a chequered blanket in Vera's linen cupboard and spread it over the mattress. Dry walnut leaves fell from the blanket folds where his mother had laid them against moth. He swept them up and crumbled them in his hands then dropped them into an ashtray. This he carried to the kitchen. The sunlight fell at a slant over the formica table top with its old scratches and blade cuts. Was this where he had cut up that photograph? Or had it been in the old one-roomed apartment? He could not remember any more. That life seemed to belong to a different planet. Now he looked through the open kitchen door towards his bedroom. He took out a cigarette then he put it back in the pack and quickly strode across and opened the bedroom door.

Breathing fast he went directly to the bedside cupboard. He had to tug the door to get it to open. The ball bearing was rusty and he automatically rubbed it with his finger and brown oil came onto his skin and he wiped it off down his trouser leg. He would not have done that in the old days. His suit hung in the wardrobe. The two beds were neatly made with the quilts pulled up over the pillows. Spiders' webs festooned the corners of the room. His hand went into the little cupboard, feeling around without him looking. He was gazing at the window where the net curtains made a motionless haze between him and the tower blocks outside. His fingers found the stack of slim boxes. But what could he do with them? He would not bring the tapes to take part in his new life. He could not listen to them without a tape player. He had seen the latest model for sale in the market. It was as small as a book and the tape cassettes were no bigger than a cigarette pack. People had stood fingering the little tape machine. No-one could afford to buy it. Iosif's plate-sized spools belonged to that other planet where his sister had died of polio.

He closed the cupboard door, pressing it tight shut so the ball bearing clicked in. But then he gave a gasp and clenched his midriff. The old pains twisted in his gut. No, he muttered. But from the depths of his innards came the patter patter of patent leather shoes performing the rejuvenated jig of an old-ster who has just returned from a cruise to balmy, sensual climes. Now Iosif spoke aloud to his familiar, a thing he would never have done in that other life. You wait ... You just wait ... One day I'll be dead and then you'll see ... Not yet though. I'm going to live and be happy! I'm going to *have a nice day*. You can't do anything about it.

Vake Park had become a meadow of knee-high grasses and wild flowers. He stood for a moment, a lone figure in the twilight, wondering at how patiently the flower seeds must have been waiting in the earth during all those years of mowing. Then he lit his fire outside the groundsman's hut and sat on the log, staring into the flames.

Hello, my name is Iosif Dzhugashvili, I am an ethnomusicologist, he practised.

Fortunately the word for his profession was interchangeable, but his surname was difficult and they, he and Tamoona, had wondered about alternative versions. Josef Jackson, for example. *Hello, my name is Joe Jackson. What is your name?* They would marry in America and Professor Ted would sponsor their application for a green card and the right to stay indefinitely. The word, indefinitely, pleased him with its rolling landscape of easily traversed terrain. So he sat on the log by his fire and felt the warmth not just from the flames but from this surprising sense of well-being, even after what his father had done – as if a gift from the region of death, the loss of his father, was making it easier for Iosif to let go of the past and allow this glow of hope and happiness to occupy his heart.

When Alik appeared from the dark Iosif beckoned him in to the firelight. He had bread, gherkins and cheese wrapped in newspaper which he spread on the ground. He also had a bottle of home-made *chacha*. For a while they sat in companionable silence, munching the food and passing the bottle back and forth. Iosif was thinking of ways to break the news to Alik about his leaving. Alik passed him a Winston and he drew on the American smoke, hoping it would help him find the right words.

This is our last night on the ridge, said Alik. I can't stay long, I have to get back to my men. I've been given a role in the government. It's an unofficial post for now, but what isn't these days? They want me to flush out the last of the opposition leaders. We need the arrests to look correct so I have to compile criminal records for the men I'm going to take by force. That won't be difficult! Listen my friend, I've been looking through old files in the government headquarters, Soviet material from years ago. Listen, there's no other way to say this. I found a bundle of high court documents relating to the trial.

Iosif shook his head. Don't speak of that now. But Alik reached in to an inner pocket of his new camouflage jacket. He said that the papers were the final court decision. He said that Iosif would want to read them for himself. But Iosif shook his head.

Alright then, said Alik and drew in a breath of smoke and held it and let it go in a long sigh. There's no easy way to say it. Poliko was executed the day after the trial ended. This document is the death warrant and this is the notification that the execution was carried out, dated, stamped, signed. He was shot in Tbilisi's high security prison. This other document is about Maia. She was taken to a regional women's prison. Look for yourself. I seem to remember it's near the village that her father's family come from.

But we're waiting for the appeal. He can't be dead, said Iosif.

It's terrible news I know. Your brother's gone. I'm sorry ... But that was the old life. Best put it behind you. We have to think about the future. What you and Tamoona are doing at the phage clinic, that's a good example of how we can get our country back on its feet. Iosif, you came to me and asked for help and I gave it, but now I need you to help me. There are still powerful forces at work with potential to defeat everything we've achieved. Georgian independence is very fragile. There are certain opposition leaders with deep connections to Russia. You know as well as anyone how the old KGB structure will never let go willingly. I need all my men with me, I can't risk being seen to be connected to what I need you to do. You must act as an individual with a grudge. I don't think you'll find it difficult. I want you to destroy Poliko's executioner. He was a top KGB operator back then, he had a reputation for enjoying watching his victims die slowly. I know this is hard my friend, but I want you to hate him. One of my men will come later with a package. I'm asking you to plant a car bomb. Say you'll do this for Georgia, Iosif. Say you'll exterminate the bastard who made your brother's last hours an agony.

He threw more branches on the fire. As he stared into the flames he saw the dungeons where the high security prisoners were interred. The rats were not afraid of anything. The walls crawled under timeless electric light. The air was thick with the stench of open toilet pipes and the sweat-ridden dust from straw mattresses. Germs bred in the sheddings of the men who had lain there. Their shoes and sandals mouldered in corners. The walls were gouged with names, the sign of the Orthodox cross, dates, stick figures, a hanging man, a love-heart, a Communist star, caricature portraits of fellow inmates. At the end of a low passage where cables drip slime onto the heads of those passing through, is a cell with a shallow trench dug in the floor. The wall above this trench is pitted and stained with blood. The trench is slick with scum like the last scrape of a fatty stew. Half submerged in this black jelly are shoes, broken combs, house keys. Iosif stared unblinking into the flames and there he saw Poliko with his feet in that filthy slime, his back to that scarred wall, his grey eyes wide open as he returned Iosif's gaze.

He sat on by the fire and in time the fighter came with the package wrapped in oily cloth. The fighter gave him the street and the car registration and explained how to press the bomb up under the chassis, that it had a magnet and would stay. He must depress the switch on the timer and then he should get away as quickly as possible but not running. Set it just before dawn, the target always leaves home at the same time, said the fighter, then he touched his chest over his heart with a clenched fist and bowed his head in acknowledgement.

I used to know your brother, he said. He was a hero to me and my friends. I live in the tower but one from yours.

Yes, now Iosif recognised this man who used to be a boy.

Tell me, he asked the fighter. Why do you think they did it?

Hijack the plane? Pity they failed. They had the nerve to actually do something most of us just dreamed of. That wasn't a failure. It was such an insect life back then. My cousin was in Afghanistan with Poliko. He came back with no legs. We live on the fifteenth floor and we can't get him down stairs. He still wakes up screaming in the night. He said it was all a lie, there was no construction programme. He was forbidden to talk about what was really happening. So he woke up screaming about it every night. But I don't think that's why your brother decided to go with a bang. He and Maia were twin comets. They didn't care if they were going to shatter. They couldn't put up with being boxed in any more. That's all. That's what I think.

He turned to go.

If you'd been given the name I have, what would you have done? called Iosif.

Me? Nothing! He's history. Adopt a nick-name if it bothers you. Take it easy. I'm off home now.

And the fighter walked away into the dark.

After a while he went into the hut and lay on the pallet watching the stars twinkle between the slats in the roof. He did not need to sleep. He had been sleeping all his life and now at last he was awake. He saw how far the starlight had travelled to reach him. Poliko was gone but Maia was so near. She was here, right next to him.

A pack of wild dogs fell in with him as he walked. Their leader cantered ahead showing its tail like a white flag. He was not afraid of the dogs. The old white leader of the pack knew the way to the street Iosif needed. The dog paused and cocked a hind leg against the car. The mongrels stood watching, stepping from paw to paw and panting as he lay down in the gutter, reached up into the grimy undercarriage, pressed the package to a metallic part and felt the magnet clamp on.

The pack followed him back to Vake Park where they slipped away into the shadow of trees. First light showing grey through the branches. Birds cheeping softly and meadow flowers stirring with the dawn breeze. The dull boom of an explosion. Ravens flying out from the ridge above the park. He could see that their beaks were wide open, but the prehistoric calls they made did not belong only to the birds.

He had downed the rest of the *chacha* that Alik had left. There was enough in the bottle to do the job. He deliberately did not shave or wash. He marched in to the waiting room and made a great deal of rapping on the sliding hatch to the clinic and calling loudly for Tamoona. He turned and grinned to the waiting patients and they watched him with impassive faces. She slid the hatch open and peered through. He glimpsed the starched white V of her lab coat and the skin between her breasts. When she saw it was him she gave him an intimate smile but murmured that she was busy right now.

Not too busy for your American professor though! he slurred.

Her smile froze. Her eyes flicked to the patients.

He swung round and addressed them belligerently. Better make the most of it while you can. Your doctor is going to sell your phage to America. She thinks they need it more than you do.

What are you doing? Tamoona gasped.

What am I doing? I'm telling your patients the truth!

Get in here and be quiet!

She slid the hatch shut and in a moment the clinic door flung open and there she stood, glaring at him, her lips compressed into a dark red line, her hands planted on her hips. He swayed over to her and made as if to show off this fine figure of a woman to the bemused patients.

Sweeping his hand he bowed to her and called her the Phage Queen and said, Her Majesty is running away to America. She's in love with one of them, a Professor of some kind, rich of course, fat, terrible breath as well. A good fuck though. She likes it from behind. Haha. She won't have to look as his ugly mug that way! Take your filthy sores somewhere else comrades. Her Highness isn't interested in you now that she's been paid in dollars. Haven't you my dear? Got an account with *mister have a nice day?*

Now the patients turned their eyes to Tamoona and they were not disappointed by the enraged expression, the bitten back words.

How dare you come to my clinic in this state!

I should never have come back to you in the first place.

I didn't ask you to.

You seemed happy enough to let me screw you.

If this is the way you're going to behave . . .

Like a real Georgian man. But you prefer 'Mericans now. You're a fool.

What took you so long?

The patients' heads were turning from side to side with expressions ranging from amusement to mild impatience. But now this drunkard was flourishing a Georgian passport. And it was obvious that he meant it harm.

No! shouted many of the patients, refugees all, some rising from their seats, others putting a hand to their mouth in horror.

He ripped off the cover and tore the inner pages in half and threw the pieces into the air. Tamoona slapped him across the face. He smiled and bowed and walked unsteadily from the clinic.

Outside he could go no further than the immediate wall where he leant and gasped and closed his eyes. He dragged himself upright and a few steps on but then he bent over and retched. His legs were like two logs but he forced them to take him away. Had he made her hate him enough? It had been too theatrical. He should have done it in private. He should have said more clever things to make her fully despise him for ever. It had not been as he had planned it. He fell to his knees and retched into the gutter again. With spittle hanging from his lips he groaned his own name again and again as if by doing so he would bring up the other owner of it with the next heave. His groans had the sound of hollow laughter made by an offstage ghost. This haunting was demanding his attention. Billowing in his basement. Throwing bits and pieces from his nooks and crannies. Spinning round and round and knocking his tidy shelves all over the place. He was a child with a big man stuck inside his little body. A boy with a bloated boss in his works. He was always going to be guided by double vision. Always suffer from this tummy bug. Always have a rotten voice. Oooff, he gasped as his life-long pal scooped the last slop of spew out of his stomach.

How would he manage to get far enough away so that he did not rush back and beg Tamoona's forgiveness? Doubt came flooding in. He was sick to the soles of his feet. He was a liar. A coward. But she would have brushed away his plan to rescue Maia. She would have applied her logic to his gut emotion. And she would have won. This he knew for certain. Because he still wanted to be in love with her. It was not that simple to give up the peace of mind he had found with her. He forced himself to believe that Tamoona would be better off without him in America. Ted or no Ted, she would find someone worthy of her. A man who was not disabled by out-of-date anxieties. A man who would take care of her. A man who did not have a bullying lodger to take care of.

PART III

her grandmother's walnut tree

He wasted no time in getting his suit from the wardrobe and checking the seams. He found no loose threads or gaps in the stitching. When he entered his parents' bedroom he went straight to the chest of drawers and pulled one open and rummaged beneath the clothes. These were Vera's things tumbling beneath his fingers. He did not look at them but searched with his fingers until they found something papery. Now he needed to look. Inside the envelope he saw the severed edges of a photograph and he quickly folded the envelope closed and slipped it back beneath the clothing. He flung open the next drawer. Father's work shirts lay neatly folded. He lifted them one by one, hurriedly feeling amongst them. The envelope lay at the bottom, near the back of the drawer. Written on the outside, *For Poliko and Maia*. He ripped it open and withdrew the roubles and put the envelope back under the shirts. Then he closed the drawer.

He did not count the money but it felt like plenty. Although Georgian coupons had been issued as temporary currency, he knew he would have no trouble using these old roubles. He stood breathing slowly over the turbulence in his guts. He wished something had been different in the apartment. Some change to mark his waking. But there were not even dead flies below the windows. He took his suit over one arm and slipped the money into the jacket pocket.

He had not planned what he was going to do when he met Victor on the stairs. They stood on the seventeenth landing smoking their cigarettes.

257

Poliko's dead, he said.

Victor looked away and then looked back at Iosif. I thought as much, he said.

I know where Maia is.

And you're going to find her.

That's right.

It's chaos out there.

Yes.

You'll need this, said Victor reaching into his jacket.

I don't know how to use it.

This is the ammo clip. It goes here. This is the safety catch. The trigger. A child could shoot this with no trouble.

Thanks.

No, thank you for taking it from me. I fought my friends. I made the wrong choice. It doesn't matter now. I just want to go to a lake and sit and fish and not think. Do you like fishing?

I've never tried.

Well, good luck. I'm sorry about Poliko.

Victor bowed his head in farewell and went on up. Iosif waited for a moment as he got used to holding the Beretta. He watched a rat emerge from the stinking rubbish chute. Someone had gouged *METALLICA* into the stairwell wall.

In his grey suit, with his money and the handgun hidden in the pockets, Iosif looked determined as he pushed through the crowded bus station. It always seemed to be springtime when he thought of Maia. The bus was jammed with peasants and their goods. The aisle stacked with bulging nylon bags and jute sacks. He found the last empty seat next to an elderly woman in black. She took him for a new-style entrepreneur and began a rambling story about a house and land for sale. The tattered curtains swung to and fro as the bus lurched onwards, swerving around the potholes and bumping over the ruts. The sun was on their side. The window glass too filthy to see through. He had the aisle seat but there was no leg room because of the bundles in the way.

His throat throbbed and his ears were singing. He leant his forehead on the seat in front and closed his eyes and within minutes began to feel nauseous. The old woman jabbed him with her elbow and offered him half a peeled orange. But he could not eat it. She pushed her sack to the floor between them where it wriggled and clucked. He leant his forehead on the seat again and closed his eyes.

He had time to think about what he had done to Tamoona. He hated himself for hurting her. But at the back of his guilty mind, and somehow connected to this throbbing in his head, he was being hurled around on a terrifying storm of joy. He began to formulate the plan. He would take on the guise of a business man who was head of an NGO. (Tamoona had used that term and he knew it meant something foreign and moneyed). Never mind the details though, his NGO was on the lookout for talented singers to re-establish Georgian culture, especially for those victims who had been locked up under the old repressive regime. In return for the release of such a singer he would donate a large sum to the prison for educational purposes – meaning to the chief warden for personal use.

Iosif did not really think his story held water. But it was all he could come up with in the hot queasy rattle of that journey. And if that plan failed he would use the handgun to force his way past the guards. There was no question in his mind that he would not come away from Surami prison with Maia.

The bus came to a halt.

Where are we? he asked.

This is the place they call Surami's Shadow, replied the old woman.

He leant over her and peered from the window. Dimly through the dirt he saw a black hilltop where a group of twisted pillars stood against the sky.

Surami Fortress, the old woman said.

He scrambled over the baggage.

We're not at the village yet! cried the old woman.

But Iosif had already jumped from the bus and was climbing up a sheep track on the side of the hill.

The pillars were the limbless hollow trunks of long dead oaks. Fallen blocks of stone lay everywhere. Fragments of broken wall jutted from the long grass. He sat and rested his back against the warmth of a smooth grey slab. Within minutes he had fallen asleep. Sunset came quickly. Shadows rolled out over vermillion hillocks and pastel orchards. In the lowering light the ruined outlines of industrial structures merged with the lengthening shadows. Black snakes of stilted troughs and high-legged conveyor belts slid over a blacker geography of forests and gulleys. There was no moon that night. Iosif slept on. His eyes flickered as if dreaming but he did not know his dreams. He slept, drugged with joy. Oil lamps burned in the village below the hill. He did not move a muscle all night.

When he finally woke he was stiff and cold. He relieved himself against one of the hollow trees. He smoked a cigarette and walked about, shaking life back into his arms and legs. He wanted to sing but his throat was too sore. He watched the early trucks wheeling along the road below. Turkish number plates. On the far side of the hilltop he looked down to the smoky village. Cattle plodding along the lanes between terra-cotta rooftops. Her grandmother's house somewhere amongst them. He circumnavigated the hill-top once more, waiting for the sunlight. He did not want to appear like a crazy from the night. He ran his fingers through his hair and brushed grass seeds from his suit.

The road he had arrived on went past the village and con-tinued towards a walled complex of barracks. There the road branched sharply away and on to other villages. A single con-crete track led to the compound gates. As befits a prison the high walls were crowned with tangled barbed wire and there were watch towers. But he could not see any guards. He walked slowly closer, clutching the Beretta in his pocket. Swallows came darting down to the rooftops of the barracks beyond the wall.

He pushed on a small door set into the massive steel gate. It swung open and he stepped through onto a deep litter of papers, slithering beneath his feet and strewn over every bit of ground. The barracks were arranged in rows with walkways between but the walkways were also strewn with these aban-doned documents. Faded scraps of clothing fluttered from the barrack window bars. The early morning sun blazed in a clear blue sky. Everything was silent. Something glinted from amongst the documents around his feet. He picked up a powder compact, rubbed the gold coloured case to a shine on his jacket front, flicked it open and saw himself in the little round mirror. The powder puff was intact and the unused disc of powder gave out a delicately fresh perfume.

Nobody here, he croaked.

The Surami village spring had long ago been piped to a tap set on a paved terrace. There were always one or two women collecting this favoured water and lingering to gossip. But at this early hour the tap was busy and the women impatient to get back to their kitchens. When Iosif came they were not in the mood to let him through. Thirst made him careless though, and he pushed a way to the tap and knelt to put his mouth under the flow.

The water was icy. It gushed down his throat half choking him. He put his head under it and let it wash over him. It was so cold that his ears lost all feeling and his skull became numb. He was aware of the women clustering around him with their buckets swinging. Their black skirts brushing him and their odour of salted fish. He attempted to stand up but now a woman had got in his way. He slipped on the wet paving and accidentally grasped her skirt. She gave an exclamation and he turned his head to look up and apologise.

Their eyes met for the shortest moment and then she twisted away and was gone. Iosif staggered to his feet. The village women jostled him, blocking his way and glowering at him. All were black clad. Black scarved. Black lines grooving their faces. He saw her running down a lane from the spring. Black headscarf. Dark cardigan and long skirt flapping. Rubber sandals and grey socks.

He tugged the pistol from his pocket and the women stepped back and let him through. They were not shocked. They had seen plenty of unhinged men waving guns recently. He ran after her down a leafy lane where steel-panelled gardens were overhung with lilac and fruit trees. His heart was thudding in his brain. Maia! Maia!

When he came to the garden where she had turned in he

suddenly doubted himself. The house was shabby and low. The yard was unkempt and heaped with rusted scrap. He gasped for breath. His head was spinning but he forced himself to stand upright and quiet.

If he had made a mistake he would have to back out of the situation. There might be a husband or brother in the house. He stood on the threshold at the open gate. When something came hurtling toward him he could not tell what it was at first. A low pale bulk. A snorting force to it. An enormous sow! Charging straight at him with anger in her tiny eyes. Iosif had no time to turn and flee. He raised his hand and squeezed the trigger. The sow veered away and ran round and round in circles making an awful human sounding scream.

The air was strangely dark and yet things were shimmering brightly. The house was draped in a cloak of iridescent silken silver and the pomegranate bushes around it shed crystallised droplets of blood red as they swayed in the breeze. He saw two figures emerge from the house, one covering his face with his hands – and Iosif understood that some almighty tragedy had overtaken that stumbling, hiding man. The other ran towards the crying pig. To his fevered eyes it seemed that she would never reach the wounded pig, and then when she knelt and held it still with her arms wrapped around its neck, he thought he had never seen such tender love as that woman gave to the animal. He wanted this to last forever. This sight of a woman he had once known giving her love to an innocent creature. The man wobbled away and out of sight. The woman led the sow to a sty and they both went in. Iosif stood where he was. He thought he would never move again. He had arrived at the place where everything ceased. But then he was overtaken by fear. The woman was not really here. None of this was real.

He felt terribly sick. His legs were weak. He stumbled to the pigsty. A giggle broke from his dry lips as someone tickled at his insides. Unbearable. He opened the pigsty door, could not stop giggling as he called out a hello.

Ah, there you are, he continued mirthfully. Been looking all over . . . Pig alright? My mistake . . . Oh yes, I brought a present. Just a little joke . . . D'you like it?

He dropped to his knees and held out the powder compact. Black spots circled at the edges of his vision. Her hair is cropped to nothing. She looks so much older. I have always loved her. The pistol fell from his fingers. He toppled sideways.

In his battle with the thing that had made its lair inside him, Iosif almost perished. He came back to the world through narrow slits of light where he crawled forwards, always terrified that the thing would catch him before he could get to the place where he crouched over a long drop into an earth that smelled sweetly of human dung, and was home to hand-sized beetles who gathered the dung into perfect spheres and rolled it away. He crouched in this safe place out of sight. The stuff he expelled was sulphurous. His body hurt all over, inside and out. His skin was unbearably sensitive and he felt bruised under his armpits. Breathing was an effort almost not worth making. Then he would find himself crouched over the long drop into the earth. His stinking stools fouling the sweet dank air. He wanted to die for the shame which caused his face to flush and perspire. His poisonous gasses were leaking from this safe place and were spreading to the house and its inmates. Someone chuckled inside him. He found himself squatting over the deep dark hole. He had nothing left to give the beetles. But his intestines went into spasm and his muscles contracted with the effort of expulsion. He was a little boy. A helpless baby. He peered down between his thighs. Naked. The woman in the luminous house. He squeezed his eyes shut. He crawled along the slit of light to the safe place where the earth opened up and huge black beetles slowly rolled their perfect spheres away. He understood that this was the final stand. Squat, he giggled. A serious person, whom he seemed to know very well but could not quite put a name to, was parading up and down with his chest puffed out. Parading up and down the years with his big fat moustache bristling. His legs could not hold him in the squat and so he sat himself over the drop, foolishly, his legs stuck out in front of him, his back bent over, his fingers digging into the earth on either side. The woman with the beautiful old face. His hellish emissions. If I'm a baby, he reasoned, I can't be blamed. He longed to be a baby. To be cradled. To be tiny and protected. He had been in this darkened place all his life. The slit of light was gone. The woman with cropped hair was gone. It was just him and the moustachioed person. He reached towards the plank walls and traced his name with his muddy finger. He stared at the scrawl. Ants climbed across it. A stream of tiny beings. He felt very peculiar. Something happening to his eyes. Wetness coming out. I'm bleeding, he panicked. But he had no strength to call out for help. He raised a hand to his face and stared at his fingers. They were just wet. No blood. He got himself up from the ground. He was weightless. The slit of light guided him back to where the woman would be waiting.

A piece of green cloth sucked in and out against a bright square of light. A fly buzzed against the cloth and then flew away and then returned. He lay watching the cloth and the fly.

He heard chickens clucking, sparrows, a distant cow bell. He lay at peace, watching the green cloth and hearing the pleasant sounds. And then someone interrupted this calm by shouting something he could not quite catch. He was super-sensitive to everything around him, so he absorbed and understood the other world of false tears, petty demands, the implied wrath in that petulant female voice.

He tried to sit up but found that he was very weak. He made an effort to take in his surroundings apart from that green illuminated cloth. Cinder block walls. A sloping corrugated tin roof. An earthen floor. He lay on a low pallet spread with a straw mattress. He was covered with an ordinary black and white chequered blanket. He had no idea where he was. The voice called out again with the same bossy petulant tone. Someone replied, low, subdued.

Later he woke and looked once more at the lime green square of cloth. A shadow moved across it. The cloth lifted away. A face peered in and then disappeared. He remembered everything in an instant. He was mortally afraid that she had looked in at him and gone away and would never return again. But the door opened and Maia came in carrying a plate of thinly sliced apple.

She put her hand on his forehead. You've been very ill but you're getting better now, she said. She set the plate of apple on the blanket and turned to go. But he held on to her wrist.

Sorry, he said.

She stood staring at his fingers around her wrist.

For what? she asked in a level tone.

I hurt the pig.

She's alright.

I didn't mean to . . .

The same petulant voice called out. Maia looked at the wall where the voice was coming from, and he understood that he was in a storeroom extension and the house was on the other side of that wall. She pulled away from his fingers.

Is that Eliso? he asked, already knowing the answer.

But Maia had hurried out.

He nibbled a slice of apple and drank from the clay jug of water on the floor. He got out of the bed and found that he was wearing faded pyjamas. He could not see his clothes anywhere. He was not strong enough to do more than stand at the open square and lift the green cloth away. Despite feeling weak and confused at finding Maia in this way, he felt a deep content. Lilac blooms hung low over the metal panelled fence. Their heady scent wafted towards him on the warm air. He took in the untidy yard, the rusty buckets, the overgrown vegetable plot where bean stalks grew confused with columbine. His gaze lingered on the earth closet. He did not remember the details of the final stand. Squat, he murmured without knowing why. He smiled a smile which was unique to him alone.

A night passed. He woke to find she had left a plate of bread, hard boiled eggs and cheese and he wolfed it down and drank a lot of water. On the opposite wall a shelf held several garden implements so he got up and began examining their condition. Some needed a nut and bolt tightening, others a wooden handle jamming back in place. The scythe was blunt and he found the whetstone and began running it rhythmically up and down the blade. He was absorbed in this when Maia came in with his clothes.

I've washed the shirt and socks and your underwear, she said.

He put away the scythe and whetstone.

You needn't have done that, he said, taking his clothes.

You'd better hurry, the bus leaves in fifteen minutes, she said.

He stood there clutching his clothes, gazing at her. She wore a red and black printed headscarf knotted at the nape of her neck. The same dowdy cardigan and skirt. Those dreary rubber sandals and grey socks.

Maia, he began.

There's nothing to say. Go back to Tbilisi. You shouldn't have come here. I'm going out and I don't want to find you here when I get back.

She looked at him with expressionless eyes. Her face immobile, hollow-cheeked, severe. Her chin raised to dare him to defy her. Her nostrils flared slightly with the will of her words.

When she was gone he dressed. It was too warm to wear the suit jacket but he found the roubles in its pocket. The Beretta and powder compact were missing. Well, he did not need them any more. He drank some water and went back to sharpening the scythe.

She must have known he had not gone. She must have heard him tinkering with the tools in the cinder block extension. He had arranged the green cloth so he could see the gateway and had seen her coming back. She had not looked over to the extension. Eliso was calling out for her and she went into the house and he heard the door shutting.

When he went to use the earth closet – a thing he had put off doing until he really had to and then found that it was alright, everything was ordinary, the huge black beetles were still rolling their spheres, the air was dank and sweet, the mud scrawl he had made had dried and dusted away, the walls were just plain wood planks – he got a good look at the house through the heart-shaped ventilation hole cut into the door. A typical single-storey wooden village house with a pan-tiled roof. The remains of a decorative veranda along the front. Many of the roof tiles were broken and slipping, the walls were bowed, the windows twisting in the rotted frames. Heavy lace curtains hung at the windows on either side of the door. The wide cracks in the glass were stuffed with yellowed newsprint. The old house just needs mending, Iosif thought.

He peered through the ventilation hole for a while longer. He had never known such solitude as then in that earth closet with the outer world framed by the roughly shaped heart. Is this how it is to stand alone? This insurmountable air between me and others who breathe it? This chasm of mind where only my own voice echoes in my own silence? My flesh and bones bearing only the weight of my unique solitary form? He felt a moment of fear. The world beyond the sweetly carved heart was peopled with Maia and her mother and father. He was not a world. He was not peopled. Not a lodging house. Not a name. He was just a man standing alone in dank privacy. It did not occur to him to catch that bus. He was going to stay with Maia.

Later that day he walked to the village shop and bought tinned meat and fish, cheese, bread, yoghurt, spring onions and beetroots and carrots. He bought tea and a jar of local wine. Sugar and salt. He left these on the rotting veranda by the door. He did not knock or call out for her. He spent the rest of that day sitting on the pallet smoking the cigarettes he had bought. He was not fully recovered and he slept early after his exertions.

When he woke sometime in the night he heard Eliso sobbing loudly and breaking off with cries of *My heart!* He felt that blade of fear again. The past was not escapable. His forty years of life was a dead weight which he must always carry. He dare not believe in this new order, this weightless bubble of his skin enclosing nothing but the dust of what seemed now a dream – and if his life up until now had been a dream, if his long-term lodger had suffocated on his own bile and had been evacuated, gone, poof, forever, leaving Iosif with only the trace of a bad taste on his tongue, something that would wash away with a few sips of water as one sips after waking from a dawn nightmare with the deathly bogey stalking the outskirts of memory, then had the dream belonged to his sleeping partner, his celibate bed-mate, his quilt-stealing snorer or had it been Iosif's, and what was he to do next, awake and perpetually dreamless now, a man who had been infested with a smiling portrait of tyrannical happiness? He did not think he could ever be happy. He could not put his trust in happy-habits. His dream of rescuing Maia was a fantasy. She had not needed to be rescued. And worse, she hated him. Of course she did. He represented everything that she and Poliko had hated.

But when he woke the next day he was calm again. If happiness was never going to suit him he would find other balms. He would study this new language of his lone voice, his lone ear. Maybe he would even learn to hold a note in pitch. He washed at the outside tap beneath the rain tank. A piece of mirror leant on the shelf above the tap and next to it, country style, a mug and shaving brush, a razor, a slab of yellow soap. He shaved and used the comb. Dato came with a wandering step to the tap and Iosif stood aside.

Good morning. It's me, Iosif. How are you Mr Dolidze?
But Dato's mouth slipped to one side and his eyes were blank.

Iosif had cleared the vegetable bed of weeds and hoed the earth between the beetroot leaves and bean stalks. He had raked a patch ready to sow the seeds he had found in the extension. He found a plate of food on the pallet at the end of each day, but he never caught sight of Maia taking it there. He knew that Eliso was keeping watch on him. He had glimpsed her peering round the net curtain. He had raised a hand in greeting but the pale face did not move.

He was afraid of her, this woman who had become the sobbing whinging voice of the night. By day he heard her ranting at Maia. He heard crockery smashing. He heard a sound like a stick thwacking a table top. When this happened it was all he could do to prevent himself rushing into the house. But then what? He had no right to interfere. Maia did not want him here. She acted as though he did not exist and was only feeding him because of the law of hospitality.

Time blurred in the routine of gardening, plucking the burgeoning fruit from the trees, absorbing the sunlight and flickering shade, the evening wood smoke.

One day he collected a great heap of brush wood from round the back of the house. He broke it into bundles and left it at the door for kindling. That same day he sharpened the axe blade and split logs into stove-sized lengths.

He often forgot about the city. The fire-blackened ruins around the old Communist Party headquarters. The dead gas taps and power switches. The lack of running water. It was easier in the country. If only Maia ... But his thoughts were interrupted by a commotion in the house.

His bundle of kindling came flying from the opened door and with it Eliso's wailing.

He's going to steal you from me. I'll die alone. You don't care about me anymore.

Dato, stricken by a brain haemorrhage, began his own keening and moaning. Iosif clenched his fists, stepped towards the house and then retreated. She would not thank him for making matters worse with her mother.

One part of Maia's history Iosif felt a special attachment to, and even allowed himself to feel part of. There were many walnut trees in other gardens along the lane but her grandmother's tree was no more, not a sign of it. This made him feel even closer to that part of her life, because he would not forget the story she had told him, he would keep it safe in his store of facts. One hot afternoon when he was pulling the sheets of scrap metal aside, intending to stack them in an orderly way, he discovered the tree stump beneath a rusted tin bath. Etiolated shoots sprouted around the base of the stump and pale leaf buds half unfolded, not doing well in the twilight they had been consigned to. He brushed these shoots with his fingertips, whispering to them, a foolish smile on his lips. Grandmother's walnut tree, he whispered. After all you've seen and heard you still want to live. He crouched there for a moment more, wondering at his life thus far, at the rusty steel lid which had clattered over his soul to shelter the false pride of a nasty-minded strutter. He pictured in his mind the little cartoon of the cockerel with the tyranical boss's head. Then he sprang up and rushed to get his spade and dug at the earth around the stump. It was rock hard but he persisted and each strike gave him a jolt of joy and he became pink in the face as he worked on in the heat.

He went to fill a bucket at the outside tap but the tap would not turn. It needed him to cut a fresh washer from some leather he had found. He did this every so often and he knew it would take time and patience which he could not manage right now because all he could think of was that her walnut tree must have a drink. He had seen Maia going out a while ago. She had crossed the yard looking straight ahead as she always did.

She had not been wearing her headscarf these last hot weeks. Her hair was now a dark fuzzy cap on her finely boned skull. He wondered where she went. Did she have female friends in the village? A lover? He pushed this thought aside and, taking the bucket, he strode to the house.

As he had hoped Dato was sleeping on a bed by the stove. He stood quietly as his eyes adjusted to the gloom. He was fairly certain that Eliso would also be taking a siesta somewhere, and all was quiet and still. He closed the door softly and stepped carefully to a door that must lead to the back scullery. Everything spoke of poverty. But it was clean and orderly. The bare wooden table was scrubbed white. The floor was washed grey. The tin stove stood by a neat pile of faggots which Maia chopped herself. He let himself in to the scullery where it was dark with only a dingy grey light at the end over the sink where a small hole had been cut in the asbestos roof and covered with plastic sheeting. He barely noticed the couch bed and the heap of quilts, the few clothes on hooks, the side table and piece of scratched mirror and ivory handled hairbrush. These he hurried past, set his bucket in the sink and watched the screw of rusty water coming from the rain tank.

He was not thinking of anything except pouring this water around the walnut tree stump. This libation was more than the practical need of the tree. The old walnut tree had a massive root system and did not really need his help to survive. Now that it had the sunlight the tree would flourish all by itself. Iosif was picturing Maia as a child, and this water was to restore her back to that innocence. Or so he might have said if he had had time to interpret the music of joy in the depths of his mind.

The bucket was almost full when a low laughing made him spin around in alarm and there in the gloom was Eliso resting on the couch amongst the quilts. In the same instant he saw a tapestry on the wall above her and the silvery black threads of mountains and stony plain and the figure of a man like a shadow unravelling. Eliso smoothed the quilts and touched her hair and gave that conspiratorial laugh. She was altered, but not so much in the twilight at least, thicker in the flesh yes, but her black hair fell in waves over her shoulders and her eyes and the brows were theatrically dark. He stood there gaping. Then he stuttered, Sorry to intrude. I was just getting water. I'll be going now.

As he passed close by her couch Eliso made a grab for his arm, the water swilled onto her and Iosif was caught with her holding onto him and saying, Look what you've done. He jerked away, losing his balance as he tried to prevent more water spilling, righting himself, half kneeling on the edge of the couch bed because she still had not let go of her grip on his arm. I'm soaking wet, she said. He dabbed with an automatic gesture at the damp quilt. In that moment she tried to draw him closer. He recoiled, pulling free from her clutching hand and she lashed out at him, her fingernails catching his cheek. He still had the bucket as he fled, blindly, running on tip-toes past the sleeping Dato.

He went to the cinder block extension and pulled the door shut. For a long time he stood with his head bowed, his shoulders shaking. The tears could not stop by themselves and he did not know how to stop them. He heard the strange sound of his sobs and was disgusted and dismayed and he thought that it was time now for him to leave this place where he was not wanted and did not belong and return to his real life in the city. But he did not move until the sun left the square of green cloth.

In these southerly climes darkness falls quickly and by the time Iosif had almost finished mending the garden tap he was working by starlight. He had not noticed Maia coming from the house with his plate of food. She had returned while he was shut away with the sound of his tears and that sound finally fading into a sort of song in his quiet heart, a little ditty, a nursery round where fear and laughter took their part in equal share and the more the round was sung the more the two were indistinguishable. She stood in the blue-black of the ancient light, a slender figure with finely chiselled features and a dark cap of curling hair. She watched Iosif working.

She had been on the fortress mound in the sun and was tired to her bones. She glanced around the dim garden, saw the cleared away scrap, the freshly bare earth, the tree stump. She went softly to the extension and set the plate on the ground outside the door. She spread a clean cloth over it. She paused and her hand went to the door handle, hovered, fell away. She stole back to the house.

Maia shared the couch bed with her mother. It meant that when Eliso woke, Maia could slip from the quilts to get what she needed without disturbing Dato. By day she had household tasks to see to. By night she must massage her mother, bring her tea, brush her hair.

Maia had not slept a full night for what seemed to her a lifetime. In prison sleep came fitfully and was constantly broken by the other inmates' snores or nightmares. She had become used to operating on little sleep. It meant that her thoughts flew bat-like in the topmost quarters of her skull.

The women had fled from their prison like winged mice on that day when the makeshift brigade of fighters had killed the guards and unlocked the doors, laughing gallantly, asking for sex, but not raping. They had scurried out, none talking, none smiling. A horde of small female bat things who wanted to hide their half-blind eyes from the world. They had become used to the upside-down life inside. They had recited their contrite re-integration speeches in meek squeaks over the prison tannoys.

Set free, they scattered into the landscape. Maia had been lucky that her grandmother's village was nearby. She hid in the empty house for days. Only coming out to dig up vegetables that had self-seeded over the years. When the neighbours, Nino and Valeria, eventually discovered her they were kindly, seeing at once the look of loss in her eyes. Nino had been Dato's childhood playmate. She had always been fond of him and she remembered how his pretty little daughter Maia used to come and stay with her grandmother in the summer, until the grandmother had passed away.

They told Maia that there was no Soviet Union any more. Nino fed her with stew and gave her hot bath water and a clean set of clothes. Without Maia knowing she telephoned Dato. But Dato had had a stroke, or as Eliso said when she answered the call, had become a mental case. In no time Maia's parents arrived and Eliso decided to stay on in the village house where life was easier than in the anarchic city. And where she had Maia to herself.

This night with the earth of the fortress mound still between her toes, Maia lay awake waiting for Eliso to ask for her tea. She could not stop seeing Iosif as he had looked in the starlight. He had aged but was still handsome with that taut bowstring way he had of holding himself. He always seemed to be listening to something she could not hear. He was the opposite to Poliko who had taken everything as a series of ludicrous party games. We both did, she thought. Except when we were singing the old songs. That was the only time when anything felt worthwhile. But Maia did not go any further along the paths of memories. She knew from experience that memories do not change anything.

Prison may have tall walls and barbed wire but prison gossip passes from ear to ear, mouth to mouth in an instant. Through this unofficial network Maia had heard about Poliko's execution the day after being sentenced – but not of how it had been carried out. In some ways, although she could not stand it, it was better that he was no more from the very beginning. At least he had died instantly. He would not have survived prison. He would have taken heroin. He would have caught hepatitis, typhoid, tuberculosis. He would have slowly perished to death. So she had tried to comfort herself in those dark months after the trial and in the years of her confinement.

She shifted away from Eliso, hoping to rise and catch a moment to herself while she was still asleep.

Where are you going? asked her mother.

Would you like tea?

Not yet. We have to make plans.

Eliso sat up and pulled the quilts around herself.

Bring a candle, she said. I'm afraid of the dark now.

There's nothing to be afraid of, I'm here.

But you weren't here this afternoon. I don't know how to tell you . . .

What's the matter? Shall I massage your back?

No! I can't bear to be touched. After what he did to me . . . Why did you let him stay here? He came when you were out. I tried to fight him off. I managed to scratch his face. But he just laughed and did what he wanted. We must get the police first thing. He's got to be arrested. You'll go for them won't you?

Eliso buried her face in her hands.

What happened exactly? asked Maia.

Her mother peeped at her through her fingers and shuddered. Maia set the candle on the side-table, then took it up and walked away.

She tapped at his door. He had been sleeping but her knock woke him instantly and he rose and opened the door still half asleep. The white cotton of her night dress billowed softly in the night air. He reached out to her. But in the same moment she held the candle up to his face. So it's true, she whispered. Then she span around and ran back to the house leaving him with the impression that the white gown had been an apparition.

Maia sat all night on the chair by the stove. Eliso did not make another sound. Dato snored softly. The room darkened as clouds gathered and rain fell on the roof and clattered down the zinc drain pipe into the water butt.

The cattle were coming from the opened gates of their home gardens, each following the hoof prints of the beast in front, churning the muddy lane as they processed from the village to the pasture. The little bells around their necks tinkled, muted in the soaking air, and Iosif thought of the fabled cities that were drowned in the depths of the Black Sea. There were sunken towers with flattened bells, and stones were rolling and ringing against them beneath the lifeless waters. He bowed his head, his suit wet through already, rain dripping from his black hair over his solemn face. He was going to collect drinking water for her. He was out early before her mother woke and found that he had helped her.

At the spring he dutifully emptied out the rain that had collected in the bucket and filled it from the tap. He thought about finding her here. The shock of seeing her. He still did not know how long she had been free. But last night, he had dared to believe she wanted him. He had been wrong. He was here to watch over her and not to want her. With the bucket full, he began to slip and slither home in his sodden city shoes. His money would not last forever. He was worried that she had come to depend on his bringing provisions from the village shop. He would have to return to Tbilisi and find a way to get more cash for her. Maybe try to sell some things from the apartment. Lost in thought he did not see her as she came towards him holding an old khaki army cape.

The rain had fallen relentlessly, washing through her mind as she sat awake all night, feeding logs into the smoky stove. She thought it quite possible that Iosif was capable of violent action. Everything she had known had this harsh potential, this agenda of violence. The history that had followed her from the tower blocks to this quiet village had been fuelled with cruelty and oppression. Nations had been forced to leave their birth lands. Husbands had been dragged from their beds. Wives had never come home from the market. Children had betrayed their parents. Friends had been forced to denounce each other. But as the night wore on and the rain acted like a balm on her tortured thoughts, she chose to disbelieve her mother's accusation of rape. No, Iosif was not capable of such debasement. She relived that fraction of a second when she had stood at his open door. Only the bending candle flame between them. His hands reaching for her.

When she heard the soft clank of a bucket on the veranda she peeped from the window and watched him leaving the yard. She stood without moving for several minutes and then she went to the hook and took down a cape, slung it over her shoulders and reached for the other.

She had pulled the heavy hood over her head and he did not recognise her until they came together in the lane. She pushed the spare cape at him.

Put it on, you're soaking wet, she said.

He set the bucket down and pulled the cape over his shoulders.

Put the hood up, she said.

Shrouded in these oilskin cloaks they walked along the lane. The hood blinkered his vision. Only dripping foliage. Sucking mud. He could not see her trudging next to him until the lane narrowed and she pressed ahead and they walked in single file with the rain-laden branches sweeping them on either side. The way became steep and difficult. He watched her feet in the rubber sandals as she pushed on up the track. He felt an intense loathing for these useless things, the single cracked band, the way her socks slipped down to her heels. He hardly noticed where they were going. His heart was pounding with the climb. The rain came from all directions. The army cape was heavy and his clothes wet and cold on his clammy skin. But he did not think of turning back or trying to stop Maia.

As the track levelled off a mist descended around them and they were inside the rain cloud. Underfoot was slippery grass and hidden rocks and he stumbled more than once. In one moment he lost sight of her so he hurried on, certain she would appear in the next step. But he could see nothing beyond arms' reach now. The rain came sideways into his face and whichever way he turned the wind whipped around and blinded him.

Maia! he called. Where are you!

Nothing but the patter of rain on wet ground.

Maia! he called again but his voice was swallowed in the mist.

He reached out in front of him, walked on a few steps. His fingertips came to some smooth solid surface and he could go no further. Through the wisping cloud he saw a tall jet black wall. He turned around, his heart beating fearfully as the shining jet wall encircled him. From afar he heard a singing voice, a child's voice, and he knew it was her and that she had been singing the legend for him when she was a little girl visiting her grandmother for the summer.

Maia circled the fortress ruins and criss-crossed the top of the mound. Even with this dense cloud she would not get lost, she knew the shape of every stone by heart. She called out his name several times but heard no reply. She slithered back down the muddy track, expecting to see him looming in the mist ahead of her. She wanted to reach him, overtake him, warn him about Eliso's plan to call the police. She had been a fool to lead him to the fortress. What had she been hoping for? A return to that innocent hour when they had first sat together looking out over the wheat? His ardent attention while she sang of the mother who had buried her son alive? His arms around her in the chill of the rain cloud? She was an ugly old stick who had been locked up for years. She did not deserve even a glance from any man. She slipped down the track to the village and her garden gate. She went straight to the cinder block extension but he was not there.

The cockerels were just beginning to crow. Neither Dato nor Eliso were awake yet. She went into the scullery and opened the side-table drawer, quietly so as not to disturb her mother. At the back were the pistol and the powder compact where she had hidden them. She took the compact first. It fell open and she caught a waft of the fresh powdery perfume. She snapped it back shut. Now she took the Beretta. Her breath caught at the touch of the gun-metal.

Poliko had shown her how to use a firearm. They had laughed over its ever-so-stern simplicity. But we won't have to really use them, it's just to make us look serious, so they'll believe us, said Poliko. Yes, she had replied. And as soon as we've crossed the border we'll throw them down the toilet. So she stood now, with this weapon in her hand, their laughter at the joke of their pistols falling through space to land on some peasant's plot – and the things that had really happened – the never ending gunshots, the screams of terror, the smell of blood in the dark – a film looped forever on the screen of every passing moment, in every breath, in all her dreams and in each heartbeat of her waking life.

She would return these things to Iosif. He would be able to

sell them. She was going to make him go back to Tbilisi today. He must never come to find her again. At the back of her mind she heard her father's dragging steps as he rose and tended the stove. She understood that the few little things which Dato could manage gave him pleasure, and she was in the habit of tidying up after him, clearing away the dry kindling, closing the stove door. She stood lost in her thoughts, unwilling just yet to summon up the cruel words that must send Iosif away.

Smoke came drifting into the scullery. She hurried to see to the stove. She found a heap of twigs flaring on the floor. Flames came flickering along the surface of the splintery boards. Dato moaned and held his hands over his face. The smoke was thickening as a flame ran along a board and caught the edge of a blanket on the bed and the stench of scorching wool filled the room. She took her father by the arm and steered him to the door but he pushed her away and stumbled back into the smoke. Eliso! she called as she ran towards the scullery. The tinder dry floor was aflame. The net curtains burning at the windows.

He heard the fire before he saw it. Wood that was dry as bone beneath the surface wetness of rain burned with that manic crackle of a fire set free. When he saw the smoke rising from her garden he ran as he had never run before. He went straight into the house but was beaten back by the heat. He held his soaking cape over his face and ran back in. Someone shambling in the smoke. He grabbed Dato, hauled him out and entered the burning house once more. He could hardly breathe and could not call for her. The flames were around the edges of the room, creeping up the walls and flaring in the herbs she had hung there. He found her in the smoke filled tunnel of the scullery. He dragged and carried her out to the yard. She was choking and covered in soot. He held her upright and patted her on the back and she clung to him as she gradually got her breath back. In the briefest of moments he noticed that the rain had stopped. The lilac blooms were covered with sparkling droplets. The sun was breaking through the cloud. He told Maia to stay with Dato and he went towards the blazing door-way. But he could not enter that inferno. He ran round to the back of the house. It was aflame. Eliso! he called.

The neighbours had come running with buckets of water. They hurled the water into the fire and the flames roared. A handful of minutes had passed. Minutes in which he took Maia and Dato by their hands and led them away from the sight of the blackened timber frames teetering in the flames. He took them to the neighbours' house.

Nino, who had been so kind to Maia when she first arrived, brought a wet cloth and wiped Maia's face. She led Dato to a bench by the stove and sat him next to an elderly man who patted his arm and murmured, That's right son, you sit by me.

They drank water and sipped brandy and smoked cigarettes. Valeria returned with the news that the fire had almost died down. Iosif looked at him and he shook his head. Nothing to be done. The poor woman has perished in the smoke. Nino took Maia to wash and change her clothes. She understood that her mother had died but she felt nothing. She fumbled in the pocket of her dress and handed the compact and the pistol to Nino. Nino nodded and left her to bathe. She gave Iosif a bowl of water at the kitchen table and he sluiced his face and arms. She made no comment on the things Maia had given her, simply laid them on the table by the bowl of water. Valeria took Iosif to a back room and sorted out an old-fashioned collarless shirt of stiff white linen and a pair of black trousers threaded with a dark blue stripe. Iosif bundled up his filthy suit. Would you throw it away for me? he asked. Nino will use it for rags, Valeria replied. Iosif put on the new clothes. That's better, said Valeria.

He sat back at the kitchen table and smoked another cigarette. Nino warmed some broth and set a plate in front of him. She sat opposite him and gave him a shrewd look.

Dato can stay with us, she said.

He glanced over his shoulder looking for Maia.

She's washing, said Nino.

I couldn't save Eliso, he said.

Maia's going to need a lot of love, said Nino pressing her hands flat on the table. Best if you stay indoors with her today, she's seen enough without seeing her mother's last resting place in the ashes. Sleep the night with us. There's a bus to the city first thing in the morning.

What about the pig and the chickens? asked Valeria.

Take them, said Maia as she came in to the kitchen.

They turned to look at her. Her hands fluttered nervily over the skirt of a faded green dress with cream polka dots.

Come and sit here with me, said Nino. You did all you could. It wasn't your fault. There there, you have a good cry and let it out.

Maia did not cry. She sat smoothing down the full skirt. Iosif watched her but everything he saw was encircled with flames and smoke. It was the same for Maia. Flames were licking at her green dress and the cream polka dots were shrivelling in the heat. Only Dato seemed to have recovered the few wits he had. He had been given a wash. He was allowing the old man to spoon soup into his mouth.

Your father can stay with us, said Nino. He'll be safe here.
Come back to visit when you can.

Maia looked at Iosif. He nodded.

A man came to the door to say that the fire was out. There
was nothing left. Nothing but red hot cinders.

So that's that, said Nino glancing at her husband.

Aye, Valeria replied. That's the end of it.

The last of his money bought them tickets on the bus. The
sky had cleared and it was hot and humid. The bus was filled
to capacity with extra passengers sitting on their sacks in the
aisle. Maia and Iosif had hardly spoken all the rest of the day
of the fire until they had each been led to their separate
makeshift beds and had lain staring into a smoke filled darkness. Now they sat in mute continuation. Iosif took a handful
of walnuts from the bag of food Nino had given them. He
broke the shells in his hands and passed Maia the wrinkled
oily nuts. Some he ate himself. The sun shone through their
window. A luminous warmth which, as the bus trundled
slowly onwards, gradually eased the shock of that other
smoke filled heat. She leant her head on his shoulder and
slept.

He could not take her to the apartment, not yet, not with
Poliko between them, so he took her to the hut in Vake Park.

They acted as though they had always lived here together.
He went to collect wild flowers for the table. She swept the
earthen floor with the twig broom. He made a fire outside and
when it had died down he cooked Nino's chicken on a spit of
green wood. He set the potatoes in the cinders. They sat outside in the balmy evening air, drinking the home made wine
Valeria had siphoned off for them.

After a while Maia drew in a breath and said, They executed him.

I know, he cut in.

I want . . .

Stop. It's alright now. He raised his glass and she raised hers. To Poliko's victory, he said. His victory, she replied. They sipped their wine watching the sun sink below the ridge above the park. Iosif tended to the meat. It was ready so he took bread and used it to pull the succulent pieces from the spit onto a plate. They ate with their fingers. He was ravenous. When it was all gone Maia yawned.

He showed her the place in the bushes where she could be private. While she was away he filled a basin with water and left it on the table in the hut. He put a clean towel next to it.

He sat at the fireside, smoking a cigarette. A sliver of moon showed between the trees on the ridge. He sat on until the crescent moon hung amongst the topmost stars. Then he went in and undressed, and without allowing himself to think about it he got under the quilt and lay next to her.

He thought she was asleep, curled away from him. He lay very still, feeling the curve of her spine against his chest and stomach and the softness of her buttocks against his groin. She wore a silky slip and he had kept his underclothes on. He wondered if for her they were just brother and sister. But he could not resist allowing his lips to graze the back of her neck.

I can't, she whispered.

Alright then, he murmured. And curled himself around her back.

But in the deep night she turned to embrace him. He had

287

been asleep. He woke and caught his breath as their lips met in the dark.

He stood on the street and soon sold the Beretta and the powder compact. On that same day he had gone to the phage clinic and to his relief it was being run by two brisk clinicians, who in reply to his question had said that Tamoona had emigrated.

They convalesced all that summer, two invalids who could not speak of the dread disease they had escaped. The vegetable plot needed tending. Maia made the hut more comfortable with cushions and a new quilt that she sewed and stuffed with fabric and wool which she bought at the market for next to nothing. They had not ventured back to Nutzubidze Plateau.

They got to know the boys who lived under the trees in Vake Park. They had run away from State orphanages and none of them cared to speak about their history. They had started coming to the fire like stray dogs will in the evenings. Adolescents with adult eyes and sharp noses, they would spit and curse and flare up in angry face-offs at the drop of a hat. Iosif saved water so they could wash and he always gave them food.

Maia did not attempt to mother them. But one warm night, when the three boys were chain smoking a pack of cigarettes and bragging about pick-pocketing, she clapped her hands together and said, That's all very well, but can you do this?

The boys might be feral but they had not forgotten the formal respect for women, the bedrock of a Georgian man's pride. So they held their tongues and watched her curiously. She stood in the firelight, wearing her green polka-dot dress. She sang the first few bars of an old-time Tbilisi city song and then, waving her hand to encourage the boys, they joined in, one at a time, until the four-part melody was complete. After the first verse the boys gained confidence and began improvising harmonies. Maia sang an octave above them. The boy with the lowest voice took the part of bass drone. They sang through the short summer's night, Maia teaching the tunes, and some they already knew and had not sung since forever.

Iosif did not try to sing with them. He stoked the fire and sat quietly watching her giving these lost youths their stolen childhood. From the city came the sound of gunfire shooting only at the stars, the howling dogs and other human voices singing into the balmy night. At daybreak, as Maia led the way through their final song, a young priest climbed the steps in a belfry, took hold of the short rope and whipped the clapper back and forth. The boys fell silent but she continued singing with the bell, *nau nani nau nani nau nani nana nau . . .*

Author's Note

In 1983 a group of young 'intellectual' Georgians hijacked an Aeroflot plane with the intention of crossing the border to live in the West. Their plan failed with tragic consequences. A novel is not real life, it is always a fiction. The story I have written is not theirs, although I have been inspired by and have borrowed something of their mad, sad dream.